THE Hurricanes OF WEAKERVILLE

ALSO BY CHRIS RYLANDER

The Fourth Stall Saga

The Fourth Stall

The Fourth Stall, Part II

The Fourth Stall, Part III

The Codename Conspiracy

Codename Zero

Countdown Zero

Crisis Zero

THE Hurricanes OF WEAKERVILLE

CHRIS RYLANDER

WALDEN POND PRESS
An Imprint of HarperCollins*Publishers*

Walden Pond Press is an imprint of HarperCollins Publishers.

The Hurricanes of Weakerville

www.harpercollinschildrens.com

Library of Congress Cataloging-in-Publication Data
[TK]
Library of Congress Control Number:
ISBN 978-0-06-232750-5

Typography by Michelle Gengaro-Kokmen
22 23 24 25 26 PC/LSCH 10 9 8 7 6 5 4 3 2 1
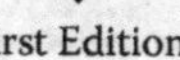
First Edition

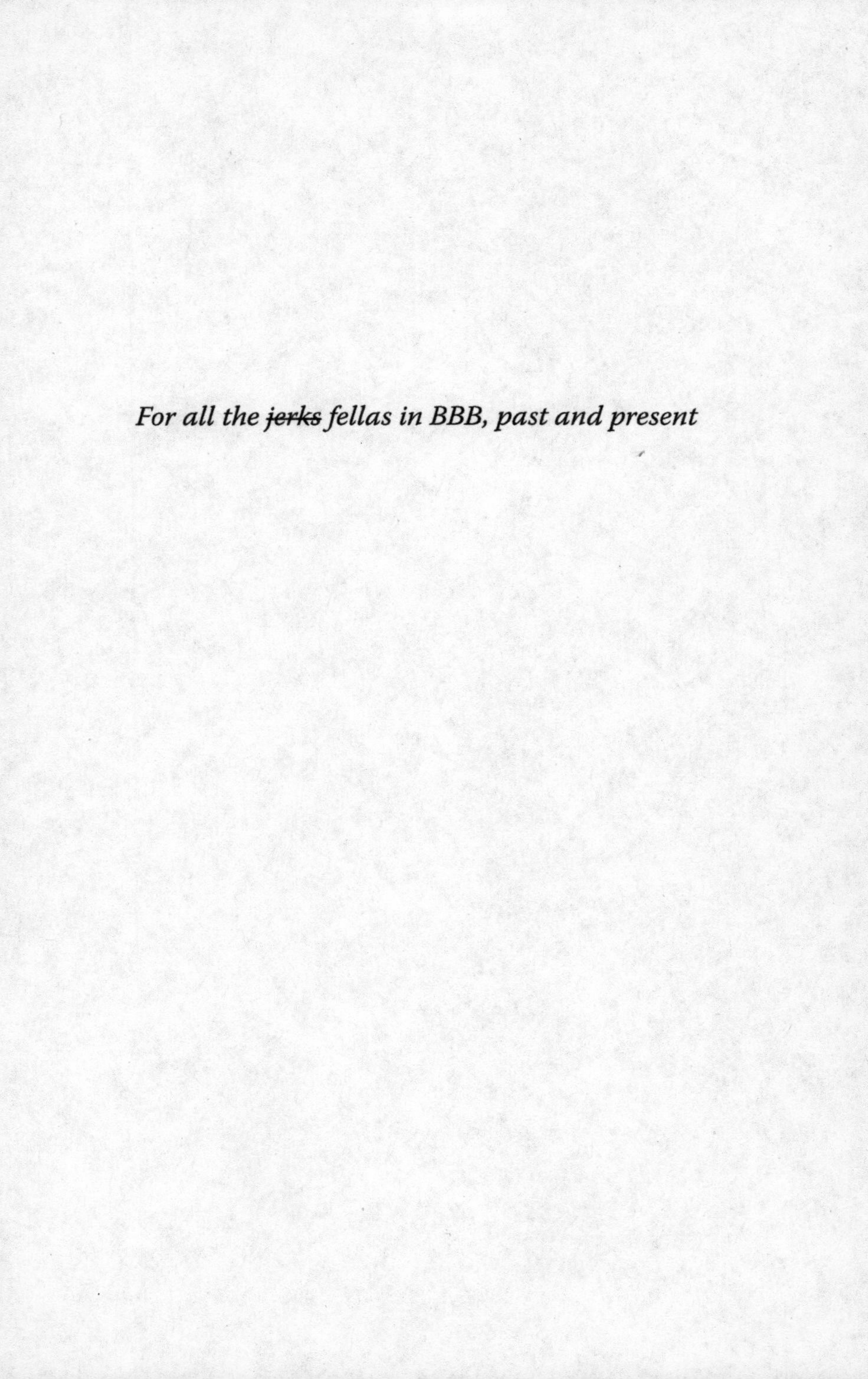

For all the ~~jerks~~ fellas in BBB, past and present

Chapter 1

MY NAME IS ALEX WEAKERMAN, AND THE FIRST THING ANYONE SHOULD know about me is that I love baseball.

The second thing is that I'm probably the worst in all of Iowa at actually *playing* it.

"It's your pick, Noah."

It's the second-to-last week of seventh grade and we're playing baseball in gym class. Now that it's nearly summer, I thought we might get to do something a bit more relaxing, like Ping-Pong or checkers. But our gym teacher, Mr. Muskel—a.k.a. Mr. Muscles—is obsessed with stuff like "hustling" and sayings that go "sweat is just your fat crying." So there's no way he was going to be so merciful.

As usual, Mr. Muscles picked his two favorite students to be team captains: Noah Figgins, a mouth-breather who speaks only in single-word sentences but is awesome at every sport imaginable, and Aliyah Perkins. For the record, Aliyah isn't, like, that girl who makes my legs unsteady and hands shake every time I see her or anything. Okay, well, that's not entirely true. But it has nothing to do with how popular she is. It's because she's the ace pitcher of the regional Little League team. Aliyah is probably the best thirteen-year-old pitcher in the state of Iowa, and possibly even the whole country. She played in the Little League World Series last summer, which means she pitched live on national TV with millions of people watching. She even got to be in a Nike commercial. Her team lost in the semifinals, but Aliyah pitched lights out. She threw nine scoreless innings between two games and had an absurd swinging-strike rate of 68 percent. So, yeah, I admire her quite a bit, from a baseball perspective.

Now she and Noah are mulling over who they're going to select for their teams. I'm always one of the last two picked. No matter the sport, it always comes down to me or Emma Driver, a.k.a. the girl who literally eats her own dandruff instead of actually trying to participate.

And it's not because I'm fat. Which I am. Always have been. My mom says I even set a record at the Weakerville Family Clinic for the largest baby ever delivered. She brings this up a lot, for some reason. I think maybe she's proud for surviving such an incident. But that's not why I'm picked last. There have been a lot of successful overweight baseball players, after all. Bartolo Colon, Tony Gwynn, Prince and Cecil Fielder, Matt Stairs, Rod Beck, Pablo Sandoval, and, of course, the Great Bambino, Babe Ruth himself. The difference is those guys were coordinated. They had natural athletic instincts. Being overweight isn't why I can't catch or throw or swing a bat without injuring myself.

But, honestly, how good you are isn't even the most important criteria for getting picked in gym. For example, there's a kid even bigger than me in our class: Brandon Sussman. He wouldn't be able to run a lap around the bases if there were a rabid hyena chasing him. And yet he always gets picked second or third. He even has a nickname teammates chant when he steps up to the plate.

"BRAN-DO! BRAN-DO! BRAN-DO!"

I definitely don't get a nickname.

And there's a reason for that. See, some kids make friends easily and some don't. It's that simple. And I just happened to be born with that weird trait that's the total opposite of charisma. A trait so awkward, it doesn't even have a real name. So, I just call it *Flumpo*. It's that thing inside some of us that makes us stutter around classmates instead of cracking witty jokes. Or clouds our vision of what the new cool clothes will be when school starts in the fall, even though everyone else already seems to know. Having Flumpo means when you're called on in class, you'll probably accidently burp, fart, and sneeze at the same time, nearly killing the kid sitting next to you, instead of being able to simply and calmly recite the correct answer.

Like last year, when I brought some lemon cookies my dad made to class for my birthday, as is tradition, and nobody wanted one. Everyone said they looked like "pee cookies." But then, two months later, Grayson Wu brought the exact same kind of cookies for *his* birthday, and he was basically crowned the class Snack King right there on the spot.

Well, that's just Flumpo at work.

I can't explain it; nobody can.

But I've learned to work around my Flumpo well

enough to get by. I have a hilarious best friend, I have the coolest grandpa in the world, and, most of all, I have baseball. All in all, that's not so bad. I mean, there are worse things to be born with (or without) than Flumpo.

But Flumpo obviously has downsides, and gym class is one of them. Specifically, being picked last, or second to last, every single time.

Today Noah has the second-to-last pick, meaning he'll technically decide who gets picked last. His half-opened eyes drift from me to Emma—who's already suspiciously chewing on her own hair—and back again. His expression is totally blank, almost as if his brain has switched off and gone into Sports Mode.

One of his teammates prods him in the back. "Come on, just pick one, so we can play."

He finally throws his chin in my direction.

"Weakerman. I guess."

I walk over to my team. Nobody acknowledges me—they're already busy arguing over who gets to play what position. I stay quiet and await my inevitable fate.

Once all the other positions are picked, Noah glances at me.

"You got right."

I always get stuck in right field. But I don't blame

them—it's where I'd put myself if I were manager. Most kids are right-handed batters, which means very few balls get hit to right field. The whole ordeal is degrading, sure, but I can't fault their statistical analysis. Besides, it means less chances for my Flumpo to make an unwanted appearance.

The game is mostly uneventful. The ball ends up in right only once, a dribbling grounder that squeaks through the infield. But our second baseman runs out to the ball first, so I don't even have to embarrass myself trying to throw it in. In fact, I don't touch the baseball the whole game.

But then comes my final trip to the plate.

At this point, I've learned to not even swing the bat at all. I just let Mr. Muscles, who's always the pitcher for both teams, strike me out looking. It gets fewer laughs—and results in fewer self-inflicted injuries—than if I actually try to make contact. And sure enough, the opposing players are kicking at the dirt and joking around as I step into the batter's box. They know I'm an easy out. But Mr. Muscles has apparently decided I should reach base at least once during my seventh-grade year. Because on the first pitch, he lobs the ball right at me.

I'm too startled to even move. The baseball bounces

off my thigh and lands in the dirt near my feet.

Mr. Muscles's expression doesn't change, but I swear I see a sadistic glint in his eye.

"Take your base, Weaker-*Man*," he says, pointing at first.

Mr. Muscles loves to pronounce my name with an emphasis on the second part. And I think we all know exactly why.

I put the bat down and start walking.

"Come on, Weaker-*Man*, hustle!" he yells.

I pick up the pace to something of a scurry, but still nothing close to actual running. Running, in my experience, is just an invitation for Flumpo to come out.

Aliyah Perkins is playing first base. She's pretending she isn't awkwardly looking away as I approach. When I finally reach the base, I don't even dare glance in her direction. I don't want to know whether she knows I'm already as sweaty as a damp towel.

"Nice job stepping into that pitch," Aliyah says.

"Huh?"

I finally look at her. Her hair is tucked under a Chicago Cubs hat. She chomps on a massive hunk of Big League Chew bubble gum as I stare with my mouth hanging open like a largemouth bass.

"You're down by three," Aliyah says. "You need base runners. With nobody on, it's as good as getting a base hit. You took one for the team. I like it."

I can't tell if she's being serious or mocking me.

And now, see, right here is where if I *didn't* have Flumpo, I'd pat my leg and smile to let her know I'm comfortable with my baseball ineptitude, then say something like:

Honestly, I've been training to get hit by that pitch for years. Three hundred squats, every morning. Three hundred more at lunch. Never once skip leg day. It's not easy, doing squats in the cafeteria line, doing lunges while everybody around me is just trying to grab their burgers. But I knew I had to do it, for a moment just like this. To withstand Mr. Muscles' fastball hitting my thigh. I did it for the sake of this team. Because you're right: having a runner on first with no outs statistically doubles our chances to tie the game.

But when I open my mouth to try and actually say that, all that comes out is a faint wheeze that the wind picks up and carries away like an empty candy wrapper.

I take another breath and try again:

"Squatburgers, uh, I mean, skiplunge, you know?" My

face starts burning. "Mr. Cafeteria . . . statistically doubles our . . . Muscles . . ."

Aliyah stares at me for a second, her mouth hinging open like she might laugh. But she says nothing. After a brief moment that feels like hours, she finally gives me a funny look and turns away, embarrassed for the both of us.

But then the next hitter steps to the plate, and I realize I have a more immediate problem than figuring out if there's a way to save face in front of Aliyah.

Noah's up next, and he's probably the fastest kid in our class. He'll almost definitely get a hit, and then will be running right behind me. In baseball, it's against the rules to pass the base runner in front of you.

My chest cavity constricts like a dried fruit. I start breathing heavily. More sweat streams down my cheeks like tears. Am I having a heart attack? Can thirteen-year-olds have heart attacks?

Can they?!

Mr. Muscles lobs in the first pitch.

CLANK!

Noah crushes it.

My first mistake is just standing there watching as

the ball rockets into the left-center-field gap. The school baseball field doesn't have a fence, so any ball that gets past the outfielders will just keep rolling. It *should* be an easy inside-the-park home run.

Noah's voice rips me back to reality.

"Come on! Run, Weakerman!"

He's already nearly to first base.

I start moving toward second. It's definitely not something anyone would call "running." I'm too busy trying not to fall face-first into the dirt to *run* run. And so I'm not even close to second base when I feel Noah on my heels. He shoves me slightly. I stumble, slowing down to keep from tripping. He must realize pushing won't help, because he just curses a few times while jogging in place as I regain my footing.

I round second base a few moments later. No idea where the ball is, but I keep going, desperate to get out of Noah's way. To get off the base paths. To get out of sight.

After what feels like several decades, I finally round third base. At this point, I've finally gotten my legs to move in a pattern that could be called running by some. I'm still not moving all that quickly, but everyone is yelling my name, so I don't stop.

Honestly, it's a minor miracle that Flumpo hasn't tripped me up yet. I should be sprawled on the ground somewhere between first and second with a mouthful of dirt.

It isn't until I'm approaching home plate that I see the catcher, Giada Rivera, standing in my way. She holds up the ball casually in one hand.

I stop and look back, my chest heaving as I gulp for air.

Noah is standing on second base, shaking his head in disgust. He and everyone else must have been shouting at me to stop at third, not encouraging me to keep going.

Giada smirks and taps my shoulder gently with the ball.

"You're out, Weaker-*Man*," Mr. Muscles says, taking off his hat and rubbing his shiny bald head. "Take a seat."

I keep my head down and find a spot at the end of the bench. Aliyah is saying something to Noah—probably telling him he could have had a home run if I hadn't been in the way. My team quickly moves on to cheering for the next batter, having expected nothing short of disaster from me all along.

But I can't blame them.

Baseball, like everything else, is a game of numbers.

The statistics would have told anyone that this was the most likely outcome when I ended up on first base. Numbers don't lie.

Unfortunately, that doesn't mean you don't still have to play out the game.

Chapter 2

FOR MOST PEOPLE, HOME IS THE PLACE THEY SLEEP EVERY NIGHT.

But for me, home is a place that smells like boiled hot dogs, fresh popcorn, and mustard. A place where people cheer and shout obscenities in equal measure. A place where the constant buzz of a crowd is sometimes broken up by the loud *CRACK* of a bat hitting a baseball.

I'm talking about Mustard Park. Home field of the Hurricanes of Weakerville, Iowa, the greatest independent professional baseball team in the whole world. In my opinion, anyway.

There's nowhere else I'd rather be.

The Hurricanes are down 6–0 to the Laredo Salt Dogs on opening day for the Midwestern Association Baseball League—which fans simply call "the Mabel." There are two outs with bases loaded in the bottom of the third inning and it feels like the most important moment of the game. Because it is. *Every moment* in baseball is the most important. That might not seem like it makes sense, but if you know baseball, then it's the only thing that makes sense.

That's part of why baseball is special. There's no clock, so any moment could last for a second or for a lifetime. And each one becomes a statistic that can be recorded. Individually, most moments, most solitary stats, maybe don't mean much. But if you track them all, add them all up over time, then you can extrapolate models that will help you predict the outcome of a whole season, a series, a game, or even just one single pitch.

Like right now.

The Hurricanes' best player, Oliver "Big Fish" Salmon, might come through with the bases loaded and knock home a few runs, changing the trajectory of the game entirely. Or he might strike out, and the team will remain down by six, deflated, knowing they missed their best moment to start a comeback.

And the thing is: I *know* which one will happen.

Because I've been keeping track of each and every pitch for each and every player, pretty much since I could read and write. Which means I usually have enough data to predict likely outcomes.

It's all in the numbers.

Big Fish steps to the plate and taps it with his bat before crouching into his stance. He's going to swing at the first pitch, that's for sure. When Big Fish is up with men on base, he takes a home run swing on the first pitch 89.2 percent of the time. If *I* know this, that means the opposing pitcher probably does too. And sure enough, the first pitch is out of the strike zone, a fastball up near Big Fish's shoulders. He swings anyway, taking a hack so colossal it's a miracle his spine is still intact by the time the ump yells out, "Steerriiike!"

Just like that, Big Fish is down in the count. He fouls off the next pitch, and it's now zero balls and two strikes. In his career, Big Fish gets on base only 12.3 percent of the time after being down 0–2. But I'm pretty sure he will get on base *this* time. Because what everyone else here *doesn't know* is that Big Fish hits a ridiculous .573 with base runners in the month of May in his career. And that somehow even goes *up* to .682 when he's down in the count. It's a statistical anomaly most mathematicians would dismiss as an outlier. But in baseball, results like this just happen sometimes, and you gotta trust the numbers either way.

The next pitch is a curveball in the dirt in front of home plate. Big Fish flinches but ultimately lays off, bringing the count to 1–2. His normal odds of reaching base are now up to 19.2 percent. But since it's May with runners on base, it's actually 74.6 percent.

The small crowd gets to their feet.

The Salt Dogs pitcher stands tall on the mound, nodding at the first sign he gets from his catcher. Then he fires a rocket toward home plate. It registers at 94 miles per hour on the radar gun, which is pretty serious heat for the Mabel.

Big Fish winds up for another monster swing.

CRACK!

The ball is on its way out of the stadium before the

sound of its seams being split apart by the bat even hits my ears. Big Fish drops to a knee at the end of the swing, a showcase of the raw power that helped him lead the league in home runs last season. The baseball's exit velocity is likely over 110 miles per hour as it soars into the blue sky, perhaps never to return to earth.

It's a grand slam.

The small crowd celebrates as the Hurricanes cut the deficit to two runs. I calmly record the outcome on my scorecard with a pencil. I'm as elated as they are, but what the rest of the fans are forgetting is that this is baseball. Which means this is just one statistic among many.

There's still a lot of baseball left to play.

A lot of moments for things to change.

For better or for worse.

Unlike most of this town, I will never give up on the Hurricanes.

As a baseball fan, there's nothing like living in a small town with its own semiprofessional team. For one, people can actually afford to go to the games. Plus, rooting for a small-town team isn't as anonymous as being part of an MLB fan base of millions. Instead it feels like being part of an exclusive secret society or something.

After Big Fish's grand slam, I fall back into my seat, just nine rows behind home plate.

When I say my seat, I mean *my seat.* The same one I've had for the past three seasons, ever since I got season tickets. And it's not because my grandpa Ira owns the Hurricanes and hooked me up with them. I actually pay for these two seats every year on my own, with the money I've made playing fantasy baseball (two thousand dollars last year alone playing under my dad's name).

The second seat belongs to my best buddy, Szymon Zajac—who everyone just calls "Slips." And who is finally plopping down next to me, late as usual.

"Okay, so it's the third inning," Slips says, checking the clock on his phone for the first of what is sure to be hundreds of times. "Which means there's only another ten hours and forty-two minutes left in the game? And then another seventeen years until the season is over?"

"Yeah, but it will go by so fast you'll feel like you're at Six Flags," I say. "I mean, every pitch is a whole chess match wrapped inside a staring contest involving a ball hurtling through the air faster than a car on a freeway. Every swing is a subconscious neuroelectric muscle-twitch reaction happening faster than a lightning strike. Then there're the *sounds*: the ball smacking a mitt, the umpire screaming out calls—"

"And don't forget the pitcher *stealing* three minutes of my life between *every* pitch," Slips interrupts with a grin. "While he takes off his hat and puts it back on again. Wipes his hands on his butt. Gratuitously *adjusts himself* thirteen or fourteen times . . ."

Yeah, so, Slips hates baseball. To be fair, he doesn't like *any* sports. He thinks they're a complete waste of time and energy—*inconsequential* is the word he uses. He says all sports boil down to a bunch of egos trying to show dominance by literally prancing around fields and playing with toys like show dogs. But he still comes to games with me. Partly because he likes to joke around with the high school girls who work the concession stands, but mostly because he's my best—and, well, *only*—friend.

"Silence," I say. "I need to finish filling in my scorecard for the at bat you just missed."

"You can always just fill it in later."

"Yeah, but the team website box score is laughably insufficient for my advanced metrics," I say. "I need to record every *pitch* Big Fish saw *and* his reaction to that pitch and the pitcher's reaction to those reactions. Those details aren't found in any box scores. Plus, there's the pitcher's routine and any variations—"

"Okay, okay, I get it," Slips says, laughing, as he scans the ballpark. "Man, look at this place! *Nobody* is here."

It *is* a pretty tepid crowd for opening day. Fewer than 1,000 of Mustard Park's 4,884 seats are occupied. Most residents of Weakerville, Iowa, haven't cared about the Hurricanes in decades. Not since back when the legendary Early "Eights" Foster, the best of the Big Four, became a hometown hero and the first Hurricane to make it all the way to the major leagues. The team's popularity has gradually declined since then. The last few seasons had the lowest attendance in the franchise's very long history.

"Yeah, well, they're missing out," I say.

"Or, *or,* and hear me out," Slips says, looking straight into my eyes, "maybe they're not. Maybe they're doing something that *doesn't* suck five hours of your life from your soul like a ghastly white demon with red stitches running across her face."

"*You're* here," I remind him, recording the third out of the inning on my scorecard—a weak groundout by our shortstop.

"Only because I like hanging out with you," Slips says.

"Plus, the hot dogs. *The hot dogs.* Oh, *man*, the hot dogs are sooooo good."

"Speaking of hot dogs . . ." I say, pushing myself up out of my seat. "I'm gonna go grab a few before next inning. Want anything?"

"I'll wait until I get *really* bored," Slips says, taking out his phone.

"If I'm not back by the time the game resumes—" I start.

But Slips finishes for me: "I'll make a video for you, yeah, yeah, I got it." He rolls his eyes dramatically.

I keep a scorecard by hand for every game—even away games, which I can usually watch online. My small bedroom is stuffed with piles of binders and stacks of notebooks, filled with stats, trends, and analysis on various players and pitching matchups. I know putting everything into a computer would be more efficient. But keeping stats by hand is how my grandpa Ira showed me how to do it. He loves writing down every little thing that happens—he always says the in-between moments are where baseball *really* sings.

That's my favorite part of baseball. All I need is a game and my stat sheet. Hot dogs and hilarious-but-irritating best friends, optional. When I'm at Mustard Park,

I'm no longer just that Flumpo kid who *struck out* playing T-ball. Instead, I'm Alex Weakerman, baseball genius and the most devoted Hurricanes superfan in team history.

Well, the second-most devoted.

Chapter 3

GRANDPA IRA HAS ALWAYS STOOD OUT IN A CROWD.

At six feet six in his prime, he used to tower over most people. Then there's his smile. Based on old photos, people in the past apparently didn't smile much. But Grandpa Ira's large white teeth are visible in *every* picture. Plus, he just dominates a room, always making wild gestures and passionate speeches about anything and everything, from his favorite baseball player of all time (Roberto Clemente) to how delicious the apple he just ate was. Grandpa Ira is the exact opposite of Flumpo.

Now, at eighty-six years old, with a thin frame that hunches so much he's barely over six feet tall, Grandpa Ira still stands out—even if part of that is just the portable oxygen concentrator he wheels around.

I spot him right away in the mostly empty concession concourse of Mustard Park. He never uses the owner's box, preferring to walk around talking to fans during games. His face lights up with a toothy smile when he spots me. Even though I see him every day—he's been living with me and my parents for a few years now—I can never get enough of his smile.

"Alex!" he wheezes excitedly as he makes his way over, the oxygen concentrator doubling as a walker. "Rough opening game, huh?"

"Yeah, but Big Fish's grand slam helped. And since then the opposing pitcher has only thrown two fastballs, so if—"

"No, not that," Ira says, shaking his head. "I mean, it's the first game of the season, and there's no one here!"

"Oh, sure," I say. "That's a bummer too."

He looks around the empty concourse.

"I just don't get it! We *almost* had a winning record last year, and yet these are still the lowest opening day numbers in Mustard Park history." His smile disappears for a moment, then he shakes his head and it's back. "But more fans will return. We'll win again. The old Hurricane Magic will come back, I'm sure of it."

That's Grandpa Ira. He's never sad longer than a few seconds. It's one of the things I love about him. But I can't be as optimistic about the future of the Hurricanes. Back when Grandpa Ira was younger, I suppose the town had nothing else to do but come out to Mustard Park for a day. Plus, the Hurricanes were one of the best teams in the Mabel back then. But now, I hear what the kids at school really care about: superhero movies, basketball, music, video games, social media. . . . Except for me and the kids who play it, nobody seems to care much about baseball. Especially not the Hurricanes. It doesn't help that we haven't made the playoffs in fourteen seasons. Plus, there's just a lot more to do in Weakerville now than back in the day: the IMAX theater, the go-cart track, the new Fun Zone complex a few towns over, complete with an indoor waterpark, golf simulator, arcade games, a VR room, and more. Weakerville has doubled in population since the Hurricanes' glory days thirty years ago, yet ticket sales are a quarter of what they were then. The numbers don't lie.

But I can't bear to say any of this to Grandpa Ira.

What I say instead is, "When school's out, I'm sure more kids will start coming."

Ira smiles and nods.

"Would you be willing to hand out free tickets to your classmates again? That helped more than usual last season."

"Sure."

Every year since third grade, Ira gives me a stack of bleacher seat tickets to give away the final week of school. And it gets a little harder every year to hand out the whole stack. Mostly I just see them scattered on the floor throughout the halls by the end of the day.

"Oh!" Ira adds, his eyes wide. "And maybe try to spread a rumor around the schoolhouse that the Hurricanes aim to compete for the title this year!"

"Grandpa . . ." But before I can answer, someone calls out my grandpa's name from down the wide concourse, saving me from needing to say anything at all.

It's his old friend, and the Hurricanes field/equipment manager, Paulie "Peez" Paulsen.

Grandpa Ira pats my shoulder and shuffles past me.

"Peez!" he shouts with a cough as he moves slowly toward him. "Got any more of those cookies Hazel made last week?"

I sigh and continue toward the concessions. There are at least three hot dogs with my name on them. They might be the only thing aside from a Hurricanes win that can cheer me up now.

The line at the nearest hot dog stand is nonexistent, one of the few benefits of poor attendance.

"Hey, Alex!" Gloria says with a huge smile as I step up to the counter. She's worked for the Hurricanes for almost two decades and probably makes me meals nearly as often as my mom during the baseball season. "How are you doing this evening, honey?"

"Pretty good. You?"

"You know me, same as always. The usual?"

I nod. "And a pretzel too, please."

She places three hot dogs and a big soft pretzel into a brown cardboard box.

"There you go, honey."

I pay her and then head to the condiment station. All three dogs get hit with ketchup, onions, mustard, and relish. I stay vigilant to get a balanced distribution. Well, except for the mustard. Everything in my box, including the pretzel, gets *doused* with mustard. It's a *must* here. We're at Mustard Park, hallowed ground for the condiment in more ways than one. I put almost as much care into dressing up my hot dogs as I do in keeping game stats. The aroma makes my stomach rumble like an earthquake is brewing.

I pivot to head back toward my seat.

Then stop dead.

It's Aliyah Perkins. She's standing with a bunch of friends near the stairs for my section. To get to my seat, I'll have to squeeze past her and half the most popular kids in school, while holding a huge box of hot dogs drenched with enough condiments to sink a small boat. That might not seem like a big deal, but most kids don't understand the power of Flumpo and the things it sometimes makes me do. If I try to slip past them, it's surely going to end with all that ketchup and mustard smeared all over Aliyah and her friends' clothes like a four-year-old's finger painting.

I move against the wall, thinking I'll just wait until they're done talking. But then a voice over the PA announces the next hitter. The fourth inning is starting. I really don't want to miss the first pitch. Slips is easily distracted when recording game action for me. Like the time he spent two whole batters zoomed in on a fan who was dipping french fries into a side cup of mayo. He even added his own commentary, correctly predicting that, once finished, the man would use his finger as a spoon to consume the remaining mayo.

I can't move past them with all this food.

But I also can't miss the next at bat.

So I make a quick decision and dump the entire box into the trash can beside me. Seeing those loaded hot dogs tumble into the garbage is like witnessing a car full of adorable puppies snuggling on piles of cash plunging off a cliff in slow motion.

Knowing I'll regret it, I quickly try to squeeze past Aliyah and her friends, doing my best to look invisible.

"Hey, Weakerman," Aliyah says, and I stop, my heart slamming against my chest, sweat beading on my forehead. Despite being in two of her classes, I didn't know Aliyah even knew my name, let alone had any reason to talk to me. I always assumed that to her I was just Anonymous Weird Fat Kid Who Definitely Has Lots of Whatever the Opposite of Charisma Is. "What's your grandpa think about the team's chances this year?"

Everyone is staring at me, waiting for some kind of normal response. And as always, the sort of thing a normal kid might say flashes through my brain.

Well, you know, we made a few nice acquisitions, and Big Fish is primed for another big season, so who knows? And hey, why don't I talk to my grandpa about getting you and your friends some tickets to the next home series? Right behind home plate sound good?

Instead, when I open my mouth, this comes out:

"Prime fish is big," I mumble. "Grandpa sits at home plate?"

Aliyah's eyes go wide. Her friends giggle with their hands over their mouths.

I quickly look away and hurry past them, back down to my seats, red-faced and empty-handed.

"Where are your hot dogs?" Slips asks as I sit down. "Did you finish them on the walk here?"

I shake my head sadly.

"It was a . . . a *massacre,*" I say. "A tragedy of the highest order. A catastrophic event that will be passed down from generation to generation. Something people will call The Day the Hot Dogs Died. Or The Sausage Incident at Mustard Park."

"What happened?" Slips asks, turning in his seat to face me. He doesn't even glance back when the hitter smacks a single and the few people around us cheer. I snag my scorecard and mark it down.

"I bought my dogs, prepared them perfectly," I say. "And then . . ."

"And then . . . ?"

"And then I saw Aliyah Perkins."

Slips laughs. "So you gave her your hot dogs?"

"No, I . . . I threw them away."

"You *dumped* your dogs?" Slips shakes his head. *"Koleś."*

Slips breaks out Polish words only for matters of utmost seriousness. And the fact that he always understands is why I knew I could tell him the truth about what just happened.

Slips and I first met in second grade, right after he moved to America. Back then he wasn't nearly as popular. Second graders are automatically mean to kids from Poland who speak little English and have funny names. Even meaner than they are to pudgy, socially awkward kids like me. As two kids who didn't fit in anywhere else, we hit it off. It helped that I didn't talk much, so the language barrier wasn't a problem. Once he got better at English, we realized we found the same types of things funny. So, for a few years, it was just the two of us, making up our own inside jokes. But as we got older, other kids saw just how funny and cool Slips actually is. Now he has no problem making friends. But he hasn't left me in the dust, even though he could easily trade me in for a best friend upgrade anytime he wanted.

"I'm not proud of it," I admit. "I was just . . . y'know, the Flump—"

"Don't even get started with that," he says, cutting me off and shaking his head.

Slips knows all about my Flumpo theory. When I first told him about it a few years ago, he dismissed it immediately as "*Glupota!*" Which is Polish for total hogwash.

Now, though, Slips just puts a hand on my shoulder and grins.

"All this talk about hot dogs is making me hungry," he says. "I'm going to go get a few. And unlike you, I won't send them to an immediate, undeserved death. I've got morals. Sausage-based principles, you see."

I roll my eyes as my stomach growls.

"And don't worry," Slips says. "I'll grab you some too. Just promise you won't throw them onto the field in a panic if Aliyah walks by again."

"*Harcerze* honor," I say, raising my hand like a Boy Scout.

Slips laughs and heads up toward the concessions.

And that's what having *the best* best friend is all about: inside jokes, and buying you more hot dogs after you foolishly throw your own away.

Chapter 4

IT'S STILL LIGHT OUTSIDE WHEN THE HURRICANES' VICTORY SONG PLAYS over the PA at Mustard Park.

Slips suggests we celebrate the win at Cheese'N Stuff Pizza. Well, for him it's less about the win and more about just wanting to eat pizza.

"This is the first time in four years we've started the season with a win," I announce as we walk toward Slips's scooter in the nearly empty parking lot.

Slips's dad, Jerzy, found this 1967 Vespa VLB in a heap of pieces somewhere in Davenport and brought it back to his junkyard last fall. Slips became obsessed with the old thing. He paid his dad a hundred dollars for the scooter—nothing at Zajac's Junk and Salvage is free, not even for the owner's son—then spent all last summer fixing it up. He painted it pale green, which is how it earned its name: Yoda.

Technically, Slips isn't old enough to drive. But in rural places like Weakerville, a lot of kids are driving tractors by age twelve. So enforcing such laws would result in mobs of angry farmers storming the county sheriff's office with pitchforks and garden hoes. Besides, *everyone* loves Slips, so he can get away with just about anything. He could probably wear a severed head on top of his own head, and the deputy county sheriff would just say, "Nice hat, Slips!"

I put on a helmet Slips hands me and climb onto the back of Yoda, and he heads toward Cheese'N Stuff.

Cheese'N Stuff Pizza is, in my opinion, the best restaurant in Weakerville. Even counting the newer and fancier pizza chain that opened recently. But to call Cheese'N Stuff a "restaurant" is a bit of a stretch. It's basically just a back room attached to one of Weakerville's small gas stations. It consists of a few booths and tables and a small kitchen where glazed-eyed teenagers feed premade pizzas through an automated conveyor belt oven. It's my favorite place to eat. The combination of the sauce (garlicky), the crust (golden and buttery), the cheese (plentiful), the price (cheap), and the lines (nonexistent) make it hard to resist.

Slips and I eat there as much as we can. In addition to it being the best pizza in town, we're afraid we're going to show up one day and find it's closed down forever. As far as I know, Slips, me, and a few teenagers who get free pizza from their friends who work there are the only people who still eat at Cheese'N Stuff.

"Hey," Slips yells back over his shoulder. "Did you see that the parking lot is finally done for the new A-Mart that's opening?"

"Yeah, I guess."

"It's a bunch of donkey dung," he says, following it up with a string of Polish curse words. "Weakerville doesn't need an A-Mart. Don't you know where it's at? Right across the street from Hagen Family General!"

Hagen Family General is basically a smaller version of an A-Mart, but with more random, odd stuff. I've never seen it busy. Pretty much only old people shop there. People whose families have probably been going there since it first opened back in 1902. Everyone else drives the forty extra minutes to the Bullseye Mega Store in Maple Park, or fifty minutes to the A-Mart over in Riverdale, rather than shop at Family General just down the street.

"My dad says the A-Mart will create more jobs," I say. "Besides, competition never hurt anyone. It keeps prices down."

"Ugh," Slips says. "Now you actually *sound* like your dad."

"But isn't it kind of inevitable?" I ask. "It's like baseball: it's just numbers. The bigger a store gets, the lower the prices they charge. The lower the prices, the more people shop there. The more people shop there, the more stores they can open. I mean, what can any of us do about it? The numbers are the numbers."

"Can't Ira do something?" Slips says. "I mean, he basically owns the whole town."

I roll my eyes, even though he can't see my face while driving Yoda.

"*Owns the town?* He doesn't even buy his own socks anymore."

Grandpa Ira moved in with us a few years ago, when he could no longer take care of the family ranch a few miles outside town. He may still own the Hurricanes, but my mom has to buy his clothes, cook his meals, run his errands, and sometimes even help dress him in the morning. I know it's hard for him. Ira thinks he's the one who's supposed to be taking care of everyone else, not the other way around. He's always tried to take care of *the whole town* of Weakerville. It's in his blood, after all.

You may have noticed my last name, Weakerman, is similar to Weakerville. That's not a coincidence. My grandpa's grandpa's grandpa Powell Weakerman founded Weakerville way back in 1868. At the time, he was just a simple farmer who bought a small plot of prairie land, right where the Hurricanes ballpark sits today.

During my great-great-great-great-grandpa's second winter here, a young Englishman with a funny accent named Jeremiah Colman passed through and introduced Powell to something that would change his life forever:

Mustard.

Colman didn't invent mustard spread. It had already been around for centuries. But he had invented a new recipe for it and offered some to Powell to try. Powell became instantly obsessed with the exotic, tangy substance. But back then it was nearly impossible to find a specialty item like mustard in the Middle of Nowhere,

Iowa. So Powell thought to himself: *I've got land. I know how to farm. Why don't I plant my own mustard?*

And that's how America got its very first mustard field, right here in Weakerville.

Powell spent years perfecting his own homegrown mustard recipe. He sold a few jars here and there to neighbors, but he longed to introduce more people to his own version of mustard spread. And then a fateful trip back east gave him just the idea he was looking for.

Powell went to see a game taking the country by storm: baseball. He attended a 37–16 drubbing of the New York Mutuals by the Troy Haymakers. Powell quickly grew tired of the game itself, which he found incredibly boring. He was much more fascinated by the hundreds of spectators devouring small sausages that they called "hot dogs." He immediately recognized the potential for a marriage between these hot dogs and his own handcrafted mustard.

Which is why he founded his own professional baseball club back in Iowa the following spring: the Weakerman Farm Cowpies. Having his own team and baseball field meant Powell could sell hundreds of mustard-covered hot dogs at every game. Powell's bright yellow mustard—which was quite different from European brown mustards—became legendary in the Midwest. Teams traveled from all over to play in Weakerville, and they often stuck around after the game to try Powell's famous mustard, the unfortunately named Powell's Tasty Tangy Yellow Sauce—or PoTTY Sauce, for short. Sadly, no living person today knows what PoTTY Sauce tastes like, because Powell took the recipe with him to his grave in 1905.

But it wasn't the mustard that eventually made the Weakerman family famous—it was the baseball team. While Powell never even bothered learning the rules of the game, his son, Rancid Oval Weakerman, fell in love with the sport and oversaw a local baseball dynasty that has lasted nearly 150 years. Eventually, Rancid and his son, Magnum, used the proceeds from the team to open a service station. Then a bank and a grocery store and more, building a modern township from the ground up. By the time my grandpa Ira was born, the Weakerman family owned a dozen businesses in the thriving town of Weakerville.

But over the years, things changed. Every economic downturn that hit the country seemed to hit Weakerville even harder. And as much as Grandpa Ira loved his family and the town, the only family business he focused on keeping afloat during the past five decades was the baseball team. Since then, all the other businesses were bought out or went bankrupt. By the time I was born, the Weakerman family had lost everything, save for the old family ranch, Mustard Park, and the baseball team. It has changed names and leagues many times over the years, but through all the ups and downs for our family and Weakerville, it's the only thing that has survived.

I suppose this is why I don't feel the same way as Slips about what's happening to the town today. Weakerville is a different town than it used to be, it's true—but that happened a long time ago. My family is evidence of that. The Weakermans used to own dozens of businesses in a thriving town; now my parents need to work multiple jobs just to get by.

"Nothing lasts forever," is what I shout at Slips now, over the rumble of Yoda's motor. "Old things get left behind or forgotten as new things move in. It's inevitable. There's no sense fighting it."

"I don't think your grandpa would agree," he says as he pulls into the small parking lot of the gas station connected to Cheese'N Stuff.

He's right. It's why Ira is so devastated to see everyone in Weakerville ignoring the Hurricanes. To him, it's more than just a baseball team. It represents the history of our town and our family. It's all that's left. Everything else is gone, just like my great-great-great-great-grandpa's mustard recipe.

Slips parks Yoda, and I step unsteadily off the back.

"Hey, either of you Scurvy Waffles got some change?"

An old man is slouched on a bench, holding out a gloved hand.

What he said might sound weird to anyone outside of Weakerville. But the whole town is used to his insults by now, despite not knowing his real name. We all just call him Gloves, since he's always wearing old leather gloves, even in the summer. He looks like he could be a hundred years old, and even though he's not technically homeless—he supposedly lives in a small apartment above the vacant movie theater downtown—he's always drooped somewhere near Main Street, asking people for money and hurling bizarre insults at anyone who refuses. And sometimes even the people who don't.

Slips hands Gloves a crumpled dollar bill. The old man stuffs it into his breast pocket with a crooked grin plastered on his wrinkled face.

"Your dad is going to be mad if he finds out you gave him money," I tell Slips.

"Whatever." Slips shrugs. "I'm not going to tell him if you don't."

"Don't go tattling on your little friend." Gloves sneers at me. "You Rat-Knuckled Glob of Water-Trash."

I smirk awkwardly. Being insulted by Gloves is a rite of passage in Weakerville. Repeating his unique brand of slurs at school is a pastime with as much reverence as the homecoming dance and the seventh-grade bake-off. Still, even though the guy curses like a sixteenth-century Dutch sailor and insults everyone, including small children, dogs, and the elderly, there's something empty behind it all that makes me kinda sad.

"Bring me your leftovers, you Rotting Diaper Jackets!" Gloves yells as we head inside.

"What the heck is a diaper jacket?" Slips whispers.

"No idea." I laugh.

We order a pizza at the counter and squeeze into our usual booth near the back.

"Why do you always give that guy money?"

"Can't I just be a generous fellow?" Slips shrugs. "He

needs it more than me. Isn't that enough?"

"I guess."

"You're the one who threw away a whole box of hot dogs at the game," Slips reminds me. "Gloves would *definitely* murder you if he ever found out. Then he'd, like, he'd use your skin to make a *new* pair of gloves. 'Mittens by Alex,' he'd call them."

"Gross," I say, laughing.

"You know," he continues, "when Aliyah talks to you, instead of freaking out, you should actually just *respond* to her."

"That's easy for you to say. Everyone likes you. You don't have Flumpo."

Slips rolls his eyes. "Don't even get started with that nonsense. The only reason no one talks to you is that they don't *know* you. In fact, Aliyah's probably the one kid in school that should be *easiest* for you to talk to. You both love baseball. To an unhealthy degree, if you want my opinion."

"I just . . . I know it would play out poorly. I'll freeze up. Or accidently spill the contents of my backpack all over my feet. Or panic and say something totally inane, like 'I put hot sauce in my oatmeal and then I ate the oatmeal.' That's how it always goes."

Slips looks like he's about to say more, but then our pizza arrives. He immediately picks up a slice and shoves the entire thing into his mouth. I laugh and grab a slice for myself, taking a comparably smaller bite, while he chews in silence for three full minutes.

"People aren't just statistics, you know," he says after finally finishing his epic whole-slice bite.

"Huh?" I mumble.

"People aren't as predictable as you think," he continues. "Just because a certain player has always struck out every time they've faced a left-handed pitcher at home on a Tuesday with runners on base and more than one out and it's between sixty and sixty-four degrees during a waxing gibbous moon, or whatever, doesn't mean they're going to strike out *this time*."

"That is literally the longest baseball-related sentence you've ever spoken."

"Laugh if you want," he says, grabbing another slice, "but I'm right. And just because you might strike out every time you try to talk to anyone at school, it doesn't mean that's how it always has to be."

I take a second slice of my own and stare at a pepperoni left behind on the pan. Slips might not be wrong. But I don't know that it really makes a difference. I have an awesome grandpa, I have an awesome best friend, I have baseball—also awesome. That's more than a lot of people have.

It's also about as much as anyone can count on.

Chapter 5

WHEN OUR PIZZA IS FINISHED, WE JOKE AROUND FOR A BIT WHILE enjoying a few free Pepsi refills.

When we eventually leave, Slips steers Yoda in the opposite direction of my house.

"Where are we going?"

"I want to stop by Hagen Family General," he says. "Might be our last chance."

I know he's pretty hung up on this whole thing, so I just nod.

Eight minutes later, Slips is parking Yoda in Family General's gravel parking lot, across the street from where the new A-Mart is going up. The exterior is already painted the trademarked neon orange of an Always-Mart UltraSave, and the bright AMUS sign lights up the slick new asphalt of their massive parking lot.

A large banner hangs across the front doors:

OPENING SOON—NOW HIRING!

Once we're inside Hagen's, I head directly to the sports apparel section. Hagen's is secretly a great place to buy Hurricanes gear. Well, it's probably the *only* place other than the official team store at Mustard Park—which is just a small kiosk near the ballpark's front entrance. Sure enough, I make a nice find: an Early Eights Foster T-shirt in my size.

"Who's 'Foster Eight'?" Slips asks, looking at the back of the shirt.

I would laugh, except I know he's not joking.

"Come on, Slips. The greatest Hurricane to ever play the game?"

He just shrugs and shakes his head.

"You've lived here for six years. And have been my best friend that whole time. I've talked about Early Eights Foster literally dozens of times."

"Alex, I don't even know the names of two players *on the team right now.*"

"Okay," I say with an exaggerated sigh. "Early Eights Foster is one of the Big Four, and the only Hurricane to ever make it all the way to the major leagues."

"The Big Four?"

"Yeah, the four players that anchored the Hurricanes Dream Team."

"Dream Team?"

I sigh as loudly and obnoxiously as I can, which only makes Slips smirk.

"Probably the best team Weakerville ever had," I explain. "About thirty years ago, the Dream Team won the Mabel Championship three straight seasons, going ninety and ten, ninety-three and seven, and ninety-one and nine, the best three-season stretch in league history. And the Big Four were the heart of the team, each a bona fide Mabel superstar. There was team ace Lefty 'Seven Fingers' Bowman, who ironically was a righty with exactly ten fingers. Then there was the closer Luis 'Dirty Ball' Mendez, who used to bean hitters on purpose to lead off the inning just to set up double plays with his devastating splitter. There was cleanup hitter Bernie 'BAM' Morgan, who had a swing so powerful his homers sounded like cannon blasts.

"And then, of course, Early Eights Foster, the best of them all."

"Okay," Slips says, like I just told him that broccoli is healthy to eat.

I continue, pretending he's interested.

"He was the only one of the Big Four who was a Weakerville native; hence the huge billboard that used to be on Highway thirty-five. 'Weakerville: Proud Hometown of Early Eights Foster.'" I use my hands to emphasize the grand scale of the billboard's display.

"Never seen it," Slips says.

"That's because it's not there anymore. Anyway, when my grandpa signed him, a high school dropout from Weakerville who had never even made the varsity team, everyone said he was nuts. But Grandpa just had a feeling about him. 'Numbers can be deceiving,' is what he told the local paper. 'Some players just got a special quality that can't be measured.' And Ira was right: Early Foster quickly became one of the Hurricanes' most exciting players. He earned his nickname, Eights, that first year with the team when he scored eight runs, stole eight bases, and recorded eight RBI in a single game, the infamous twenty-six-to-one blowout of the Joplin Railcats. He played three seasons in the Mabel with the Hurricanes, the Dream Team years, then had his contract bought out by the Angels' MLB organization. He finally made it to the bigs a couple years after that and went on to score the winning run in game two of the World Series."

"I assume all of that is good?"

"You assume right," I say, refusing to let Slips's intentional ignorance annoy me. "But then his career came to an abrupt end in what would eventually be called the Eights Scandal. They say he took money to lose games on purpose. He got banned from baseball for life. In the majors, he was never a superstar or anything, so most people didn't give him another thought after the scandal died down. But here in Weakerville, it was a different story. The town was devastated. No one was more upset than Ira. I think he felt personally responsible somehow."

"Okay, so Eights was a decent baseball player, then he cheated," Slips summarizes.

"Right, but the worst part is what happened *after* the scandal," I say, looking at the T-shirt in my hands. "A few years after the lifetime ban, Eights died in a plane crash."

"Heavy."

"Yeah. He was piloting a small plane over the Atlantic Ocean, and it disappeared. Because the wreckage was never found, conspiracy theorists think he's still alive. ESPN even made a documentary about it, *The Search for Early Eights Foster.* But they concluded what the radar records and eyewitness accounts support: Eights was flying carelessly and crashed. He was declared legally dead a few years later."

"Sad," Slips says. "So, you're pretty obsessed with this guy?"

"Well, yeah," I say, pulling on the shirt. "What he did and how it ended totally sucks. But he's also the best player in Weakerville history. He still holds nineteen Mabel records. I can't figure out why he'd cheat and throw it all away."

"What does Ira think?"

"He doesn't talk about him anymore. Whenever I bring up Eights, Ira gets really quiet and changes the subject."

"Well," Slips says as we start making our way toward the cashier, "I certainly hope you find out why he cheated someday. Then nobody ever has to hear that long story again."

I glare at him for a second but then can't help but burst out laughing. I'm still laughing as I hand the shirt to the lady working the register. Her name tag says *Carla.*

Carla holds up the shirt and stares at the back of it for a few moments, as if reading the name Foster over and over again. But then she seems to snap out of it and grabs the barcode scanner.

"Eights was something else. That whole team was," she says, shaking her head with a thin smile as she rings up the shirt. "Eighteen-sixty, please."

"He sure was," I say, handing her a twenty.

"I went to almost all those Dream Team games as a kid," Carla says. "It's a shame what happened. . . . Not him throwing games. Or even the lifetime ban. But the way he just . . . ran away on us. Gave up."

"What do you mean?" Slips asks.

Carla shakes her head.

"Eights made a mistake, and he had to pay for that mistake. But he turned his back on Weakerville. After the ban, he still had a lot of people here who cared about him, you know. But instead, he just ran away to Florida to drink and fly planes, and eventually, well, you know . . ."

"But . . . ," I say, "if he *had* come back, wouldn't everyone just have been really mad at him?"

"Maybe. For a while. But not forever. People can surprise you. Anyway, I guess we'll never know."

Carla takes a deep breath; her face is lit up orange by

the giant A-Mart sign across the street. I glance at Slips, who shrugs. Carla keeps staring at the number eight on the back of the shirt. I really hope she isn't going to cry. I never know what to do when grown-ups cry.

"Anyway, it's good to know his spirit isn't totally dead with you kids nowadays," she says, finally putting the T-shirt in a bag.

I take the bag.

"Well, uh, thank you," Slips says.

"Yeah, thanks for shopping at Family," she says. "You guys have a good night."

Chapter 6

THE LAST DAY OF SCHOOL IS USUALLY MY FAVORITE DAY OF THE YEAR.

It's the end of another long year of pointless schoolwork. The end of awkward gym-class moments. But most important: the start of summer and days at Mustard Park watching Hurricanes baseball.

This year, though, it feels like a funeral. I managed to give away only ten of the two hundred Hurricanes tickets Grandpa Ira wanted me to hand out. I just can't get that look on Grandpa Ira's face out of my head as he stared at the nearly empty ballpark on opening day. I can't bear the thought of telling him about the stack of unwanted tickets beneath my chemistry textbook in my backpack.

I try to avoid him when I get home from school. But that's pretty much impossible with Grandpa Ira.

"Alex, is that you?" he calls out excitedly the moment I open the front door.

"Yeah, Grandpa," I reluctantly shout back.

"Get in here!" he shouts through a coughing fit. "I want to talk about tomorrow's game!"

On my way to Ira's bedroom, I pass my mom and dad on the living room couch. They both work two jobs and so it's rare to see them home together at all, especially before 5:00 p.m.

"What are you guys doing home so early?"

"Your grandpa had another doctor's appointment today," my dad says. "Your mother needed my *emotional support*."

I don't really like the way he says this, but that's just kind of how my dad is. You get used to it. About the only time he seems truly happy is when he's grilling or smoking meat.

"Please don't get Grandpa too excited," my mom says to me. "The doctor said he really needs his rest."

"Is he okay?"

"*Of course* he's not okay," my dad says. "Illnesses like this don't just get better. It's not helping that he's at that ballpark every day, stressing himself out even more. He needs to let that team go. Should have sold it years ago, like I always said."

"*Andy!*" my mom scolds him.

"You know I'm right," he shoots back. "The doctor specifically said he needs to rest. Stay home more. That team isn't helping."

My mom makes a face, but she doesn't disagree with him.

"He can still go to the games, though, right?" I ask.

Mom gets up and wraps an arm around me.

"Of course," she says. "Your grandpa is as tough as they come."

I hug her back, knowing how hard taking Ira to the doctor is for her.

"Alex, you coming?" Ira yells.

"I better go."

My mom nods and sits back down.

Ira's room is crammed full of boxes. There's barely even space for the sagging twin bed in the corner and small desk strewn with sheets of paper and pencils.

His grin fades when he sees me.

"What's wrong?"

"Nothing," I say quickly.

"What happened?" he insists. "Come on, out with it."

I clutch at the backpack strap dangling behind me. I can't bring myself to explain how his own grandson is so bad at talking to other people that he failed to give away *free* tickets. But maybe that would be more comforting than telling him kids simply didn't want them. Either way, he'll be disappointed. I can't let him down like that, not now.

"It's nothing . . . got a bad final grade, that's all."

That part's the truth: I did get a C– in phys ed. But the grade didn't really bother me at all.

"What?" Ira says, his thin eyebrows forming arches. "Your mom says you're doing very well in school."

"I am," I say. "You know, my gym teacher can just kinda be a jerk sometimes. It's really no big deal."

Ira frowns, and I can tell he knows I'm hiding something. But all he says is, "Yeah, every school seems to have one, don't they?"

With that, we do what we do every day during baseball season: talk about the next game. Calling our upcoming series against the Duluth Harbor Pirates a "tough matchup" would be a massive understatement. They're the best team in the league. They've won six of the last eight Mabel Championships and have made the playoffs for fourteen straight seasons. We've won just four games against them the last ten seasons combined.

Phil "the Law" Sheriff, one of our veteran pitchers, will be making his first start of the season. He's our oldest player but still our most talented pitcher. He actually got picked in the first round of the MLB draft by the Baltimore Orioles nearly twenty years ago, and everyone believed he'd one day become their staff ace. But it never happened. The Law always had an impressive fastball—even now he routinely hits 96 miles per hour—but he never developed a good secondary pitch that he could throw consistently for strikes. Instead of improving in the minors, he got steadily worse. He played in the Orioles system for only a few years, got traded several times, and was eventually released. After playing in a couple international leagues, the Law eventually signed a contract to play for the only team left in professional baseball that wanted him: the Hurricanes of Weakerville, Iowa.

He can still be good at times, but he's too inconsistent to ever be the ace that we desperately need. Grandpa Ira, though, loves him.

"So, Grandpa, I've been thinking . . ." I say, pulling out

my notebook for the Law.

I have at least one notebook dedicated to every player on the team. I flip to his career stats page. His terrible 5.68 earned run average from last season jumps out at me immediately. Probably because I've circled it a dozen times in red marker.

"I know what you're going to say, buddy boy," Grandpa Ira says, "and you can forget it."

"Maybe we can at least *think* about moving the Law to the bullpen?" I try anyway. "His opponent's batting average the first time through the order is kind of not-terrible—it's that second and third time through when it jumps way up. If he doesn't have to face batters more than once a game, he *might* be more effective."

Grandpa Ira waves his hand dismissively but smiles.

"I have a feeling about the Law," he says. "I think this is going to be his season."

"He's almost forty years old and his WHIP has risen every season he's been with the team!"

"First of all, what's a WHIP?" Ira asks with a sly grin. I've explained what the walks/hits per inning pitched stat means to him a hundred times and he knows it. "And second, all these scorecards we keep? They just tell us what *has* happened. What *will* happen, well, we don't know, do we? If we did, we wouldn't have to play the game!" He coughs, takes off his Hurricanes cap, and pats down his thin hair. "Besides, I'm not the manager, so it's not my call."

"Ugh, don't even get me started on old Buddy LeForge," I say, referring to the team's longtime manager. He's a bit too old-school for my tastes. Doesn't play the metrics at all.

"Say, is that a new Hurricanes shirt?" Ira asks suddenly. "Where'd you find that?"

"Hagen Family General," I say, looking down at my new Eights shirt. "Hiding out on the clearance rack."

"Mrs. Hagen actually called me today," Ira says. "She's really worried about her store, what with that new A-Hole-Mart opening."

"It's just A-Mart, Grandpa," I say.

He winks at me, but there isn't a smile in it. In fact, he's looking as sad as I've seen him in a long time.

"I think . . . I think it's *my fault* her store is at risk."

"Grandpa, don't be ridiculous," I say. "There's nothing you could have done—"

"No, I . . ." He stops and looks down at his large, knobby hands folded in his lap. "Alex, you know, there's something . . . well, your mom and dad might have told you I went to the doctor today, and . . . there's something I need to tell you. Something I maybe should have said a while ago."

It's unlike him to stumble over his words. I almost fall off my chair waiting for what he'll say next.

"I guess I just used to think we could save Weakerville from places like A-Mart." He sighs. "I never gave up hope, even for a second, that Weakerville would bounce back someday. But that dream, it's getting harder to hold on to now."

He falls silent and looks down at his shaking hands again.

"Grandpa . . ."

"I'm just . . . worried about the future of the town, I suppose," he says finally.

I don't doubt any of that is true. Ira is the most positive person I know, but even he must get down sometimes. Still . . . I know this isn't what he was *going to* say, in the same way he knew that my C– in gym wasn't what's bothering me. Whatever he really wanted to say, he'd apparently changed his mind. Part of me wants to press him for more. To find out if there really is some dark secret he's been keeping from me. But I know Grandpa Ira better than anyone, and I know that if there's something he needs to say, he'll tell me in his own time.

"It's not your job to save the town, Grandpa," I finally say. "A-Marts are everywhere now. It's kind of inevitable we'd eventually get one."

"I know. I just sometimes miss what Weakerville was like before you were born," he says. "Everyone in town knew everyone else, it seemed. And at the heart of it all was the Hurricanes. Half the town would cram into Mustard Park to root for the team. The rest would tailgate in the parking lot or gather in one of the local bars and listen to the radio with pints of cheap beer in their hands. It brought everyone together. It created a community. We knew we could rely on one another. Which really matters when times get tough, like after the Great Hurricane of 1933."

Back in 1933, a series of epic thunderstorms and torrential downpours raged through Weakerville, flooding half the town and destroying a whole season of crops. The excitable newspaper editor of the *Weakerville Herald* mistakenly called it a hurricane on the front-page headline the next day. Of course, the Great Hurricane of 1933 was, in fact, not actually a hurricane—it isn't possible to have a hurricane in Iowa. Hurricanes develop over an ocean, and Iowa is smack in the middle of the country. But once the idea got in their heads, the townsfolk became convinced it actually *was* a freak hurricane. Years later, after everyone kinda realized the truth, it became something of a running joke around town. And, soon thereafter, the new name of our baseball team.

"My grandfather would tell me stories about how the town got together to rebuild after the storm, which was also during the Great Depression," Ira continues. "That's how Weakerville has been my entire life. No matter our other differences, we were still all in this, as a town, *together.* Now, though, there doesn't seem to be a darned thing that we can all agree on anymore—not even the hometown baseball team."

"That's not true, Grandpa," I say quietly, even though I suspect it actually is.

"We're supposed to take care of one another. That's what it means to be a Hurricane. To be in Weakerville."

I pat his hand because I don't know what else to say. This isn't the first time Grandpa Ira has spoken about Weakerville like this, but it's the first time he's sounded so hopeless while doing it. I think he always believed that if the Hurricanes could only inspire the town the way they used to, everything else would fall back into place.

But like always, I can't tell him what I really think: that

the world doesn't work that way anymore, if it ever did. I love the Hurricanes more than anyone else in the world, but they're just a baseball team in a league that almost nobody has heard of. I've seen the news. I know what the world is like. It's not like a baseball team can magically make people ignore reality, forget their differences, shop at Family General instead of A-Mart. A baseball team can't make people, like . . . I don't know, hold hands and sing songs together in a sunny meadow.

Still, I can't bear to say any of this to Grandpa Ira. I can't let him down like that. In fact, I'd do anything to find a way to somehow *make* that true again for him.

I just don't know if that's even possible.

Chapter 7

I'M AT MUSTARD PARK THE DAY EVERYTHING CHANGES.

It feels like any other game. I arrive with high hopes, in spite of the team's 19–28 record. Not that they'll suddenly turn things around—the numbers alone could tell anyone that's not happening—but I'm hopeful that I'll at least get to see some snippets of decent baseball, and get some raw data for my metrics.

Slips isn't here; now that summer vacation has started, he has to spend at least two afternoons a week working at his dad's junkyard. But it's probably for the best, since the stands are too deserted to keep him entertained. And Mustard Park feels especially empty today, because Ira isn't here—he hasn't been able to leave the house all week. It's the first time he's ever missed a home series. But he insisted that I still be here.

"Can't have a game without a Weakerman in the park," he'd said that morning with a thin smile.

At least he's still keeping his scorecards, sick in bed or not, while listening to the game on the radio. Neither of us will ever miss a single pitch of a Hurricanes game.

Or so I thought.

During the fifth inning, my phone buzzes with a voicemail.

My ringer is always off during games, and I normally wait until the end to check any messages. But then a series of texts invades my screen:

Mom: Alex, meet us out front.

Mom: We're picking you up in 5 min

Mom: It's grandpa

There are only two ways I'd leave a Hurricanes game early:

Unconscious or dead on a stretcher
Getting told my grandpa has just been rushed to the
hospital

My parents pick me up outside Mustard Park and we speed toward the county hospital. My mom barely speaks on the way, except to ask if I'm okay.

"No," I say, sweating. *"No."*

My dad just grips the steering wheel with two hands and stays quiet. My mom sobs quietly the rest of the drive. That short, nearly silent car ride tells me all I need to know before we even get there.

I don't need to overhear the doctor telling my mom it will be only "a matter of hours, maybe a day at most, I'm sorry," to know just how dire the situation is.

I don't need my dad's hand on my shoulder, him saying, "I'm sorry, Alex, I'm really sorry," over and over again to know this won't end well.

I don't need to see my grandpa in the hospital bed to know this will probably be the last time I ever see him.

"He hasn't been very responsive," my mom says softly from the chair in the corner. "But you can talk to him if you'd like."

Now that we're here, and this is actually happening, I'm sad, for Grandpa Ira and for me. But at the same time,

I'm calm in a way I hadn't expected. Maybe it's because I've been thinking about this moment since his diagnosis a few years ago. Or maybe I'm calm because I know he's lived an amazing eighty-six years, which is all anyone can ask for. Ira has actually said those exact words many times since moving in with us.

At this moment, losing the only person who loves the Hurricanes as much as I do, I feel a peaceful melancholy. And it doesn't feel selfish or callous, thinking about baseball. I know it's what Ira would want me to be sad about. I know if he's dreaming his last dream right now, it's probably about a sold-out Mustard Park, full of Weakervillians cheering on the team.

His hands are outside the covers, resting at his sides. I touch his left hand—it somehow feels both cold and warm at the same time. I squeeze it more tightly and Ira stirs just a bit and shifts his head, a wheezing sigh escaping from his pale lips.

"Grandpa," I say quietly. "It's going to be okay. The Hurricanes will be fine."

"*Alex!*" my mom gasps. "That's not—"

Her words are cut short, though, when we see Ira smiling. It's not his signature smile from every photograph ever taken of him. His eyes are still closed, and his lips haven't parted, but he's definitely grinning. It's unmistakable, and my mom sobs again. Then Ira's hand closes around mine. He gives it a single, firm squeeze.

I'm not sure what, if anything, it means. But for some reason I can't possibly begin to explain, I suddenly know everything is going to be fine. It's the most comforting moment of my life, and all I can do is smile back.

Maybe a lot of people would cry right about now, but that's the last thing I feel like doing.

I'm actually smiling when I let go of his hand and leave the room so my mom can say goodbye.

And still smiling, on the inside, when Ira finally passes away an hour later.

Chapter 8

"ARE YOU SURE YOU'RE OKAY?" SLIPS ASKS AGAIN, LOOKING AT ME LIKE I'm the one who died.

"Don't I look okay?" I dig into my second slice of Cheese'N Stuff pizza at our usual booth.

"Yeah . . . I mean, well, no," Slips stammers. He looks down at his plate. He has taken exactly one bite since we got here. "That's sort of the problem. You seem, like, *too okay*. Know what I mean?"

"No, I don't," I mumble through a huge bite of pizza. "*Too okay* isn't even possible, by definition."

"That's not what I meant. . . ."

"Just say what you want to say."

"Fine." Slips takes a deep breath. "Ira died only *two days* ago. You guys were super close. And you don't even seem sad."

"Everyone grieves in their own way," I say, repeating some line I'd heard at least a dozen times in movies.

Slips leans back in his seat.

"If you want to throw clichés at me, fine. I've got one too: I feel like you're not facing what happened. You're closing yourself off to emotions, bottling stuff up, or whatever. It's the same thing the school counselor said *I* was doing when my mom died, remember?"

Of course I do—it was only four years ago. For a while Slips had acted like nothing was wrong. Then that shifted to him being irritable all the time, which wasn't like him. When he started failing class, the school made him see the counselor twice a week. And then, after a month of him crying himself to sleep at night, Slips was, well, not back to normal exactly, but he at least felt like a slightly different version of the old Slips again.

I understand why he thinks the same thing is happening now. But this is different. My grandpa lived a long life and was sick for years. I'd been preparing for this. It wasn't sudden like his mom. I got to say goodbye. And Ira got to say goodbye back. In his way.

How can I explain all this to Slips?

"Come on, Alex," he says. "Now it's your turn to just say it. I'll listen. You can even cry if you need to. Here, use my pizza as a tissue. . . ."

I look at the greasy slice of pizza in his outstretched hand, the nervous, earnest grin on his face, and I can't help but laugh. At first he probably thinks I *am* crying, but when he sees I'm laughing, he cautiously joins in.

"I'm not bottling anything up," I finally say. "Sure, I'm sad . . . but, just, in a different way."

Slips nods. Unlike my parents, he seems to believe me. "Well, I guess I'm just glad you're okay."

"Thanks," I say, touched by his awkward concern.

Being serious is not Slips's specialty, but he does it admirably. I tell him so, and he nods and pretends to dab away tears with his greasy pizza slice. This sets off another bout of laughter, and just like that we're done talking about Grandpa Ira's death.

"Honestly, though, there is one thing bothering me," I say.

"Okay," he says cautiously.

I tell him about the last day of school, about how Ira

was going to tell me something, but then didn't. Almost like he had a secret. But then he never brought it up again.

"Now I'll never know."

"Maybe it will be in his will or something?" Slips says. "Did he have one?"

"I guess." I shrug.

"What about the team? What's going to happen to them?"

"My dad said that for now someone in Grandpa's front office staff is taking care of running things at Mustard Park. After that—"

"*Hey,*" Slips says suddenly. "What if *you're* getting the team? Like in *Little Big League*?"

That was this old movie I made Slips watch once, where the main character's grandpa owns the Minnesota Twins, and after he dies, he leaves the team to the kid. And I can't deny that the thought has crossed my mind at least once the past few days. But . . .

"I don't think that kind of stuff happens in real life," I say.

"Why not? Maybe *that* was his big secret?"

"*Because* Grandpa knew this day was coming. He definitely left behind a plan for the Hurricanes that was better than: 'Eh, I guess my thirteen-year-old grandson can be the owner of a professional baseball team.'"

"Yeah, I suppose," Slips relents. Then his gaze drifts behind me. "Hey, check it out."

I spin around. It's Gloves. He's actually inside Cheese'N Stuff Pizza. He's usually hanging out near the entrance, or in the alley, but I don't think I've ever seen him *inside* the restaurant.

"What's he doing?" I whisper.

"He's coming this way," Slips whispers back.

Gloves shuffles toward us, his head down. I figure he's heading for the restroom, but then he stops at our table and looks down at me calmly. He hesitates, his gloved hands in his pockets, like he's got something he wants to say. He takes a hand from his pocket and holds it out.

Then a scowl appears on his haggard face.

"Give me some money, you Festering Gut Wound," he sneers. "Ira would have wanted you to!"

I'm too shocked that he knew Ira's name to say anything. Though, Ira knew everyone in town, so he'd probably talked to Gloves tons of times over the years. Probably took him out for lunch and coffee too, knowing Grandpa.

"Hey, mister," the teenager working the register says, walking over. "Are you planning to buy anything?"

"Here." Slips holds out a five-dollar bill. "Take this and get out, before they call the cops or something."

Gloves quickly snaps up the cash and stuffs it into his pocket.

"I'm not afraid of the cops," he says. "Those Dripping Bucket Flaps."

Bucket flaps? Slips mouths at me.

"Come on, guy," the employee says, putting his hand on Gloves's arm. "I've told you before, you can't be in here if you're not going to order anything."

Gloves shakes off the cashier's hand and starts walking toward the exit on his own. He's muttering something angrily to himself.

Before he leaves, he stops at the door and takes one last look back at me.

Chapter 9

IT SURPRISES NO ONE THAT GRANDPA IRA WANTED HIS MEMORIAL service to be held at Mustard Park, where his ashes will get scattered over the pitcher's mound.

What *does* surprise me is how many people show up. I haven't seen this many people at the ballpark all season. Or last season either. In fact, I'm pretty sure this is the most people I've *ever* seen at Mustard Park. Most are adults—former players, senior citizens, people from around town—but there are also more kids than I would have expected. Including pretty much the entire high school baseball team, and even a few kids in my grade.

None more surprising than Aliyah Perkins.

When I first spot her walking toward me along the third baseline, a cup of red punch in her hand, I'm so stunned that I just stand there with my jaw hanging open like an idiot. I'm still gawking when she's standing right in front of me, taking nervous sips of punch.

Thankfully, Slips is there to jab me back to reality with a sharp elbow to my gut.

"Ughng," I grunt. Classic Flumpo greeting.

"Hi, Alex," Aliyah says. "I'm, um, really sorry about your grandpa."

I'm still surprised she remembers my first name, but even more surprised that she apparently knew my grandpa well enough to be here. I'm still trying to work this out in my head when Slips steps in, so I don't seem like such an awkward goon.

"He very much appreciates your condolences," Slips says. "Don't you, buddy?"

"Oh, um, yeah," I mumble. "Thanks."

The three of us just stand there for a bit, trying not to look at one another. Aliyah takes another sip of punch, looking ready to bail on this whole thing.

"How, uh . . . do . . . uh, *did*, I mean, did you . . . uh, know Ira?" I finally manage to stutter.

She looks relieved to have something to say.

"Are you kidding? I wouldn't have gotten to pitch the Little League World Series without him."

"What do you mean?" I ask.

"When I first wanted to play baseball, the traveling team wouldn't let me," she explains. "'Softball is for girls, baseball is for boys,' the coach said to me and my dad when we tried to sign up. 'It's what she'll have to play in college, so why bother with baseball?' There's nothing wrong with softball, but I've been playing *baseball* since I was five years old. I guess no girls around here had ever tried to join the traveling team before."

"This," Slips says. "*This* is why I don't like sports."

Aliyah shrugs before continuing.

"Anyway, they weren't going to let me play, but then my dad mentioned it to your grandpa, and he pulled some strings with the local Little League commissioner and got me a tryout. Ira helped bring Little League baseball to this part of Iowa, so I guess he had a lot of influence. He's one of the few people I ever met who seemed to care about what *I wanted*, instead of just what I can do." She looks down, uncomfortable. I don't think I've ever seen her like that before. "I owe him a lot."

"Wow, that's . . . uh, wow . . . that's . . ." I stammer.

I'm still trying to figure out how Grandpa Ira did all that and I never even knew it. What else did he never tell me about? How many secrets did he have? It's hard not to feel a little . . . jealous.

"That's cool," Slips says, helping me out.

"Yeah," Aliyah agrees, finishing off her punch. "Well, I just wanted to say sorry."

"Um, right, thanks."

She hurries away.

"Wow," Slips says once she's gone. "Did you know your grandpa knew Aliyah Perkins?"

"I did not."

We stand there in silence for a moment, looking across the baseball field. Hundreds of people are gathered in dark suits and dresses on the infield, eating snacks and talking about Grandpa Ira. It's the first time since he died that I feel like crying. Not because I'm sad, but because I'm proud to be his grandson. There's a reason why people liked him so much—a lot of reasons, apparently.

"Why am I not more like Ira?" I suddenly wonder aloud.

"Nobody could be," Slips says. "He was the *best*."

I just nod and keep trying not to cry.

* * *

I expect Grandpa's will reading to be this big thing where a bunch of people gather in a room filled with thick law books and uncomfortable wood chairs, while some lawyerly guy in a dark suit reads aloud who gets what from Grandpa Ira's estate.

But that's not even close to what happens. Instead, Ira's lawyer, wearing jeans and a yellow polo shirt, stops by our house the night after the service to drop off a copy of the will. He goes over it with my parents, and then asks if they have any questions. They talk for a few more minutes. He leaves. And that's it.

Once the lawyer is gone, I creep out toward the kitchen. My parents are still sitting at the table, gripping half-empty mugs of coffee with two hands, like they're holding up crosses to ward off vampires. I expect them to tell me to go back to bed, but instead, my mom smiles.

"Have a seat," my dad says, pushing out the chair across from him with his foot.

I sit and we look at one another solemnly.

"Your grandpa left you all of his old notebooks and scorecards," my dad says, breaking the silence. "We can leave them in his room for now, but eventually they need to go. So, it'd be helpful if you could go through them and decide what you want to keep."

"I'm keeping it all," I say immediately. I can't believe my dad would suggest throwing away a single one of my grandpa's scorecards.

"We don't have the space, Alex—" my dad starts, but my mom cuts him off.

"You can keep as many as you want," she says. "As long as you know you're responsible for storing them in your own room."

"That's fair," I say. "So . . ."

My mom and dad look at each other.

"So . . . what?" my dad finally says.

"What about the team?"

"Alex . . ." my dad says, and sighs.

"Your grandfather . . ." my mom begins. "Well, I don't know how to say this, Alex, except to just say it. It turns out Grandpa Ira didn't technically *own* the Hurricanes."

"What? What do you mean?" I say. "I don't—I don't understand. . . . If he didn't own the team, then who does?"

"Ira's brother-in-law," my dad says. "A man named Parnell Cohaagen."

"*What?* Brother-in-law?" I'm in a complete stupor now.

As far as I knew, the three of us were my grandpa's only remaining family. I never heard of a brother-in-law before. All my aunts, uncles, and cousins are from my dad's side. Grandpa Ira had a sister once, but she died a long time ago, back when my mom was still in high school. Nobody ever talked about her; I don't even know her name.

"He and Ira weren't very close," my mom says.

"Understatement of the decade," my dad mutters under his breath.

"How can Grandpa not own the team?" I ask, still not getting it. "His great-great-great-grandpa founded them! And it was Ira who kept them alive and going. *He* got them into the Mabel! *He* built the new stadium! *He's* been running the team his entire life!"

"Your grandfather's finances are a lot more complicated than we knew," my dad says.

"Well, then tell me."

And so they do.

Apparently, Grandpa Ira was flat broke. He moved in with us not just because he'd gotten sick but also because the bank had foreclosed on the family ranch years ago, and he couldn't afford an assisted living facility. By the time he died, he barely had a single penny to his name.

In fact, the opposite: he was deeply in debt.

And it's all because of the Hurricanes.

Twenty-five years ago, Grandpa Ira still had a small fortune stashed away from all the businesses the family once owned. And the Hurricanes were turning a modest profit, just a few years removed from the Dream Team seasons. But during the decade that followed, the town gradually lost interest—Early Eights Foster's cheating scandal being one of many reasons. The team's profits dwindled until they were gone entirely. For the last twelve seasons, the team has been losing money. A lot of it. Grandpa Ira, my parents explained, spent every dollar he had, and a lot that he didn't, keeping the team alive. He amassed substantial debts, and five years ago one of Ira's creditors finally threatened to take the team away from him.

"This next part," my mom explains, "gets a little fuzzy."

"We don't know when, exactly, Ira reached out to this guy, Parnell 'Tex' Cohaagen, his estranged brother-in-law," my dad elaborates. "Or even what sort of arrangement they agreed to. What we were just told, however, is that this fella, who has probably never set foot in Iowa, bought out Ira's debts in exchange for ownership of the team and the land Mustard Park is built on. Why a rich businessman would purchase an unprofitable baseball team and keep funding it for a brother-in-law he barely knew . . . well, that part is a mystery. Except to Ira and his brother-in-law."

"So, what will this Parnell Tex guy do with the team?" I ask, my stomach already churning.

"We don't know for sure," my dad says while my mom takes my hand and rubs it. "But as far as we know, he can do whatever he'd like with it. I'm sorry, buddy."

I grunt audibly, like a hired goon just punched me in the gut.

Then it all clicks into place. *This* is clearly what Ira had been trying to tell me on the last day of school. And I sort of get now why he didn't. It was basically for the same reasons I never told him what I thought the chances were that the town would ever turn out to watch the Hurricanes again.

"Grandpa's attorney thinks this Tex person will probably sell the team," my mom says.

"If he's got any sense, he definitely will," my dad says.

My mom elbows him sharply, and he grunts an apology.

"If there's a silver lining," my mom adds, "it's that we

inherited the small remaining portion of the land Ira still owned. If the team and ballpark *do* get sold, it will be a little help in paying off some of our own debts. Or maybe we can use it to finally take that trip to Chicago, for a Cubs game, like you've always wanted?"

I don't want to seem ungrateful, so I nod slowly. "Yeah, that'd be fun."

But the reality is I'm trying not to barf all over the dining room table. Of course, I *have* always wanted to see Wrigley Field, a bucket list Must for any baseball fan. And I've always known the Hurricanes won't be around forever. Kinda like Family General. So why does the sudden prospect of losing them hurt so much? Why does it feel like I'm being gutted like a fish at a fillet station? Like my world is ending?

Is it because I never considered losing them so soon and suddenly? I'd always figured I'd be able to watch their games every summer until I finally left Weakerville to go to college or something. I figured there would be time to come to terms with losing the team.

But losing them now, I don't know if I can.

Chapter 10

I WANT TO SAY MUSTARD PARK IS STILL THE HAPPIEST PLACE ON EARTH, but I'm not sure that's true anymore.

How can I keep coming here and watch the games knowing this might be the Hurricanes' last season ever?

And I also can't stop thinking about my final moments with Grandpa Ira. He had seemed so peaceful, like he knew everything would be okay. But how could he have thought that, knowing what a mess he was leaving behind?

But I'm still here. I'm still going to attend every game

this year. Because as hard as it is to imagine a world without the Hurricanes, it'd be even worse to skip out on the last half of their final season ever.

It's the third inning, and for once, I'm having a tough time concentrating on the game. The Hurricanes are currently 18–30 and in last place, with home crowds that don't even hit 20 percent of Mustard Park's 4,800-seat capacity. Part of me has been hoping that maybe this Tex guy will decide to keep the team after all, but as I look around the park, I know how unlikely that is.

I'm trying to focus on Big Fish standing at the plate, a runner on second, two outs, and a 2–1 count, when I'm suddenly enveloped in a huge shadow.

The huge shadow is actually two moderately large shadows, cast by two big, muscular guys in black polo shirts. Walkie-talkies and Tasers hang from their belts.

"Sir, we need you to come with us," the larger one says.

"I paid for these seats," I blurt out. "I have my ticket!" I start digging around inside my backpack for my phone.

"Sir, please," he says.

"Let's not make this difficult," the other one adds.

"What about my stuff?" I motion to the stack of binders and notes sitting next to me.

"Bring it. You won't be coming back."

It feels like my heart is melting into my belly as I quickly collect my things and follow the security guys up to the concessions concourse. They lead me to a door blocked off by velvet rope. Another security guy stands next to it.

A gleaming new sign hangs there:

OWNER'S BOX—INVITATION ONLY

They pull aside the rope, but I don't move.

"Kid, don't make us carry you in," the guard says. "Because we will."

I hurry through the door and up the steps without looking back.

Since finding out Ira had a brother-in-law who technically owns my favorite baseball team, I've done a bit of research on him.

Parnell "Tex" Cohaagen is *rich*. The sort of rich where his money makes *even more money* without him even doing anything. And he's got a big personality to match his fortune. One of the first results when I typed his name into Google was a series of TV commercials from the 1980s posted to YouTube with the title: "Hilarious

Vintage Car Commercials." In the videos, Tex wears a variety of loud suits, ranging from orange to yellow to teal, and always a bright white Stetson cowboy hat. Every video ends with him barking out what was apparently the Cohaagen Dealership catchphrase: "If you ain't got the *sense* to buy at Cohaagen, then you're wasting all your *cents*." The line is then punctuated, each time, by a barrage of hoarse laughter.

Based on a few articles about his business endeavors, I deduced that he's from Arkansas. But there's no record of when or where he was born, his family or educational background, or how he made most of his money in the first place.

I also had no idea he had arrived in Weakerville until this very moment.

Tex Cohaagen is not facing me, but I'm sure there's no one else who could be under the big white cowboy hat in front of me. He's sitting in the middle seat of the newly furnished owner's box. There never used to be an "owner's box" at Mustard Park. Grandpa Ira used this space, which overlooks the field from right behind home plate, to host elementary school field trips during the first few weeks of every season. "The best seats in the house!" Ira would say as he led the kids and their chaperones up the stairs and into this room.

A guy in a business suit sits a few rows in front of Tex, but the other fourteen seats are empty. They both turn and look at me as I close the door behind me.

"*Boy!*" Tex barks at me. "What are you doing dawdling there? Git on in here!"

He lets loose a fit of the same hoarse laughter from his old commercials. It sounds like a 1993 Honda Accord trying to desperately start up one final time. That might seem random, but when you have a best friend whose dad owns a junkyard, you get to know the exact sound of such things.

I shuffle into Tex's row, already feeling the Flumpo flooding my brain.

Tex looks me up and down, an unlit, worn, hand-rolled cigarette clamped in his teeth. Then he grins again and waves a hand covered in huge gold rings at the seat next to him.

"Well, have a seat, son!" he says. "Don't just stand there gawking like a heifer gettin' milked, for Lucy's sake."

I have no idea who Lucy is, but I sit down, leaving one seat between us.

Tex leans back and watches me shift uncomfortably. He's not smiling, exactly, but he looks like he wants to. It's hard to tell how old he is. He could be just a little older than my parents, or he could be 105. His face is waxy and puffy and overly tan, smooth in some places and heavily wrinkled in others. His hands are huge and knotted with massive veins and coarse hair. His movements are quick and bold, like he's going to live for another fifty years at least, no matter how old he technically is.

"Do you know the average life span of an independent professional baseball team, son?" he finally asks.

"Um . . . what?"

Tex laughs like I told a joke. "You got blueberry muffins in your ears or something?"

"Uh, no . . . sir?" I have no idea what else to say, but I'm shocked when the fuzzy Flumpo cloud in my head starts fading, as if I've known Tex for years.

"No, what?" Tex asks. "No, you don't got blueberry muffins in your ears? Or, no, you don't know the life span of a semipro baseball team?"

"Um, both?"

"Four years," Tex declares, the unlit cigarette bobbing up and down between his teeth. "The average team lasts just four seasons. And that's only because of the rare leagues, like this one, that have somehow made it longer than a decade. Many independent leagues don't even make it past two seasons. You know *why* teams die so young?"

I know the answer he's looking for, but I shake my head anyway.

"Because they don't make no money, that's why!" Tex says, so emphatically that I think he might accidentally swallow his unlit cigarette. "Your grandpa and his kin kept this team going for one hunnert and forty-some seasons, through fourteen different league changes."

As both a direct descendant of Powell Weakerman and a Hurricanes superfan, I already know this.

I just nod.

"But this team ain't been profitable for a long time," Tex continues. "And I didn't bail out your grandpappy because I wanted to own a failing team in a failing sport. I don't care about baseball, if I'm being straight with you. All I care about is net revenue. And even though this baseball team ain't valuable, the *land* the stadium sits on sure is. When I bought this sinkhole team, I knew the investment would eventually pay off, one way or another."

It's true, then: Tex is going to sell the team. If I were still standing, my knees would have buckled, and I'd be plopping onto the floor like a scoop of ice cream falling off a waffle cone.

"But, but . . . why *now*?" I ask. "My parents told me you've owned the team for years. Why keep it going this long? Why not sell it right away?"

Tex studies me for a moment.

"Well, son," he says, "that there's a private matter between me and Ira. And *nobody else*." He gestures toward the man in the business suit. "In fact, this fella here scolded me something fierce back when I signed that agreement with your granddaddy, as unconventional as it was. Rick's my accountant, you see. It's his job to holler at me for spending money."

The man in the suit nods while Tex assaults us both with hoarse laughter.

"But, anyway," Tex eventually continues. "The agreement I signed with Ira had a lot of peculiar stipulations in the event of his passing. One of which is the very reason I invited you up here."

"Um, okay."

"His first contractual death rider was that I fire the current manager, Buddy LeForge."

"Um, okay."

In my opinion, old Buddy LeForge should have been fired years ago. He rarely adjusts his lineup to take advantage of pitching matchups, never shifts the infield, and generally ignores advanced statistical metrics. But Ira was extremely loyal, so firing Buddy had always been out of the question. Until now, apparently.

"The second stipulation was pursuant to who his replacement would be," Tex says with a huge grin, holding out a hand doused in gaudy gold rings. "So, I guess congratulations are in order to *you*, the new manager of the Hurricanes."

Chapter 11

I'M TOO STUNNED TO SAY ANYTHING.

Manager?

Me?

I'm the new manager of the Hurricanes?

"I don't understand," I finally manage to mumble.

"I guess your grandpappy thought you could save this sinking ship," Tex says. "Win some games, attract some fans, revitalize the team, what have you. That's what I assume, anyway. He wasn't too keen on fully explaining his bizarre predilections, as I'm sure you know."

"Huh?"

Tex smiles patiently, takes the cigarette from his mouth, and, seeming to see for the first time it's not lit, quickly puts it back in place at the corner of his lips.

"Now, I should let you know that I negotiated for my own stipulation to our little agreement," Tex says. "And that is this: now that Ira has passed, may he rest in peace, at the conclusion of any season during which the team fails to make the playoffs, including this one, I'm free to disband the organization however I see fit, and sell the land. Which I rightly intend to do."

It feels like my heart is skipping beats.

Make the playoffs.

I'm not sure whether to laugh or cry. I've just been handed a chance to save the team. But the only way to do it is to somehow find a way to do what a real, actual professional baseball manager has failed to do for the past *fourteen* straight seasons: take a team that's 18–30 to the playoffs. Or else the Hurricanes will be finished forever.

"But I . . . I still don't understand why Grandpa Ira wanted *me* to be the manager," I say. "I don't know how to manage a real baseball team."

"You sure about that, son?" Tex asks.

Of course, I'm not sure about *anything* anymore. But

working the numbers to predict outcomes for fantasy baseball and stuff is one thing. Managing a *real* team probably involves a lot more than just analyzing numbers. Especially with the literal fate of that team resting on my shoulders. Not to mention all the unwanted attention it would bring. And the Flumpo . . . it'd be a miracle for me to even remember to put on pants every morning. Worst of all, if I failed, there's no one I'd be letting down more than Ira.

"I just . . . I don't get what Grandpa Ira expects me to do," I say aloud. "How can I do what *he* couldn't?"

Tex laughs. "Son, I understand you're a bit trepidatious. If you weren't, *then* I'd be worried. A man that is all confidence and no discernment, a man that has no ability to question his own abilities, is a man who is incapable of learning from mistakes, from improving. And we ain't got no use for a man like that, right?"

I nod.

"You're right as rain to be concerned," Tex continues. "If there was an easy answer to turning around this team, you wouldn't be in this pickle. And I wouldn't be sitting right here, in front of you, right now, would I?"

"No, sir."

Tex nods solemnly, and I think I detect a glimmer of

pity in his squinting eyes because he sighs long and low and throws one of his meaty paws onto my shoulder. It feels like it weighs ninety pounds.

"I ever tell you about the time I nearly got ate by a gator?" he asks.

I'm not sure why he thinks he might have told me any story before, being that this is the first time we've met. But I just shake my head.

"It wasn't even in the south or a swamp or nothing!" Tex says with a laugh. "It happened in Ice-LAND of all places. You believe that?"

I shake my head again.

"Yeah, I wouldn't either if I weren't there myself, in the jaws of death," Tex says. "Anyhow, what had happened was: I'd just arrived at my hotel in Reykjavik for a business meeting with some investors. I went up to my presidential suite, opened the door, stepped inside . . . and, sure as Lucy's a saint, there's a ten-foot *alligator* right there on the end of the neatly made bed! Just sitting there like he's waitin' on room service!"

My eyes widen.

Tex leans back in his chair as I glance at his accountant, Rick. He's calmly shuffling through documents like Tex is telling a story about picking up dry cleaning.

"So, the gator starts hissing and lunging at me," Tex continues. "The bellhop pushing in my luggage cart seems just as startled to find an alligator in a hotel room in Ice-LAND as I am. He's shoutin' things like, 'He's coming at you, Mr. Cohaagen!' 'Watch out, he sees your gator-skin boots!' And cussing and hollering in Ice-LANDish and this, that, and the other. Which is only agitating the gator even more; I figure maybe the alligator never heard anyone speaking that freaky-sounding language before.

"Anyway, I got to think real quick, and do the only thing that comes to mind: I grab my bag of boots off the luggage cart, unzip it, and I start throwing 'em at this gator. Just chucking boots—most of them made from the skins of his brethren as the bellhop unhelpfully pointed out—one after the other. The gator is stunned, but also right ticked off now. He hops off the bed and lunges again, snapping, barely missing my kneecaps! But now the bell-hop is throwing some of my boots too. And pretty soon that darn gator retreats right underneath the bed. Running from us like a little salamander!"

Tex roars with laughter, clutching his stomach.

I attempt a nervous chuckle.

"Turns out, some guy I'd done business with before flew that gator in and snuck it into my room," Tex continues. "Trying to throw me off my game, get in my head, since he was competing for the same contract. We had a good laugh about it over some bourbon in the lobby bar later. And I won over them investors in the end anyway. But, here now, do you know the point of me telling you this story?"

"Um . . . no, sir."

"The point is . . ." Tex stops and chomps on the unlit cigarette. "The point is . . . ah . . . Rick! What do you suppose the point of that story was?"

The guy in the business suit clears his throat.

"I suppose, sir, it likely had something to do with acting decisively in a time of crisis?"

"Yes!" Tex cries, slapping his knee. "Yes, that's it, dagnabbit. You see, the point is, son, you're in a surprising situation that you never could have imagined, just like I was then. But that don't mean bold action isn't still in order! A gator is comin' at your grandpappy's baseball team! Are you going to run away? Or are you going to start throwing cowboy boots, do everything you can, to figure this out and do your grandpa proud? You get what I'm asking you, son?"

I nod cautiously.

Tex nods and smiles.

"To be clear, I don't anticipate you fulfilling the terms of your grandpappy's and my agreement. This team ain't had but two winning seasons in the past seventeen years, after all! But the better effort you put forth, the less money I'll likely lose this final season. So, make no mistake, I *am* pulling for you, son, even though I aim to see you fail in the end. Make sense?"

I nod, even though it doesn't. I'm too distracted by one of the millions of questions swirling in my head to make sense of anything.

"Can kids my age even have jobs like this?"

"Of course they can!" Tex shouts. "I've been working since I was knee-high! Breaking mustangs and throwing hay before I could barely walk! My lawyers can work around any legal obstacles. That's what they're paid to do. Truth is, I think Ira was hoping you'd be just a little older when he finally kicked the bucket. But the situation is what it is, here and now, so we got to deal with it as best we can."

"But—"

"Rick will handle all the paperwork," Tex says, standing. "My plane is fueling up as we speak—I need to get back to Arkansas for some other business matters. But I'll be back in Weakburger later this week."

"Weakerville," I correct.

"Whatever. I'll be here off and on throughout the season, taking meetings with commercial developers and whatnot." Tex climbs into the row behind me and takes a few steps toward the door but then stops. "I almost forgot," he says, digging into the pocket of his bright yellow suit. "Ira wanted you to have this."

He hands me a slightly crumpled white envelope. A single word is scrawled on the front in my grandpa's familiar handwriting.

Alex

All I can do is sit there, looking at the letter in my hands, wondering what in the heck I'm going to do. I *have* to find a way to save the team. Until a few days ago, I didn't even know just how badly I needed the Hurricanes. But now it feels like nothing else matters.

All I have to do is somehow achieve the impossible.

Chapter 12

"WILL WE EVER BE DONE WITH THIS TEAM?"

That's my dad's reaction to the news. He's on the back patio, preparing a brisket. Pretty much all he does when he's not working is grill and smoke meats. His constant ranting about brines, dry rubs, sauces, and tinfoil would be sort of annoying if his hobby wasn't also so delicious.

He glances up and sees the look on my face and then shakes his head. "I didn't mean it like that, Alex. I just sometimes worry about how invested you are in this team."

He steps back toward his two grills, sighs softly, and then delicately inserts a metal thermometer into a giant hunk of meat resting inside his small smoker. He's always going on about his big dream to get a huge professional-grade smoker someday.

"Well, it's probably only for one final season," I say. "Unless I can somehow find a way to pull off a miracle and make the playoffs."

My dad forces a smile and claps me on the shoulder with a hand coated in rust-colored dry rub.

"Well, I wish I could help somehow. But you know how I feel about baseball."

"Yeah, Dad, I know," I say. "I'm sure you'll be too busy smoking meats anyway."

"Well, then you shall get none of this brisket tomorrow," he snaps. "If you are so dismissive of the care and commitment that I devote to my craft."

"Daaad, c'mon," I say. "I didn't mean it like that."

"Okay, fine," he relents with a grin. "You may have *one* slice."

But we both know it'll end up being a lot more than that. It would take being a vegetarian or having superpowers to have only one slice of his famous brisket. And he'd never refuse seconds or thirds to anyone. The one thing he loves more than making barbecue is seeing how much people enjoy eating it.

After helping him get his homemade barbecue sauce ready, I retreat to my room. I have a lot to figure out. I've been tasked with getting the Hurricanes to the playoffs, a feat that already feels impossible, even ignoring the fact that I'm a kid whose brains turn to mush in the company of people I admire—people such as professional baseball players.

But I *have* to find a way to get it done. Ira, for whatever reason, actually believed I could do this. I can't let him down.

Sitting on my bed, I look at the Hurricanes schedule hanging on my wall. Maybe I *can* do this? Yeah, I know a kid being the manager of a professional baseball team is just dumb. But I *do* know more about the numbers behind baseball than probably the whole town combined. And I have access to the same advanced metrics as major league managers. I compiled the data myself, after all. Metrics and data alone can lay out a reliable path to winning, if you know how to use them. Buddy LeForge didn't. But I do. Which is, at the very least, a start.

Is this what Ira thought too? Is that what his letter says?

I still haven't opened the envelope Tex gave me. Part of me doesn't want to. Once I read the last words my grandpa wrote to me, that's it. The last time I'll get to listen to him, in a way, forever. So, instead, I distract myself by taking the lid off one of the dozens of boxes of Ira's old game scorecards and notebooks he left me and pull a stack of scorecards from the box. They're slightly yellowed from age, but otherwise well cared for and safely stored since the day the games ended.

A baseball scorecard is supposed to be filled with names, numbers, and stats. My scorecards are neat and efficient; the marks are clean and simple. Anything else just distracts from the raw data indicating what transpired during the game, aside from a few notes on a pitcher's delivery or a hitch in the batter's swing.

But Grandpa Ira's scorecards are a mess. The margins are filled with writing, much of it tiny and scribbly. Almost every square inch of every scorecard is filled with notes. For instance, in the blank spaces on a scorecard for a game between the Hurricanes and Lincoln T-Bones from three years ago:

—Nigel Stern umping the dish. From Kearney. Remember: ask him after game if his house took

any tornado damage last week. Does he need time off? Maybe talk to commissioner on his behalf.

On another scorecard from later that season:

—Francisco is helluva player. Learn Spanish! I should be able to ask him how things are going with host family. Wish I could afford a translator for him . . .

From August that same season:

—Told Buddy to hold #46 from lineup. Trade to Yeti final tomorrow. Tough trade, but his sister is ill, and he needs to be closer to home. Fans will be mad at me, but it's the right move.

I remember that trade. Three years ago, Ira signed a catcher from Canada named Cormac Rader who wore number 46. He was our biggest off-season acquisition. Just two weeks into the season, he'd thrown out ten of eleven attempted base stealers and had fifteen hits in thirty-nine at bats. But then Ira inexplicably traded him to the Winnipeg Yeti. The fans were furious. An article in the *Weakerville Herald* the next day ended with this: ". . . the team's owner, Ira Weakerman, might finally be showing his age—and how out of touch he is with the game."

I was pretty angry about the trade myself—it hadn't made any sense. But when I asked my grandpa about it, all he said was, "Alex, I have my reasons. You have to trust me."

Now I finally know why he'd made one of the worst trades in the history of the team: to help a guy be closer to his sick sister. It shouldn't surprise me; that's the kind of person Ira was day in and day out.

But not all of the scorecard margin notes are so significant:

—I think lasagna for dinner tonight!

—Saw A.M. outside stadium again. Pretended he didn't know me. Again.

—Look into getting loafers. Tying shoes getting too difficult! Hah!

Grandpa Ira loved baseball and the Hurricanes. But, clearly, what he really cared about were people. The vendors, players, trainers, umpires. Their lives, their stories.

As I sit there on my bed, looking at the dozens of boxes of scorecards stacked all over my room, I realize the letter Tex gave me *won't* be Ira's final words. The notes on his scorecards weren't meant for me directly, but they're still his thoughts. And I have enough of those to last me at least through high school, probably a lot longer.

So, I finally exhale, set aside the scorecards, and tear open Ira's letter:

Alex, my boy,

I know what you're thinking right now: "Geez, thanks a lot, Grandpa, for giving me an impossible job!" Don't worry, you can be mad at me, I don't mind. I mean, I'm dead, right? Okay, bad joke, I know.

But listen: I did it because I BELIEVE in you. You know the team and this game better than anyone. If you trust yourself and your instincts, I know you can get this done. You can lead the Hurricanes to the playoffs for the first time in over a decade!

Getting this team to the playoffs would mean a lot, more than just a win for the team. When it happens (which I know it will! Because I have faith in you, Alex!), you will understand what I mean. I promise you can do this. You're smart. You got the numbers. And you got the grit, the Magic of Baseball in you, even if you don't know it yet.

I know what you're thinking: "Grandpa, pretty easy to make crazy promises when you're dead!" Okay, yes, another bad joke. Better not share this with your mother. How is she by the way? Probably not well. She'll be fine, though. She's a Weakerman, after all.

Point is: I'm sure you think this is impossible. I know you've calculated the odds, run those numbers you love so much, and they've told you there's no chance this team can become winners overnight. But if things always worked out the way everyone thinks they will, we'd never play a single game of baseball. We play the games because we don't know. We play because there's always a chance things will go differently than we expect, or even than we hope.

So I suppose I don't know whether you can succeed. But I BELIEVE you can. I've always believed in you more than you'll know.

I'm rambling now, so I'm going to say goodbye. Here, take Slips out for a J.R.'s famous old-fashioned double cheeseburger on me. For old times' sake!

Love,

Grandpa Ira

Paper-clipped to the back of the letter is a crumpled five-dollar bill. I stuff it into my pocket, trying to fight off the urge to cry or laugh or scream in frustration.

I'd been expecting some sort of sweet, encouraging note. Something about having some fun during the Hurricanes' last summer, living out some dream he thought I had of hanging out with a real baseball team before the Hurricanes were finally shut down. Or maybe, if I was lucky, he'd have had some sort of grand scheme, some logical plan that would help turn things around for the Hurricanes before the end of the season, something he wanted me to help him accomplish.

Instead, he apparently had some ridiculous notion that *I* could somehow do the impossible.

What was he thinking?

I figured he would have known I'd let him down. But apparently not. And now I was in the unenviable position of both losing the one thing he and I shared and letting him down in the worst possible way all at once.

His letter said: *We play the games because we don't*

know. We play because there's always a chance things will go differently than we expect, or even than we hope.

But he's wrong. Statistics are statistics because over time they've proven we can trust them. They can predict pretty much everything.

And the numbers definitely say that inexperienced, awkward *thirteen-year-old* managers can't turn around losing baseball teams.

There are three things I do when I'm feeling like this. Talking to Grandpa Ira was one, which is obviously out. Going to a Hurricanes game is option two, but the next home game isn't for a few days. So, that leaves me with just the third option:

I call Slips.

"Hey!" he says when he answers his house phone. "How was the game? Sorry I missed it. It was probably six or seven hours of nonstop excitement and thrills and—"

"Slips, listen," I say, and he shuts up immediately. "I'm the new manager of the Hurricanes."

I suppose most people's friends would assume this is a lame prank. But Slips knows me better than that. He knows I don't joke about the Hurricanes.

"Go on . . . ," he says.

I explain about Tex and his deal with Grandpa Ira that made me the new manager.

"Wow," Slips says at the end. "This is, like, your dream, right? You'll finally be able to put all that useless Hurricanes knowledge to use!"

"Yeah, but . . ." I stop, realizing I hadn't really thought about it like that yet. "I mean, sure, I guess that's true."

"Yeah, see?" Slips says. "It's going to be pretty awesome, to finally be able to *do something* with all that data you've got! It's pretty much the—Oh."

"What?"

"I'm on the *Weakerville Herald* website. You should check it out."

I pull up the site. On the front page is my school photo from last year—the one where Flumpo caused me to half close one eye at the exact wrong moment—and right below it, the headline:

New Manager of Local Baseball Team: Publicity Stunt or Exploitation?

I click a video embedded in the article—it's an interview with former manager Buddy LeForge, who I guess Tex has already fired. His normally stoic, unmoving face is red and sweaty as his angry voice fills my room:

". . . I've already (*bleep*) talked to the (*bleep*) players. (*Bleep*) half of 'em (*bleep*) said no way they're (*bleep*) playing for a (*bleep*) (*bleep*) (*bleep*) kid. (*Bleep*.) (*Bleep*.) Won't even (*bleep*) have a (*bleep*) team (*bleep*) (*bleep*) before the (*bleep*) end of the (*bleep*) season (*bleep*) (*bleep*) (*bleeeeeep*) and a . . ."

I hit mute as Buddy LeForge continues to spit words into the reporter's microphone. A pixel cloud appears over his mouth several times, at one point staying there for nearly ten full seconds.

"Hey, don't worry about that guy," Slips says. "Ira always knew what he was doing, right? And you know more about baseball than any person I know. You just have to manage them like you managed those baseball teams of wizards and goblins and dragons and stuff on your computer."

"Slips, fantasy baseball isn't actual—"

"Look, my point is, once the players see how much you know about the game, you'll win them over. And if the team is winning, no one's going to care if you're a kid! You're going to knock everyone's socks off."

I can tell he really believes it. He's not just trying to make me feel better.

"But the team hasn't been good in so long," I say. "And the season is already more than halfway over. . . ."

"Hey," Slips cuts in, "did you trust Ira?"

"Well, I mean—"

"Did you trust Ira, yes or no?"

"Of course," I give in. "More than anyone."

"Okay. So why can't you trust him now? He believed you could do this."

I look down at the letter. My eyes seem to find a single line on their own: *I've always believed in you more than you'll know.*

Maybe Slips is right? If Ira was convinced I could do this, maybe I actually can? After all, who was more likely to be right: *Me* or *Ira*? When I thought about it that way, just trusting the numbers meant I was actually more likely to succeed than fail.

But that still didn't tell me *how.*

How, exactly, could I pull this off?

Chapter 13

MY FIRST TEAM MEETING AS MANAGER OF THE HURRICANES IS THE NEXT morning.

I should be nervous. The fate of the team is on the line. Plus, I'm about to face a whole room of professional athletes who, if I'm being honest, already have a lot of reasons to be upset about this. I mean, who would want a thirteen-year-old boss? I don't know if they're going to laugh at me or yell at me.

It's a recipe for a Flumpo catastrophe.

But, somehow, I'm still excited. I've got some of my statistics and data from my Hurricanes archive with me in a huge backpack. I know everything about the team's lineup, their strengths and weaknesses, plus all of our opponents' as well. I'm definitely prepared, at least in the baseball sense.

I make my way through the deserted hallways of Mustard Park, eventually descending the cement stairs down into the Hurricanes locker room. It looks the same as the last time Ira brought me down here. Faded green metal lockers line the walls. The concrete floor is stained with a grimy film of history. The room is dark and quiet and smells like half a century of accumulated sweat and beer and tobacco with just a touch of leather.

I could stand here all day and smell this filthy room, but getting caught sniffing old stains on a locker room floor is probably not the best way to start my first day as team manager.

But I don't need to worry about that, because for the first twenty minutes of the meeting, no one shows up. I spend some time going through my notes again, but eventually start wondering if I'm in the wrong place or got the time wrong.

That's when I hear footsteps and hushed voices coming down the hallway. They stop just outside the locker room.

The door opens, and there they are.

Even though I've spent nearly every day of my summer thinking about these guys, it's still something else entirely to see them up close, in their Hurricanes warm-up uniforms, just a few feet away from me.

There's Phil "the Law" Sheriff, veteran pitcher and team captain, who looks much older in person than I thought he would. His brown hair is streaked with gray and white that can't be seen from the stands.

Sonny "Mayhem" Mayhew, our closer and team goofball, follows him into the room. He's known more for his antics on and off the field than actual talent. I can't help but admire his wild sideburns and tattoo-covered arms.

While Mayhem is surprisingly short in person, Oliver "Big Fish" Salmon, our best offensive weapon and my current favorite player, is the opposite. I knew he was huge, but up close, he completely fills the locker-room doorway. He looks more like a statue of a human being than an actual human being.

Eight players arrive in all and take seats on the benches around the room. I flip through one of my scorebooks, trying to remain calm. But I can already feel Flumpo making my palms sweaty and mouth dry.

I wait for the rest of the team. After a few minutes, the silence, the way everyone is looking around the room at anything but me, is getting a bit awkward. The sweat that had beaded on my forehead when the players first walked in is now trickling down my face in thin streams. My back is already soaked.

Someone without Flumpo would crack a joke right now. They'd say something like, *The rest of the team stuck in traffic?* Which is a real knee-slapper in a Midwest town with a population of just over ten thousand.

But instead, Flumpo makes me say this:

"So, um," I stammer, my voice cracking. "Rest traffic stucks . . . er, I mean, uh, where is the rest of the pla-uys . . . ?"

I get caught up between saying *players* and *guys* and instead invent a totally new word—a pretty common occurrence for those of us with Flumpo. But nobody seems to notice. They simply look like they want to be *anywhere* else but here.

"They're not coming," John Amdor, our backup catcher, finally says.

If my sweating were a dripping faucet, it now feels like someone has cranked it open all the way. "Wha . . . What?"

"They're. Not. Coming," Amdor repeats slowly.

"But . . . why?" I say stupidly, trying to rub the stinging sweat from my squinting eyes. "I mean, it's just . . . they're . . . man, it's hot in here. Is it . . . is it always this hot in here?"

They stare at me, dumbfounded.

"Why isn't the team coming?" I finally manage to say.

"Is there even a team anymore?" Mayhem asks, scratching one of his massive sideburns irritably. I notice that our closer has letters tattooed on both sets of knuckles that spell out: SAVE THIS. "First, Ira passes away—may he rest in peace—and we hear some yahoo from Texas or wherever has taken over the team. Then Coach Buddy is fired, and a kid—no offense, but what are you, like, ten years old?—a *kid* is named *manager.* It sounds to me like this *team* is finished."

"But, no, it's not," I say, suddenly aware of how whiny I sound. "I mean, um, *we're* not. My grandpa, he, like, he made me manager because he wants . . . *wanted* the team to actually win and—"

A few of the players laugh. The rest shake their heads sadly.

"I'm serious!" I say. Realizing things can't get any worse, my Flumpo actually starts to go away. "I know it sounds ridiculous, like a big joke or whatever. But I *know* baseball. And I know a lot about all of you—enough to know that we can win more games than we're winning now."

The laughter dies down, but the looks on their faces are even sadder than they were before.

I press on. "Mr. Mayhem! I mean, Mr. Mayhew. Mayhem. That's your nickname. You already know that." I stop and take a breath while our closer, still standing, raises an eyebrow at me. "You could be leading the league in save percentage. You have a solid WHIP in innings where you get the first hitter out. But you let the leadoff man on base forty-eight percent of the time, and that runner comes around to score at a thirty-six-percent rate, way above the league average. It's because you're throwing your slider too much, and the data shows it's not as effective when you're short-striding with a man on first."

If this makes any sense to Mayhem, he doesn't show

it. He just squints at me. I move on.

"Mr. Hof. Joe Hof. Joe," I stumble, turning to our shortstop. How am I supposed to address these guys? Am I allowed to use their first names? I should have thought about this before I showed up. "Your rookie year, you had a lot of opposite field hits. Sixty-three percent of them came in two-strike counts. But this season, even though your home-run rate has gone up, so have your strike-outs. And your fly-ball outs to left are off the charts. The numbers indicate you're trying to pull the ball too much. You'd be more effective shortening your swing, like you did with two strikes your rookie year."

He looks up like he's thinking about what I said, but all he says is, "Jof."

"Huh?"

"Just Jof," Joe Hof says. "That's what everyone calls me. Jof."

"Um, okay," I say, not sure how else to respond. And so I move on to the Law. "Phil—sorry, Mr. Law. I mean, Mr. Law Sheriff." It feels like my Flumpo is trying to make a return now. "I know you've been struggling to command secondary pitches, and—"

"You can stop," the Law says. "Look—Alan, is it, right?"

It's not my name, but I nod anyway.

"You seem like a good kid, and you definitely know your stuff when it comes to the team. So I'm going to level with you." He stands up, grabs a baseball off a table, works it over in his hands while he speaks. "You could be the best manager to ever walk into the Hurricanes dugout, or you could be the worst. We could win, we could lose. That's not really what we're worried about right now. I mean, it's not like we were winning games with Buddy as the manager. But you need to understand what this team means to us. For some, it's still that dream to eventually make it to the majors. For others, it's to keep playing the game we love, to use up that last bit of baseball we have left. Either way, for a lot of us, it's a job, part of how we support our families. But what I'm really saying is, we *all* depend on the team, on the idea that it'll be around every day when we show up to the ballpark."

"He's right," Mayhem adds. "We might not always win or have the biggest crowds, but Ira kept signing the checks and made sure we always had a team. What's happened since your grandpa died makes us wonder how much longer that will be the case. I'll be straight with you: most of the players who didn't show, it wasn't because this whole thing feels like a joke. Or because they don't want a kid for a manager. They just figured they needed to start looking for other teams to play for . . . or other jobs entirely."

"Baseball is what we love," the Law continues, squeezing the ball in his hand tightly. "We'll do almost anything to play. But to keep showing up for a new owner who's never even seen us play before and a manager who's still in middle school . . . believing that the people we're playing for are as serious about this as we are, well, that seems like a lot to take on faith."

"Be honest with us, kid," says James Duderkirk, one of our back-of-the-rotation pitchers. "We deserve to know the truth. . . . Is this thing over? Is Tex Cohaagen going to shut the team down?"

Eight pairs of eyes stare at me, all of them dejected, angry, and maybe above all, sad. They stare at me as if I have any idea what to say. But what can I say? I might have talked myself into believing I could help the team win some games, but this isn't about winning *some* games. The only way winning matters at all is if we make the playoffs. And at 19–30, with forty-one games left, that would require an unprecedented mid-season turnaround.

I don't know what the heck I'm supposed to do. Of

course, they deserve to know what's going on: that if we don't make the playoffs, the team is actually done for, just like they suspect.

But . . . if I actually *tell* them that, they'll probably *all* walk out, right here and now.

Helping these guys keep their jobs, not letting Grandpa Ira down, saving the Hurricanes . . . I can't do any of that if I don't have an actual team of players.

So, I do what I have to.

"No, no . . . I mean, of course not," I say. "Mr. Cohaagen—Tex—he's just as committed to the team as my grandpa. And so am I."

They're not smiling or celebrating or anything like that, but they're also not leaving either.

"But, I mean, the thing is it'd probably be better if we can, y'know, find a way to win some games and stuff."

I have no idea what I'm saying. Every word makes me feel worse. And the team doesn't look encouraged.

"So, practice tomorrow?" Mayhem asks. "Guys?"

"I guess," the Law says with a sigh. "As long as we're not going to show up and find out we have to work the hot dog stand in order to earn a paycheck."

"You will absolutely get paid for every practice and

game this season," I say. At least that part isn't a lie, since Tex legally has to support the team through the end of the season.

"What about the rest of the team?" Mayhem asks as they stand up to leave. "Most of the other guys aren't coming back."

It's the first time it dawns on me that I apparently have only eight players left. I try not to let my panic show. Their commitment already feels like it's hanging by a thread.

"Tex will fix that," I say, hoping it's true—because *I* definitely don't have a solution. "We'll have a team."

Everyone shuffles out, looking more depressed than when they came in.

Then I'm alone.

I lean over one of the benches and take a bunch of deep breaths. What the heck was I thinking? I'd expected my biggest obstacle to be convincing them I know enough about baseball to manage a team. But now I don't even have enough players to fill a lineup. You don't have to know baseball or have an advanced grasp of sabermetrics to know that you can't win games without players.

I'm definitely going to let Grandpa Ira down. There's

no denying reality here: the team is in even worse shape than I thought. I calculate our chances of winning even just ten games at about 1.1 percent. And our odds at making the playoffs are around 0.000000001 percent.

I can only hope Tex at least has an idea for getting us some more players.

Chapter 14

ON MY WAY TO MUSTARD PARK'S FRONT OFFICE, I'M INTERCEPTED BY A media swarm.

Okay, so it's just two small camera crews from the local NBC and FOX stations and one newspaper guy, Ben Reyerson, a reporter for the *Weakerville Herald* and also my dad's brother-in-law.

They start pointing cameras and aiming cell phones at me, peppering me with questions:

"Alex, care to comment on the rumor the players are boycotting the rest of the season?"

"Alex, how is Mr. Cohaagen bypassing child labor laws?"

"Alex, what do you make of people saying this is just a cheap publicity stunt to save a failing team in a dying sport?"

"Alex, people are calling Tex Cohaagen an exploitative monster. What are your thoughts?"

"Alex, Uncle Benny here, any word on your dad eventually paying me back for the money I loaned him? He won't return my calls."

Before I can stammer out any answers, Tex—apparently back already from Arkansas—shows up like a knight in shining turquoise suit and white cowboy hat, stepping between me and the reporters.

"What are y'all doing inside the ballpark on an off day?" he shouts. "Give the poor boy some space—don't you know that his *grandpappy just passed*?"

The reporters step back. Then Tex kindly asks them to leave using an assortment of swear-word combinations so colorful I'm convinced he made them up.

As the media scurries away, Tex faces me with the unlit cigarette still chomped between his teeth.

"Son!" he barks with a grin. "You look like an armadillo

that just found a dead body! Come to quit already? It's just your first day on the job!"

Tex laughs hoarsely and leads me into his office. It's the same one Grandpa Ira used, but I'd seen the inside only once or twice. Grandpa preferred to be wandering the stadium talking to people rather than sitting inside an office by himself.

Tex removes the unlit cigarette from his mouth as he sits down in a massive leather chair that definitely wasn't Ira's. He motions to the other side of a new sprawling, shiny, polished wood desk and I sit down across from him.

"What's on your mind, son?" he asks, his sharp eyes barely visible beneath the brim of his huge white cowboy hat.

"Well, um . . ." I start. "I—I think we have to forfeit our next game. . . ."

"*What?*" Tex nearly shouts. "Why on earth would we do that? Look, I know you got all sorts of newfangled baseball strategies rolling around in your noggin, but that don't make a lick of sense, no matter how you play it."

"Well, no, it's just that, uh . . . we don't have a full team."

Tex stares at me blankly for a moment. Then he taps the unlit cigarette over a clean ashtray and clamps it back in his teeth.

"We still got forty-one games we're contractually obligated to play. Forfeiting any of those games loses me even more money! I *hate* losing money. So, no. No, we ain't forfeiting any games. Now, what's all this business about not having a team?"

I quickly explain what happened at my first meeting, emphasizing the part where just eight players showed up. When I'm finished, blood is pounding in my ears, and I'm so panicked I can barely see straight.

That's when Tex bursts out laughing. It's not the reaction I expected.

"That's *all*?" he says. "Shoot, son, you actually had me worried for a second."

"Wh-what?"

Tex smiles.

"Have I ever told you about my time growing up in central Arkansas?"

"Uh . . . no?"

"Back in Arkansas," Tex says, shaking his head with a mixture of fondness, and perhaps some resentment, "my daddy used to operate a Southern revival tent church. You know what that is?"

"No, sir."

"Ain't that a shame," he says mournfully. "Well, son, it's a church inside a tent that moves from place to place. Kind of like a circus, but without the elephants." He punctuates this with a bout of hoarse belly laughs. "Revivals ain't as popular now. But back when I was about as high as you, well, you best be knowing people come from *all over* to hear my daddy preach. Shoot, son! He had a way with words that could melt the jewelry right off people's ears. And so, my daddy became right popular, so popular we was greeted in each new town by mobs of people wanting to help us set up the tent and this, that, and the other. Then we'd pack that tent full as a pregnant heifer's gut with worshippers. Thousands of folks. One time, I swear to Lucy, we had that tent so full, you couldn't see nothing but the tops of heads and mists of sweat. You ever been in a tent with three thousand people on a hunnert-and-ten-degree day?"

I shake my head, wondering if it's possible anyone could survive such a thing.

"Well, the smell . . ." Tex laughs again. "You ever want

to know the *true* smell of people, then you get yourself to a good old-fashioned tent revival in the hog's belly of an Arkansas summer. Anyway, it was none too pleasant, but the folks there didn't care so much. They hardly noticed the heat and smells and such. Now, why do you suppose that is?"

"Um . . . because they were having fun, probably?"

"Yes!" Tex says, his eyes gleaming. "More than that, though, they was *feeling* the *presence* of the Lord. They *believed*. My daddy could do that to just about anyone . . . that no good, crooked, lying old son of a . . . Well, anyway, that ain't so much the point as it is the example. You get what I'm saying, son?"

When I don't answer right away, Tex furrows his brow. I stare at him a moment and wonder if a burst of hoarse laughter will follow shortly. But it doesn't. He just looks at me like he's too busy for this.

"Um . . . maybe?" I finally say.

Then, finally, mercifully, Tex does laugh. "Well, c'mon now, think it over a second, son."

He waits.

"Umm . . ."

"Son." Tex sighs. "The point being, now, listen up here: if you can inspire people, they'll follow you *anywhere*.

And inspiration is about believing the impossible might just be possible. The root of inspiration is belief."

I don't know what else to do but nod. I can't possibly take the time to explain the intricacies of Flumpo to him. About how people like me can't inspire *anyone* to do *anything*, except maybe look away in embarrassment. Let alone get them to believe in miracles.

"Okay, good," Tex says with a nod of his own. "Now, moving on: we ain't the Atlanta Braves. The Hurricanes don't have no scouting departments or player development staff or all that rigmarole. Ain't ever been a need. Buddy had a few assistant coaches who'd been doing just fine with scouting. But here's the thing: all his assistant coaches quit this morning. So, at the present time, you're on your own. And let's be clear: ain't *nobody* alive that knows so much about any one thing that they don't need help. You understand?"

"Yeah," I say, nodding. "I think I get it."

"Great!" Tex nearly shouts, slapping the table with a massive palm. "That's a good first step. You've got full authority to cut and sign whatever coaches and players you please, at league minimum salaries of course. Just let Rick know. Remember him, from the other day? He'll take care of the financial and legal carry-on. I don't care how you find players—heck, sign golden retrievers to play if that's what it takes. We ain't forfeiting a single game! Forfeited games mean refunded tickets, which I can't abide."

"Um, yes, sir . . ." I say, standing up to leave. "And, uh, thanks. For being so nice and everything."

Tex explodes with laughter.

"Well, shoot, son!" he cries between guffaws. "I ain't no monster. Regardless of the issues that was between your grandpappy and me, kin is kin. And you and I is kin, distant or otherwise." He gets quiet for a moment, his smile disappearing. But then it's back just as quickly. "Okay, now you git on out of here. You got a job to do."

It occurs to me, as I'm leaving his office, that his story about tent church revivals might actually be the key to my salvation after all. What I need is for my team to really *believe* that we can make the playoffs. Like Tex said, I need to find a way to get them inspired. Which, obviously, won't be from me. But like Tex also said: nobody can do a job like this alone. So, it's clear I need help. Not just any help. I need someone who can keep the team's spirits high. Someone who has the sort of charisma that people are drawn to. Someone who can inspire a group of people to ignore logic, ignore all the unpleasantries of our situation, and simply believe that we can make the impossible possible.

And if I had to pick one person to lead a modern-day tent church revival, who would that one person be?

Chapter 15

SLIPS AND HIS DAD LIVE IN A JUNKYARD ON THE EDGE OF TOWN.

Their trailer literally sits in the middle of huge piles of junk, garbage, and old, rusty vehicles. Zajac's Junk and Salvage is basically a massive lot of scrap, surrounded on all sides by a barbwire fence.

My taxi, which I paid for with a team credit card Tex gave me, drops me off in front of the large double-wide trailer.

Slips's dad answers the door shortly after I knock.

"What you want?" Jerzy—pronounced Yer-Zee, but

everyone just calls him George—asks gruffly. "You come to work?"

Jerzy might make a living salvaging other people's junk, but don't let his job fool you. He's easily the most highly educated man in Weakerville, having two doctorates (engineering and biomechanics) from Gdańsk University of Technology and the University of Warsaw.

"I can't work now," I say.

"You always say this." He moves aside so I can enter. "When do you work? What is more important than working? Why do you never work?"

"Well, technically, I am working right now—"

"At what job?" he demands. "I don't see shovel in your hand. Or a computer in your satchel. What job is this that you get to stand here and do nothing? Huh?"

"I'm the new manager of the Hurricanes. . . ."

"*Baseball?*" Jerzy scoffs. "*This* is considered job? Baseball is not real job."

"Dad!" Slips shouts from the hallway. "Stop always trying to make my friends work."

"Why?" Jerzy says angrily. "Kids are lazy. You do not work enough. It builds character. And strength of mind and arm."

"Dad, go watch *Friends* or something."

Jerzy is obsessed with an old TV show called *Friends*. Whenever he's not working, he sits in front of an ancient TV and yells at the screen as fuzzy, VHS tapes play the entire series over and over. To me, the lame show looks more boring than watching the junk outside collect dust, but a lot of old people love it for some reason.

Slips turns to me. "Come on, let's get out of here. I'm hungry. You hungry?"

"Of course he is hungry, you are both always hungry," Jerzy calls out as he retreats back to his den. "Like bears waking from long hibernation."

Slips and I hop onto Yoda and head to Cheese'N Stuff Pizza. Twenty minutes later, we're settled into our usual booth near the back.

"How'd the meeting go?" Slips asks before nearly draining his 32 oz. Pepsi in one massive swig.

"Well, that's why I wanted to talk to you."

He belches so loudly a woman sitting with her toddler at a nearby table glares at us, shaking her head in disapproval.

"Sorry, ma'am," Slips says with a grin. "I did not realize there was a child present."

She rolls her eyes, but then smiles and goes back to cutting up a slice of pizza for her kid.

"I want you to be my assistant coach," I say as our large pepperoni pizza arrives.

Slips is exactly the sort of person I need. Everyone likes him: adults, teens, old people, little kids, babies, animals . . . even moms. Even, apparently, when he's belching in front of them. If anyone can win over the players, keep their spirits up, and help me convince them we can actually win, it's Slips.

"Wow," Slips says softly. "I'd be *honored*. Do I get to yell at the players when they make mistakes? Can I hit them on the shins with a cane? Is caning allowed in coaching these days?"

"Probably not," I say, laughing, as I pull three slices of pizza onto my plate. "Is that a deal breaker?"

"Nope. Do I get paid?"

"Um, I think so," I say. "I'll have to ask Rick. He's the team's director of accounting."

"Ooh, this sounds like a *fancy* job," Slips says, folding up an entire slice of pizza into a cube. Grease drips from the corners of the folds and pools onto his plate. "You're fancy now. Pretty soon you'll be wearing designer suits and polished shoes with gold-plated heels."

He stuffs the entire slice of pizza into his mouth like he always does with the first slice, and then chews it with great care, his cheeks bulging. Red grease drips down his chin.

"So . . . you're in?"

Slips's grin is warped by the obscene amount of pizza inside his mouth as he nods vigorously. He eventually finishes his massive bite, swallowing with some difficulty.

"I assume this is a lifetime appointment, and I can tender my junkyard resignation to my dad?"

"Well . . . I mean, maybe," I say, not sure just how much to tell him.

"Oh, I know that look," Slips says. "It means you're either about to unleash an SBD gasser on that poor kid over there, or you're holding something back."

"What if it's both?" I joke, trying to avoid having to tell the truth.

He pulls his shirt up over his nose. "Okay, go for it."

"Well, there's apparently this weird stipulation in the contract," I explain as he pulls his shirt back down. "If we don't make the playoffs this year, then Tex is allowed to dissolve the team and sell the stadium. No more Hurricanes."

"*Cholera!*" he says in Polish, pounding the table. "What did the players say?"

"Uhhhh . . ."

"You didn't tell them?" Slips raises his eyebrows before diving back in for another slice of pizza.

"I couldn't," I say quickly. "They were about to walk out! If they knew that Tex doesn't care and just wants to sell the team, they would have been gone, and then I'd have no players at all. You have to promise me you won't tell *anyone* about this. If we're going to have any hope of making the playoffs and saving the team, we need players."

Slips shakes his head, but I can tell he knows I'm right.

"I don't like it," he says. "I don't agree with it. I'm generally not a liar. But . . . you're the boss. The secret is safe with me."

"Thanks."

He shrugs.

"So, what's with this sudden *the team can't ever end* talk?" he asks, pointing a slice of pizza at me like a giant floppy finger.

"What do you mean? I *love* the Hurricanes. . . ."

"I know that, but at the beginning of summer when I brought up the new A-Mart, you said to me: 'nothing lasts forever, old things get left behind, and new things move in, it's inevitable.' Or something like that. What happened to *that* Alex?"

I do remember saying that. And I still feel that way, generally. But . . .

"The Hurricanes are different."

"How?" Slips challenges. "Just because it's something *you* care about?"

"No, it's not like that . . . ," I say. "I think it . . . well, to be honest, I'm even not sure myself. Maybe I just always took them for granted? Figured they'd always be around. I never thought they'd be in real danger. Not like this. Not so suddenly."

"Okay." He nods. "So, let's save this team. What's the first step?"

"We need another coach, probably. Buddy LeForge's entire coaching staff quit when he was fired, so right now it's just you and me. I feel like it would be good to have at least one coach with actual playing experience. Plus, we need another base coach besides me."

"Well, you know I'd do it, but I don't even know what all the bases are called," Slips says. "I know one is Dwelling Dinner Tray or something like that. And the one across from it is called, like, Echobase, right? And isn't one of them called Left Base?"

"Yeah, exactly." I laugh and grab another slice of pizza.

"I was thinking maybe one of the Little League coaches in town?"

Slips slams the table with his palm. Our Pepsis rattle and the lady at the next table scowls again.

"Forget that!" he shouts. "I've got a better idea. Aliyah Perkins!"

"Are you serious?" Visions pop into my head, of me trying to talk to her, of me dumping my hot dogs in the trash. "Do you think she'd even want the job?"

"Why not?"

"Well, it would be working with *me*, for one," I say. "Plus, she'd have to skip the rest of her final Little League season."

"Yeah, but you talk all the time about what an amazing pitcher she is. And if she loves this dumb, boring sport as much as you say, she'll at least consider it. Plus, remember your grandpa's memorial service? She's, like, indebted to Ira."

"I don't know . . ."

"You just don't want to ask her," Slips says. "Come on, I'll go with you. We'll ask her together."

I nod, unable to deny that having Aliyah as my pitching coach is a genius idea. Aliyah Perkins knows as much about pitching as anyone. The way she works counts, commands the zone, and repeats her delivery with such precision is masterful. Even the LLWS announcers on ABC said as much last summer.

She's perfect for the job.

But would I be able to do *my* job with her around? Flumpo already feels like a massive obstacle when it comes to coaching players. And nobody makes it flare up more than Aliyah. With her around, I'd be lucky not to somehow accidentally start my own hair on fire at the beginning of practice. Part of me actually hopes she'll turn down the offer.

But another, smarter part of me knows we need her.

Chapter 16

EVERYONE KNOWS ALIYAH PERKINS SPENDS HER FREE TIME AT THE batting cages, so it's not a surprise to find her at the rec center.

But I am surprised she greets me with an enthusiastic smile and wave.

"Hey, Weakerman," she says. "I heard about you on the news!"

My gut instantly floods with Flumpo.

"Oh, yeah," I mumble. "The news that was, um, on the news."

"Ha! Nice one, Alex," Slips says, slapping me on the shoulder like I was making an ironic joke.

"Slips!" Aliyah looks relieved to have someone with a functioning brain to talk to. "I never thought I'd see you here. You *hate* baseball, don't you?"

"Just here with this guy." Slips grins, nudging me with his elbow. "He has something to ask you."

"Um, okay . . ." Aliyah says.

She looks like she's expecting me to ask her out and she's already mentally scrambling to come up with fourteen or fifteen excuses that won't hurt my feelings. Which only muddles up my brains even more.

"I, uh, yeah," I say, staring at her sneakers. "If that's, you know, okay, and everything, to ask you a question, I mean . . . I, like, knew you'd be here . . . but not in a creepy way . . . uh—"

"Just ask her!" Slips cuts in, trying to save me.

Here, someone without Flumpo would say:

I know it's your last year of Little League eligibility, but I have a can't-miss opportunity for you. A chance to make history as the youngest pitching coach in professional baseball history. With your knowledge, we can get the Hurricanes back to the playoffs and become a dynasty again! Help me turn this team from a joke back into the stuff of legends!

But what I actually say is:

"Um, hi, hello. Er, I guess I already said hi. But double hi. Triple hi, I guess, counting the previous hello."

Slips hits me with a subtle elbow.

"I know you're busy with league eligible history, but we can, uh, make a young dynasty. From the team, I mean. The team. Help me make a joke of this team. Legend, I mean, a legendary joke . . . wait, can I start over?"

Aliyah's staring at me. Gawking, really, as if trying to figure out whether to laugh or call the hospital because I'm having some kind of medical emergency.

"Don't call the hospital!" I blurt out.

Slips finally realizes I'm not going to get it together and steps in. "What my buddy is trying to ask you is whether you'd like to *join us* on the Hurricanes coaching staff? He wants you to be the pitching and assistant coach."

"Are you serious?" she says, looking at Slips, then at me.

"Well, only if you are?" I say, knowing this makes no sense. But, unable to take the words back, I incoherently stumble on. "Um, that is, only if you want me to be? Serious, I mean . . ."

"You want *me* to help coach the Hurricanes?"

I nod, out of breath for some reason.

Aliyah grinds the end of her baseball bat into the gravel outside the batting cage.

"Man, I've never really thought about coaching," she finally says. "Right now I'm still kinda focused on playing. Plus, my dad and coach and team are depending on me. They need me. Maybe next year?"

"Well, I mean, it's sort of, well, a . . ." I'm struggling to find a way to tell her there probably won't be a next year, but Slips stops me.

"Hang on, Aliyah," he interrupts. "Can Alex and I have a second?"

She shrugs.

Slips leads me a few feet away and we huddle up with our backs to her.

"You *can't* tell her about the deal with Tex!" Slips says.

"You're the one who doesn't like us lying. . . ."

"I know, and I still don't," Slips says. "And *this* is why. Now that the lie has started, you can't tell *anyone* else. She'll never do this if we tell her it's only for one season."

"But maybe it won't be?" I suggest. "Maybe with her help we can actually pull this off?"

A smile spreads across his face.

"Yes!" he says. "I like that angle. Let's use that. It's not lying, it's just selective information."

I want to tell him that I wasn't coming up with an angle; I was being serious. I still think we can maybe pull this off. But Slips has already broken our huddle and is leading me back over to Aliyah.

"Go on, buddy, make the pitch," he says.

"Well, I was, um," I start, then take a deep breath. "I was just telling Slips that I think we can actually make the playoffs this year."

"*Playoffs?*" she scoffs, rolling her eyes. "The *Hurricanes*?"

"We know it sounds crazy," Slips says. "But that's what will make this so special. Imagine being a part of the groundbreaking coaching team full of kids that restores this team to glory! Not just making the playoffs this year, but the next, and the next!"

"A dynasty," I manage to add.

"Ira thought we could do it," Slips continues. "It was his dying wish. But we need your skills. Alex knows the numbers side of baseball, sure, but that's not enough."

"You were in my gym class," I remind her. "You saw my athletic abilities. . . ."

Aliyah grimaces apologetically, apparently remembering with excruciating detail all of my many embarrassing gym Flumpscapades.

My face is turning red.

"Ira *really* believed the Hurricanes could make the playoffs?" she finally says.

"He did," Slips and I both say in unison.

"It *would* be a dream come true to be on a real professional baseball team, even if it's just as a coach," she says. "How many people get to say they reached their dream at thirteen?" When we don't answer, she just grins and nods. "Okay, I'm in!"

She seems shocked after saying this, as if she can't believe she actually agreed.

"Really?" I say. "Are—are you sure?"

"No," she says. "Yes, I mean. Yes, I'm sure. Sorry, it's just that, normally for a decision like this I'd have to go to my dad. And my coach. They make a lot of decisions for me. But I *can't* bring this to them. They'd probably tell me not to do it. My coach for sure would. But I don't care—this time I'm deciding for *myself*. I'm in!"

I hold out Rick Larsen's business card.

"Okay, just, um, call this guy? He'll take care of the paperwork and stuff."

She takes the card and stuffs it into her pocket, then pulls out her phone.

"I can't wait to tell Ellie! Her head might literally explode!"

It's sinking in now that Aliyah is passing up her final Little League season. That adds even more pressure to find a way to make the playoffs. I'm so nervous that I almost forget our biggest problem.

"There is just one little tiny . . . issue," I say.

"Um, okay?" Aliyah says, still in the middle of texting her friend.

"We, uh, kinda, sorta . . . don't have a full team."

Aliyah finally looks up from her phone, brow scrunched. "What do you mean?"

I stumble my way through an account of how most of the team quit.

"Apparently," I explain, "twelve of the twenty-two-player roster signed separation papers, releasing them from their contracts. The Hurricanes are officially down to just ten active players. . . ."

Aliyah gasps.

Slips lets out a low, long whistle.

"But we still have our *best* player," I say desperately, holding up a crumpled sheet of paper. "Big Fish is still on the team . . . see . . ."

Aliyah examines the names on the printed roster, shaking her head slowly the whole time. Then she sighs.

"What are we going to do?" she asks. "I don't even have a full rotation. And we both know the Law needs to move to the bullpen. So, that means I'm down to Billy-freaking-Kringle and his bloated six-five-five ERA? That's not even a decent *one-man* rotation!"

Aliyah's been a coach for two minutes, and she's already at the same level of panic I am.

"Maybe I can call the players who quit and convince them to come back?" Slips suggests. "Can we double their salaries?"

"Tex would never approve that," I say.

We spend the next few moments standing there in silence. The only sound is the intermittent *crack* of someone in a batting cage.

"Well, what would Ira do?" Slips eventually asks, throwing a hand onto my shoulder.

I take a deep breath. The truth is, I have no clue how Ira would solve this problem. That's why Ira was Ira, and

I'm *me*. Some actual crickets near the batting cage fence sing out during my dumbfounded silence.

"I obviously didn't know Ira as well as you," Aliyah finally says. "But I don't think he'd care how *good* any new players were. He'd just want to find players who want to be Hurricanes. Who'd show up every day, love what they do, and try their best."

"Now you're talking!" Slips says. "How do we find people like that?"

"I know plenty of people like that around here," she says.

"Which means?" Slips leads her.

"An open tryout!" Aliyah says. "Tomorrow morning. Come one, come all—it doesn't even matter if you've played ball before. *Any* team has a better chance to win than no team. This is the only way."

"I think it sounds fun!" Slips says. "Like watching a live-action blooper real!"

"But we need to . . ." I say. "I mean, we're trying to make the playoffs! Random people off the street aren't going to make the playoffs. . ."

"Who says that random people off the street can't play?" Aliyah says, taking a step toward me. "Besides, what's the other option? Giving up? You're a quitter?

Instead of fighting to overcome obstacles, you'll walk away and come up with excuses why it was impossible? Is that really what Ira would do, Weakerman?"

It's a cheap shot, but it's effective. Plus, she's right. This is why she pitches like an ace in the biggest moments. This is why she's never lost a game as a starting pitcher her whole career. And this is why she's perfect for this job.

She's everything I'm not.

"You're right," I say. "Open tryouts it is."

"Weakerman, we're going to do this," Aliyah assure me. "If Ira said we can make the playoffs, then we will."

"Well, all I know is that you've got good taste in coaches, Alex," Slips says with a grin. "You couldn't have hired two better all-around people. Not just in baseball, I mean. Aliyah and I, we're just great kids in general. Class-A *heroes* of the working class, you know. The People's Coaches."

We all laugh.

I'm already feeling better now that I have help. Aliyah and I know baseball, and Slips is the perfect guy to convince the team to give us a chance to prove it.

But now the real question is: Can an open tryout really produce a team capable of winning a single game, let alone making the playoffs?

I can see why Aliyah would think so. She's won games on some truly terrible Little League teams. She's that good. She doesn't even know how losing happens.

But me, well, I've got a whole lifetime of failures behind me. And all that past data tells me that Ira was probably *wrong*.

Numbers don't lie, and the numbers are still saying we don't stand a chance.

Chapter 17

THE NEXT MORNING, I'M STANDING ON THE FIELD AT MUSTARD PARK FOR the first time as manager of the team.

I'm trying to make a moment of it.

"So, *this* is what it feels like to be *on* the rink court," Slips says, interrupting that moment.

"It's called a *field*," I say through a laugh. "Or *diamond* if you want to get old-school."

"Whatever, rink, court, field, gemstone . . . same thing," Slips says with a grin that makes me hope he's just joking around.

Then he starts sprinting around the bases backward, cackling like a lunatic. All I can do is laugh with him as he rounds third and heads for second, holding his arms out like an airplane.

By the time the unprecedented mid-season tryout officially begins at 8:00 a.m., I've pretty much given up hope that someone like Derek Jeter will show up out of retirement boredom. Which is unfortunate, because we could use as many real players as we can get. Five or six of the twelve players we sign today will have to *play* in a real professional baseball game tonight. It's so ridiculous, I can barely believe it's happening as Slips, Aliyah, and I face the field of candidates spread out behind home plate.

Seventy-eight people have shown up this morning, hoping to become a Hurricane.

Rick Larsen is also there with a briefcase of boilerplate contracts. So is the team's longtime equipment manager, Peez, ready to take measurements for the new players' uniforms. He promised he could get them ready by the 7:15 p.m. first pitch.

The ten current Hurricanes we've got left are here as well. Tex approved a small bonus for them to help lead the baseball activities today.

Seventy-eight is more than I expected. It also means

that 156 more eyes are directed squarely at me. Unless, of course, any of them happen to be missing an eye. Are any of them missing an eye? I can't tell.

The point is: I'm terrified.

"Here, here!" Slips shouts, waving a faded green bat in the air like a scepter. "Gather round, bring it in, people! Chop-chop! Look alive, sandworms! Et cetera! Et cetera!"

They don't look amused by Slips's tone, but cluster around in a decently orderly fashion anyway, some nervously punching the palms of their mitts with their fists. The ten current Hurricanes stand to the side, eyeing their potential new teammates and all-kid coaching staff dubiously.

The candidate pool is a ragtag bunch of people, to put it nicely. While there are a few guys who clearly have some semipro ball experience and are likely between teams at the moment, most of the group looks like they have no business being on the actual field during a baseball game. Some are older than my parents; even more are nearly as young as me. Eight are from the Weakerville Bison high school team. Several others are *middle school* classmates of mine. But at least the kids have actual baseball uniforms. Many of the older candidates are wearing sweatpants or gym shorts. One guy is actually wearing

Wrangler jeans, a belt with a huge metal buckle, a thick plaid shirt, cowboy boots, and a cowboy hat. A gray handlebar mustache is draped across his no-nonsense, sun-worn face. Of the four women who have come to try out, two appear older than my mom, and one is wearing a Hagen Family General cashier's uniform.

"I gotta get to work after this," she explains, clutching a glove to her chest. It's Carla, the cashier who rang up the Early Eights Foster shirt I found at Hagen on opening day. "Will we be done by noon?"

"We'd better be done by then," Slips says. "There's a game tonight, after all."

This sends a ripple of excitement through the crowd, cementing the fact that any one of them—or twelve, to be exact—will be a legitimate professional baseball player by the end of the day. Their excitement also confirms they're here because they love baseball and simply want to play. That kind of passion is the most important quality in a baseball player.

Well, after speed. And power. And, you know, talent.

I clear my throat, imagining myself giving a rousing introduction:

Hello, potential Hurricanes! I am the new manager, Alex Weakerman—yes, Ira Weakerman was my grandfather. And this is our pitching and assistant coach, Aliyah Perkins, and bench manager, Szymon "Slips" Zajac. Today, you have a chance to make history. Over the next three hours, you have the opportunity to show you're ready to be a professional athlete and a bigger part of this town that you probably ever imagined!

But, of course, the real thing doesn't go quite like that:

"Hello, uh, today is a day. Well, that's not what I mean. Of course, you know today *is* a day." Flumpo has already weakened my knees. A few current players groan. "But let me start over. Ahem. Hi. I'm the WeakerAlex Manager-Man. I mean, AlexMan WeakerManager . . . um . . ."

The right thoughts are there in my head, but they spill out of my mouth like they've been through a blender.

"Bench coach!" I finally manage to blurt out, pointing at Slips.

Thankfully, Slips takes his cue and saves me.

"Welcome to professional baseball's first-ever mid-season tryout!" Slips says, stepping forward. "And in case you're wondering, yes, the rumors *are* true: I do like raspberry jam better than grape. And also: by the end of the day, some of you will be pro ballplayers. Now, we have a lot to do today, so pay attention! This eloquent fellow here is the new team manager, Alex Weakerman. I'm the bench coach, Slips Zajac. And this is Aliyah Perkins, assistant manager and pitching coach. Some of you may recognize her from that rad ESPN commercial that aired last summer."

Slips is trying his best, but it's obvious he has no idea how a baseball tryout is supposed to go. So, near the end of his speech, he wisely takes a step back, leaving things to Aliyah, the only one of our managing team who has ever actually played the sport beyond T-ball.

"Okay," Aliyah barks out, sounding like a real coach. "We're going to get started with some stretching and warm-ups, then we'll break out into individual skills drills."

It all sorta seems like it's working. No thanks to me, of course. But this is precisely why I hired these two. I can handle baseball strategy. Lineups, pitching changes, the stuff where I can put my statistical knowledge to work. And Aliyah and Slips totally got all the other stuff. At the very least, things are moving along.

After stretching, everyone breaks off into pairs to do some warm-up throwing. I see more balls hitting grass than mitts, and I already know it's going to be a long day.

Next, Aliyah separates the candidates into pitchers and position players. She runs the pitching drills along with eight of the current Hurricanes, leaving Slips and me to lead the hitting drills, with the Law and Jon Amdor, his catcher.

The forty-seven hopeful position player candidates gather around us near the batting practice nets at home plate.

I motion to Slips, feeling pretty sure that if I speak right now, the Flumpo is going to make me say something insane, like reciting a recipe for rat whisker stew or step-by-step instructions on how to properly store shoes inside a toilet bowl.

Slips stands there grinning with his chipped green bat slung over his shoulder like a lumberjack with an ax.

"See here," he says. "I'm going to teach the lot of you grunts how to swing the lumber stick!"

Slips is clearly joking. Anyone who knows him would be laughing right now. But most of these guys and gals don't know Slips. So instead, they just stare at him with eyes wide and mouths open. The Law and his catcher frown, looking ready to just walk out.

But this does not deter Slips a bit.

"I call this hunk of wood here Anne of Green Gables," Slips says, slamming the barrel of the bat into his palm. "She's the bat I was using the one time I hit a home run.

Not a baseball home run, to be clear. The other kind. But she's also the bat I used to bash a dozen snakes to death last year. She's a real snake killer. All the boys down at the old shipyard call her the Snake Brainer. And the fellas down at the ole lumberyard call her the Viper Vaporizer. And of course, the crew down at them there stockyards used to call her Ol' Missus Saturday Night for some reason. Anyway, see that stain? That one, right there . . ."

A few of the players and candidates can't hide their smirks, but the majority still look pretty annoyed.

"Yup, that's snake blood," Slips says, nodding. "Viper life juice, if you will . . . good old VLJ. By the end of the summer, you'll all be expert snake bashers. Have VLJ stains on all your bats and clothes. You see, the key is to sneak up on them in the daytime, when those cold-blooded serpents like to rest out in the sun and soak up the heat. . . ."

The younger players are actually laughing—mostly the ones who know Slips from school. But the adults still look dumbfounded. They don't know that Slips is totally kidding—he'd never harm an animal of any kind.

"This is ridiculous," the Law finally says to Amdor.

"We were already a running joke around here," his catcher agrees. "And now *this*."

We can't risk losing any of the ten real players we have left, so I give Slips a look. He understands it means to cut the comedy routine.

"Okay, anyway," Slips calls out. "Gather into a line. The Law here's going to throw some batting practice to y'all, one at a time. So, let's see what you got."

The Law reluctantly takes his place in front of the mound, next to a BP net and a huge bin of baseballs, as John Amdor settles in behind the plate.

The first hitter is Josh Carlson, the star center fielder for the Weakerville varsity high school team. I have some hope—he's likely faced at least one high school pitcher who will end up in the Mabel someday. I watch with my clipboard ready.

Josh swings at and misses the first five pitches, all fastballs. The Law isn't holding anything back, and why should he? It's not like our opponents will later tonight. Josh fouls off the next two pitches, and then swings and misses at the final three.

The next nine batters don't fare much better. None of them even manage to make contact. The Mabel might not be the majors, but the Law is a professional pitcher, and his stuff is simply too good for high schoolers and people off the streets.

Still, Slips stays positive the whole time, shouting an array of empty encouragements from behind the nets. Stuff like:

"It's okay! Next time, slugger!"

"Keep your eye on the ball! But you know, not literally. Don't get hit in the eye by the ball."

"Bogey, twelve o'clock!"

Except, after the sixth or seventh batter, he just starts making random movie references.

"Stay on target . . . . stay on target . . . stay on target!"

"Doesn't *anyone* have any missiles left?!?!"

A loud groan involuntarily escapes from my mouth after the eighty-seventh consecutive swing and miss. The batters in line shoot irritated glances my way. I know what they're thinking: *Like you could do any better!* And they're not wrong. But the difference is, *I'm* not the one trying out for a professional baseball team.

It's not just me, though. By the thirteenth batter, the Law takes off his hat and angrily wipes his sweaty forehead on his shirtsleeve while sighing loudly. He may be the pitcher, but he *wants* these hitters to get hits. Some of them are going to be his teammates after all.

I let my clipboard hang at my side. What notes would I even have at this point, besides things like:

Swinging strike.

Another swinging strike.

Yet another swinging strike.

Yes, one more swinging strike.

So, instead of standing there and risking a breakdown, I stroll on over toward right field, where the pitching tryouts are taking place. I can tell things aren't going much better from Aliyah's body language alone. Specifically, how her hands keep moving from the top of her head, down to her hips, then behind her head as she looks up at the sky, down at the field, out into the bleachers, anywhere but at the people actually throwing.

I stand there just long enough to watch six or seven "pitchers" show Aliyah what they got. Or *don't* got, if we're being accurate.

Two are throwing underhand. Another, a forty-six-year-old insurance broker according to the information he gave at the beginning of the tryout, blows out his arm on his third pitch—a fastball clocked at 64 miles per hour. I'm hoping his company has insurance that covers recreational Tommy John surgery as he heads into the dugout cradling his elbow. Another guy keeps throwing the ball into the grass five feet short of the catcher. And one person's first pitch lands way up in the stands. Not on purpose.

I finally slam my clipboard down in frustration. Everyone stops for a second to stare at me, looking every bit as miserable as I'm feeling.

I'm not the kind of person who is prone to angry outbursts. But, then again, I've never felt this hopeless, with this much on the line, in my life.

"Come on, try again," Aliyah says to the guy who still hasn't thrown a pitch that's reached his catcher, trying to get his attention back. "Let's keep this going. This time square your hips first, then your shoulders, and let all the power come from your legs. You can do this!"

I need to get out of here. Everyone can tell how unhappy I am, which can't be helping. So I head down into the visitors' dugout and into the tunnel. The air is cooler down here; the humidity of the mid-summer morning hasn't seeped below ground level yet.

It finally feels like I can breathe.

But that doesn't mean I feel any better. How did Grandpa Ira think I'd be able to bring this team to the *playoffs*? I'm not even going to be able to field a team! Let alone win a single game. I'd have better luck hunting for actual unicorns and dragons.

I'm going to let my grandpa down. And Aliyah will have missed her final Little League season to be a part of this joke of an experiment. I'm going to let *everyone* down. Then lose the Hurricanes forever on top of it.

I close my eyes, lean against the cold concrete wall, and take several deep breaths.

When I finally open them again, I'm surprised to see my grandpa's familiar handwriting scrawled on the wall in front of me, on the overhang of the visitors' dugout tunnel. The message is in white paint and slightly faded, but still clear and visible. Any player on the opposing team would see it as they head out onto the field.

WELCOME TO WEAKERVILLE!

GOOD LUCK OUT THERE TONIGHT!

MAKE YOUR HOMETOWN PROUD!

I can't help but smile. It's like getting just a little piece of Grandpa Ira back. He liked winning as much as anyone. But more important, always, was that everyone was respectful of the game, their teammates, the fans, the umps, even the other team.

I'll never forget my first year with season tickets. We had this player, a washed-up former major leaguer named Victor "Big V" Valentino. He was forty-three and hadn't played in the MLB since his mid-thirties. He had plenty of money, so I suppose he was only tooling around in leagues like the Mabel for the love of the game. Which is probably why Ira signed him, despite his noted history of on-field tantrums. Anyway, Big V was a huge draw, and attendance was way up those first few weeks that year. But, like all players, he had to sign the sportsmanship waiver Ira put into every employee's contract. Then, in the tenth game of the season, Big V struck out, and after attempting and failing to break his bat over his knee, he instead proceeded to run over to the opposing team's dugout and start smashing the bats on their bat rack. This of course led to a bench-clearing brawl that took nearly thirty minutes to finally break up. And that was it. Ira cut Big V that same night, sacrificing what could have been our first profitable season in years.

What would Ira think of me right now? Slamming my clipboard down in front of players trying their best? Groaning in frustration within earshot of potential Hurricanes? Abandoning practice? All because things aren't going the way I wanted. Well, he'd be embarrassed and ashamed, that's what.

I straighten myself out, take a few more breaths, and then head back out onto the field.

Slips, Aliyah, and the Law have kept the tryout rolling

in my absence. Nobody even seems to have noticed I was gone at all as I retrieve my clipboard from right field. And I'm fine with that. I make better decisions while being ignored.

Everyone has joined back up as one group, taking batting practice, and a different Hurricane has taken over for the Law as pitcher.

I'm just in time to watch Family General cashier Carla Henderson step to the plate.

Slips is still right there by the batting cage, shouting encouragement while leaning on Anne of Green Gables like a cane.

"Let's go, Family General!" he calls out.

Carla looks nervous as she steps to the plate, making me nervous for her.

The first pitch is a fastball down the plate.

Carla's swing is cringeworthy. Everyone watching makes that *one face*. You know, the face you make when you see a YouTube video of some dude in a backward baseball hat face-planting onto the pavement while trying to jump into his swimming pool from the roof of his house.

Carla actually falls down on the follow-through. But she does generate some nice bat speed on the swing, as ill-timed and wild as it was. The next few pitches are better, in that the swings are at least watchable. But she still isn't close to making contact.

"Hey, maybe you just need a new bat?" Slips says to her.

She turns and grins at him. "What about Anne of Green Gables, there? How much is she worth to you?"

Slips gazes at the old green bat. "She's priceless," he whispers hauntingly.

A few snickers break out among the players.

Carla, still smiling, holds out her hand.

"What about I just rent her for a few swings?"

She already seems more at ease. Now it just looks like she's trying to at least have a little fun.

Slips makes a big show of "reluctantly" handing over the old green bat.

"Sorry about all the snake blood on it," he says. "Old VLJ, you know."

Carla rolls her eyes as several onlookers laugh.

Everyone holds their breath as she steps back to the plate, not expecting better results. I don't know if it's because the bat is so old and worn that we're expecting it to shatter on impact, or because Carla simply looked so outmatched the first few pitches.

But then Carla Henderson, thirty-seven-year-old Family General cashier, proves us all wrong on the very next pitch.

The ball explodes off Anne of Green Gables like it doesn't belong in this universe.

As we all watch it leave the park in stunned silence, we know it's not because the old green bat Slips probably found in his dad's junkyard has magic powers or anything. But because this is what raw talent looks like when it's utilized correctly.

Carla proceeds to hit everything the pitcher throws next—breaking pitches out of the zone, high fastballs, *everything.* She literally swings at everything and somehow manages to make contact on several pitches in the dirt and up above her shoulders. Her swing mechanics are a bit awkward, but there's no denying the natural bat speed and coordination.

Or the results. She's knocking singles through the infield, doubles down the line. She even leaves the park a couple times.

"It's the snake blood!" Slips yells with his arms in the air after she slices a line drive down the opposite field foul line.

By the end of Carla's at bat, everyone is cheering and

hollering, even the candidates with no chance of making the team.

The decision is easy: Carla Henderson is going to be our first open-tryout signee.

As far as I know, she'll also be the first non-pitcher female player in the history of the Mabel. She's not the fastest runner, and her fielding leaves a lot to be desired, but there's no denying we've found at least one legitimate offensive threat.

The rest of tryout isn't all that terrible. At the very least, there are a few bright spots scattered here and there. Like when Steven Yu, a twenty-eight-year-old financial analyst with an intuitive jump and quick feet, steals three bases in a row. Or when Josh Carlson, the player from the high school team, finally seems to catch a groove and gets a few hits during BP, then makes a spectacular diving catch in the outfield. Or when we're all shocked to find out that the real-life cowboy, dubbed "Farmer John" by Slips, can actually throw a pretty decent slider—even in cowboy boots and Wranglers.

By 11:00 a.m., we have a list of eighteen players who don't totally stink. And by noon, Aliyah and I narrow it down to twelve.

All are given contracts on the spot.

The Hurricanes are a complete team again.

Assuming there aren't any catastrophes, we'll at least be able to field a full team for our remaining forty-one games, and hopefully, maybe—just maybe—even win a few of them. But it all starts tonight, with our first game.

And I'd be lying if I said I wasn't terrified.

Chapter 18

LATER THAT EVENING, SLIPS, ALIYAH, AND I ARE ASSESSING OUR NEW team.

We're sitting in my office, which is basically just a small concrete room containing a metal desk covered in dents, chips, and rust spots, a tattered office chair with the stuffing visible in several places, two plastic chairs across from it, and a huge file cabinet in the corner.

"How did we end up with both the youngest and oldest roster in Mabel history?" Aliyah asks.

It's true: 98.2 percent of all players in the Mabel are

between ages nineteen and thirty-four. Yet nine of our twenty-two players are either *under* nineteen or *over* thirty-four. We also have the distinction of having both the Mabel's youngest player, Josh Carlson (age seventeen), and oldest, John "Farmer John" Converse (age forty-six).

"That's probably what happens when you replace eight starters with high school kids, retail cashiers, plumbers, and financial analysts," Slips says, shrugging.

"At least we have a full roster now," I say. "Last I checked that's all you need to play the game."

Sure, it may not be the best roster ever assembled for a professional sporting event. In fact, it's probably the worst. But at least it *is* a complete roster.

"Hey, is it okay that I invited a whole bunch of my friends and teammates to the game tonight?" Aliyah eventually asks, probably trying to get our minds off the team's lack of talent.

My throat suddenly clenches up. As if I needed more pressure to win this game. Unable to speak, I just nod.

"So, what's my job during the match?" Slips asks, gently tapping Anne of Green Gables on my metal desk, pounding more small dents into it.

"Where did you even get that thing, anyway?" I ask, laughing despite the mood.

"Found it in the Yard," he says with a shrug.

The Yard is how he refers to his dad's junkyard.

"I'm surprised you got it back from Carla after the way she was crushing with it," Aliyah says.

"Well, I told her she could use it anytime," he says. "But anyway, what's my job in tonight's match? I never coached a baseball match before."

"It's called a *game*," I say, even though I suspect he knows that. "Not a match."

"Hey," Slips says, grinning. "What does gingerbread have in common with a windmill?"

I ignore his rhetorical Polish idiom with a grin and continue.

"Your job is to stay in the dugout and keep the players' spirits up and their heads in the game."

"Ah, my specialty," he says, setting down Anne of Green Gables to crack his knuckles theatrically.

"This is really exciting," Aliyah says. "I'm almost as nervous as when I pitch."

"*You* get nervous when you pitch?" I ask.

"*Of course!*" she says. "Have *you* ever pitched in front of thousands of people? With a whole team depending on you? Expecting you to win the game single-handedly? And knowing that if you let them down, they probably won't even talk to you once the season's over?"

"Uh, well, I . . . I mean . . ."

"I think Alex was just implying that you always seem so cool and under control on the mound," Slips quickly adds. "Isn't that right?"

"Definitely!" I say too quickly. "You're always so amazing out there. . . ."

"Right, yeah, I'm sorry," Aliyah says. "I guess I just get tired of everyone expecting me to be great all the time. As if I don't already expect that of myself. I think that's why I'm even *more* nervous now. Being coaches, we won't have any real control over what happens on the field. I mean, I'm about to—"

My cell phone rings, cutting her off mid-sentence. "It's Tex," I say.

"Well . . . answer it!" Slips says. "Don't ignore the boss!"

I put the phone to my ear and Tex's voice explodes into my head like a tornado let off its leash.

"Son!" he shouts hoarsely. "That was quite a day! *Lucy almighty*, what a day indeed!"

"Ummm . . ."

"I *told* you, you'd find a way to fill the roster!" he says. "And my, oh my, what a stroke of genius, son. I'd never thought of something so outlandish myself. . . ."

"Huh?"

"An open tryout!" Tex yells gleefully. "I mean, for Lucy's sake, who's ever heard of such a thing? What a brilliant notion! It's as absurd as putting a rhino on roller skates! We're going to be a marvel, a disastrous wonder, a—a circus act on the diamond! Ticket sales for the next few home games are already up!"

Nervous sweat starts to bead on my forehead. I don't want to manage a team famous for being a joke. If that was the plan, I'd have picked a totally different twelve players from the tryouts. Ones without real potential. I didn't expect Tex to root for us, but I wish he'd at least take us a little more seriously.

"You know," Tex continues. "This here sort of reminds me of the time when my uncle Merle lost his hand noodling. You know what noodling is, son?"

"Uhh, yes, sir," I say, and I'm not even lying.

I once watched a show on Discovery about it. It's basically where you go fishing for catfish by sticking your arm into logs and holes underwater and such. If you're lucky, a catfish will basically bite onto your hand, and then you pull it out of the water. I remember thinking it was something I *never, ever* want to try.

"Well, how about that?" Tex says, letting loose another

barrage of raspy bellows. "A northerner that knows hisself real fishing! Well, anyway, some years ago, me and Uncle Merle were out noodling in Coal Pile Lake, which is a funny name since it ain't even near any coal or pile, and especially not piles of coal. Anyhow, you won't find it on any map, not then or now, but it's there. Some of the largest fish in Arkansas are right there in Ol' Coal Pile. So Uncle Merle and I are out one night, it's dark, even though the sky is still burnt red, like the horizon's on fire. I got the flashlight, and Uncle Merle has me shine it down on a fallen tree near a muddy inlet. He digs his arm into the water, deep into the hollowed end of the tree, so far that only his head and shoulder are sticking above the surface. Then suddenly he smiles, big and wide, like he knows a secret."

I check the clock on the wall. It's a half hour until the pregame ceremonies. But Tex seems like he's on a roll, so I just listen as Slips and Aliyah stare at me, probably trying to hear some of what Tex is yelling into my ear.

"But then Uncle Merle's face changes and he starts panicking and jerking this way and that. I think for a moment a gator has got him. But it wasn't no gator. Nossir, instead it was the largest catfish the state of Arkansas has ever seen. A feisty monster weighing over a hundred and twenty pounds! Once it had Merle's hand, it wasn't letting go for nothin'. So, he's struggling and pulling and this, that, and the other. But so is the catfish, which weighed more than scrawny Uncle Merle. His nickname back then used to be Flappy. Short for Flagpole, you see. Anyway, Merle's struggling with this fish, fighting for his life 'cause it keeps pullin' his head underwater. So Merle makes one last desperate heave and jerks his arm away and . . . POP!"

I jump nearly a foot in the air when Tex screams *POP* into the phone. Aliyah and Slips give me a look as if they're wondering whether or not they need to call 911.

"That's right," Tex says, his voice suddenly soft and low. "Pulled his hand clean off. It's still stuck in that beast's mouth to this day. But Uncle Merle was okay. He got on all right. In a lot of ways, he was *better off.* For one thing, it finally gave him a good story to tell. Merle always was the king champion of aimless stories that didn't have no point to 'em. But now he has this one, which, this here is a good one for him to tell. And I was there, so I can back it all up . . . well, that and his stump can also help verify them facts of the story."

I swallow and my throat sticks.

"What . . . what happened to the fish?"

"Oh, her?" Tex laughs. "Well, she's hanging on Merle's wall to this very day—hand and all!"

I find it hard to believe that Tex has an uncle who is still alive.

"That's not . . . wait, really?"

"Yep," Tex continues. "Turns out she bit off more than she could chew and choked to death on Merle's hand. Came bobbing to the surface lifeless as a sack of oats a few minutes later. I had the fortitude to grab her and haul her to the truck before rushing Merle to the hospital. Anyway, the thing that was to ruin Merle's life became his greatest achievement. It hangs above his dinner table, a reminder of what he done. It's a record fish, or would have been, had we ever reported it. Merle never cared about records; *he knows* what it is and that's all that matters to him."

I sit there breathing into the phone, not sure what to say, and also doubting a fish could actually choke to death on a man's fist. Or bite off a hand at all, for that matter.

"Today reminds me of that," Tex says slowly. "In more ways than one."

"Are you saying that holding an open tryout was like sticking my hand in a huge catfish's mouth? And it's probably going to get bitten off?"

Aliyah's and Slips's eyes grow wide and they glance at one another and then back at me in shock. Slips looks ready to bust a gut laughing, but he's desperately holding it in.

"Indeed, son," Tex says. "But don't forget, it turned into a great story in the end. Right?"

"I guess," I say, a little annoyed that he just likened our chances of making the playoffs to his uncle trying to catch a fish larger than himself with his bare hands.

"Well, it don't matter, I suppose," Tex says, laughing so loud the phone speaker crackles. "What matters is that you're doin' a fine job. It's *almost* a shame that this will be the final year."

The reminder of what's on the line hits me like a roundhouse to the jaw to go along with his total dismissal of our playoff chances. I'm suddenly finding it hard to breathe.

"Anyway," Tex says. "At least this last season won't be boring! Got to go now, bye-bye."

Slips and Aliyah are staring at me as my phone goes dark, likely wondering what in the heck that could have been about.

"*Well?*" Slips finally says.

"He doesn't believe in us," I say. "He thinks this is some kind of joke. That we'll be like a circus attraction or something!" I can hear the anger rising in my voice. "We have a chance; we can win games. Baseball isn't just about talent. The 1914 Boston Braves proved that. The '87 Twins did too! Those teams had no business winning the World Series. But somehow, they did. Quality players and smart managing can win games. And we have both. Sorta."

"You don't need to tell *us* that," Aliyah says, narrowing her eyes at me. "Why didn't you say all this to *Tex*, instead of sitting there quietly listening to him?"

"Well, I mean, the noodling," I say. Her yelling at me is making the Flumpo come back again. "The catfish ate his hand and I-I-I, Merle's hand . . ."

"A catfish ate some guy named Merle's hand?" Slips repeats. "I *really* need to hear more about this conversation."

But Aliyah's not finished.

"And while we're at it," she says, "why didn't you speak up more at tryouts? Aren't you supposed to be the one running things around here? What's your strategy for tonight's game?"

"I—I . . . I mean . . ."

My head slumps forward as I realize I haven't thought about any of that yet. I haven't really thought much past finding new players at tryouts. I haven't even sat down to do the math on how many of our remaining games we need to win to realistically have a shot at the postseason.

"Sorry, I didn't mean to yell," Aliyah says, looking a little embarrassed. "I'm just competitive . . . *too* competitive, a lot of my friends say . . ."

"No, but you're right," I say. "We need to find a way to win tonight. Prove to Tex and everyone else that we're not some sort of joke."

"Who are we playing?" Slips asks.

"The Heartsville Hammers," I say. "A team I know we can beat. We already swept them once this season."

"Well, let's start by heading to the locker room," Aliyah says. "You need to talk to the team. That's what my coach always does, especially when we've been playing particularly badly. Don't underestimate the power of a good rousing, inspirational speech."

She's right. It's something I'm going to have to rise up and do. And who knows? Maybe I *can* turn all my anger at Tex into a fiery, motivational pregame sermon?

"Okay, let's try it," I say.

Slips grins and nods. Aliyah smiles, but her eyes still look worried.

I stand up and head in the direction of the locker room, where the team is getting ready for the game.

And I've never been more terrified in my life.

Chapter 19

THE ROOM IS DEAD SILENT AS WE ENTER.

It's the opposite of what I expect the locker room of a professional baseball team to sound like. Shouldn't there be laughing and joking and cursing and practical jokes? But my team looks like a bunch of people getting dressed for a funeral.

Carla Henderson is next to a makeshift partition Peez set up—basically just a huge chalkboard on wheels in front of her locker in the corner. She's already in uniform, sitting on the bench, dry heaving from nerves.

My own stomach lurches, but I head over anyway.

"Doing okay?" I ask.

"Why?" she says, her skin a chalky green. "Do I not seem okay?"

"I mean, well . . . uh, you'll be fine? Everyone's nervous their first game—"

"It's not that," she shoots back, doubling over and taking a few deep breaths. "I just . . . it's this place. I haven't been here in such a long time. . . ."

I've had enough panic attacks in my day, specifically before school presentations in front of the whole class, to know one when I see it. Sounds like she hasn't even gone to a Hurricanes game in a while, so she probably feels about as much pressure as I do.

"It's okay," I try. "I mean, it's just one game, and—"

"It's not that, it's just . . . it's complicated, okay? Can I please just have some time to myself?"

"Um, yeah, okay," I say, stumbling away.

Well, my first one-on-one pregame pep talk went about as well as I expected.

Next, I spot the Law at his locker, carefully spreading a layer of some sort of clear jelly onto a piece of toast. He's about to take a bite when I notice the label on the jar into which he'd dipped his plastic knife.

"Wait!" I say, rushing over and grabbing his arm. "That's Vaseline!"

The Law looks down at me, clearly annoyed.

"No kidding?" he says, grabbing the jar off his shelf with mocking wonder. "Is that what this says? How could I have missed that before literally every game this entire season?"

The sad part is that it takes me a second to pick up on the sarcasm, even after a few of the nearby players start chuckling, which only makes me look even worse.

"No offense, Alan, but buzz off," the Law says.

I sigh and back away, letting the Law enjoy his Vaseline toast in peace.

Someone nudges me with an elbow. It's Mayhem, the team's closer.

"He does this before every game, even when he's not pitching," he whispers. "Claims it keeps him young. How many nearly forty-year-old professional pitchers do you know with no history of arm injuries? He's *never* missed a start."

I nod, dubiously eyeing the gray hairs lining the Law's neck. His elbow makes a gross clicking noise every time he lifts the toast up for another bite.

"Man, I love this job," Slips says, watching the Law eat.

"So, Weakerman, when are you going to do that big pregame speech?" Aliyah asks, joining us in the corner.

"Uh, well, yeah, I mean . . ."

Why did I ever agree to this? She knows as well as I do that the odds of me gathering everyone and delivering any sort of inspiring and cohesive thoughts are about as good as me hitting a home run versus Nolan Ryan in his prime. My Flumpo would almost certainly lead to me telling them that I like to glue dog hair on my face and pretend I'm Abraham Lincoln—which, for the record, isn't true, but is something I *may have* actually said once while panicking during a school presentation.

"Maybe I'll take the pregame speech this time?" Slips suggests. "Alex can do the next one?"

"Yeah," I say. "Yeah, that's a good plan. . . ."

Aliyah rolls her eyes but doesn't protest.

"Hey, listen up, meatballs!" Slips shouts. "I got a rousing pregame pep talk for you bums over here! So get your tissues ready, things might get emotional."

Everybody turns and stares.

"First," Slips begins, lifting Anne of Green Gables into the air like a band leader waving a baton. "Don't listen to what anyone else is saying about this team! The fact is, we know y'all got some skills! And if we manage to somehow *win*, well . . ."

He pauses here, dramatically, eyeing the room. Every player, even the oldest adults in the room, are listening now.

". . . Pork chops for all! And mutton chops for the Sagittariuses. And karate chops for the vegetarians. Chops all night! So let's, uh, go out there and try not to get embarrassed too badly! Let's prove all the haters . . . well, not wrong, but perhaps to be vastly exaggerating! Plus, if we do somehow pull off a miracle win, delicious grilled chops for the coaches too!"

A few players chuckle. Whether it's out of merciful hopelessness or actual amusement is unclear. But either way, the team goes back to tying their shoes and ritualistically frosting toast with Vaseline.

I shoot an appreciative glance at Slips.

He grins and shrugs.

Now there's nothing left to do but march back into my office to fill out my first-ever lineup card.

* * *

It's a clear Friday night at Mustard Park and the first pitch is just under an hour away.

My last-place Hurricanes of Weakerville (record: 19–30) are facing division rival Heartsville Hammers (record: 26–24) in the first of a three-game home series. We swept a three-game series against them earlier this season. But all three pitchers who started those games for us, alongside twelve other starting players, are now gone.

During pregame warm-ups, I'm standing in the dugout, looking at my lineup card, wrinkled and ink-smudged from my sweaty, shaking hands. I keep sneaking glances back at my old seats a few rows behind home plate. From here, they look small and empty. But at least up there, it was comfortable. Up there, I felt like I knew what I was doing.

I'm vaguely aware of someone shouting in the background, but it's only when Slips taps me on the shoulder that I realize it's directed my way.

The home plate ump is glaring at me.

"Come on, kid, we don't have all day!" he shouts. He reminds me a lot of Mr. Muscles. "We need your lineup. *Let's go!*"

The Heartsville Hammers manager, John Lumpkin—a dignified-looking man in his fifties with short, graying hair—is standing next to the ump, staring at me with a mixture of mean-spirited amusement and frustration. Probably everyone in the Mabel feels my employment is making a mockery of the league and the game.

They may not be wrong.

My legs are shakier than usual as I labor up the five dugout steps and start the long walk toward home plate, fairly certain I'm going to fall along the way. After all, there are probably more eyes on me now than ever before in my life. More attention in this one moment than most kids will ever get.

The buzz of the crowd has turned into a hushed silence. *Everyone* is watching me: the first kid manager in baseball history. I glance back at the stands again and am shocked to find the place over half-full—the largest regular-season crowd I've personally ever seen at Mustard Park. Could the league's first-ever kid manager, first-ever female player, and first-ever mostly open-tryout roster really be responsible for instantly doubling the usual attendance?

"Come on, move it!" the ump growls impatiently.

He and the opposing manager watch as I lumber

toward them. After what feels like nineteen miles, I finally reach home plate. I've been to enough games to recognize the ump. Tim Sharpe is one of the Mabel's most notoriously hotheaded officials. He's got a twitchy ejection thumb, wildly inconsistent strike zone, and penchant for holding grudges against managers who annoy him. Which doesn't bode well for my team, given how things have started.

"Lineup," he demands.

I hand him the card. He doesn't hide his disgust at the sweat-dampened state of it.

My combined lineup's stats are pretty sad: .243 AVG, 14 HR, 48 RBI, 5 SB, 20 BB, in just 354 total plate appearances. Well short of the Hammers' 1206 combined plate appearances and 73 HR. To be fair, though, some of the players starting for us tonight weren't even professional baseball players until a few hours ago.

The national anthem and ceremonial first pitch pass in a blur.

The next thing I know, the Law, our starting pitcher that night, is taking the mound for the first inning of my managerial career. I can't even relish the excitement of getting to work a dream job at thirteen. Instead, all I can think is how much we need to win this game and make an impression on everyone in town, Aliyah's friends, Tex, the whole league.

Which is why I decide to send a message right off the bat, so to speak.

I give our catcher, Amdor, the signal for some chin music—which is baseball code for a fastball up near the batter's head. It's designed to intimidate, to back them up off the plate, unsettle them a bit, make them feel like they don't know what we'll do next.

Amdor hesitates before facing the mound.

The Law shakes off the signal.

Our catcher looks back at me. Clearly, the Law doesn't want to go high and inside to start the game. But we need to come out strong, to show everyone we won't get pushed around. I want the Hammers to know I'm not afraid—despite actually being terrified.

I repeat the signal.

This time, the Law reluctantly nods and stands tall to begin his windup. It's easy to spot the slight hitch in his delivery, and as soon as the ball leaves his hand and hurtles toward home plate, I know this won't end well.

The pitch hits the Hammers leadoff man right in the head.

There are immediate calls from the opposing dugout

to eject the Law, who looks visibly shaken as he takes a few concerned steps toward home plate.

I bury my face in my hands as the batter gets attention from medical staff. Which means I don't see Aliyah streaking toward me, down the line, from the bullpen. But I hear her feet stomping down the dugout steps.

"Weakerman, what are you doing?" she asks angrily. "I saw you give that sign twice!"

"I . . . I don't know," I say, and it's true. In the moment, it felt right. But in hindsight, I really can't understand what I was thinking. "I think I panicked . . . the *Flumpo* . . ."

"*Flumpo?!* What the heck are you even talking about? Jeez, *Weakerman*!"

This is apparently all she has to say, because she pivots and heads out to the mound to talk to the Law before I can respond.

The good news: it was a glancing blow and the leadoff man is okay and stays in the game.

The bad news: he's now on first base.

The worse news: he promptly steals second, then scores later on a wild pitch that goes into the stands.

It's obvious the Law is still pretty shaken from almost hitting a guy in the face on a pitch he didn't even want to throw. And now, four pitches into my first game as a manager, I'm a run down without a baseball having even touched a bat once.

I wish I could say things get better, but I can't.

The rest of the inning is a disaster. The Law gives up six runs on two hits, four walks, and two errors. I'm down 6–0 after half an inning, and we're lucky it's not more. The Law is clearly upset as he stalks off the field, swearing into his glove. He won't even look in my direction as he stomps past me and drops onto the bench at the far end of the dugout.

"He's finished," Slips says.

"Our *starter* is finished? After one inning? Since when do you know anything about baseball?" I say, not meaning for it to come out like it does.

"I know *people*, Alex," Slips says, casting a worried glance at the Law.

"I agree with Slips," Aliyah says, leaning over the railing in front of me. "His mechanics were out of whack after that first batter. . . ."

I don't need to hear more. They're probably right. The Law's arm angle has dropped, and he wasn't throwing as much as *aiming* the ball the entire inning.

But, as I consult my stats, I decide I have to leave him

in. Our bullpen isn't deep enough to dip into this early. Plus, the Law's numbers in the second inning are solid across the board, even in games where the Hurricanes are down. Above all else, I'm terrified that pulling our pitcher now is like admitting defeat. Like saying: *Whelp, that's the best we have.*

"He'll figure it out," I say. I point to my compilation of the Law's second-inning stats. "We gotta trust the numbers."

Aliyah sighs and stomps back toward the bullpen.

"Whatever," Slips says with an encouraging pat on the back. "I just hope you're right, bud."

I'm not.

At the end of the second inning, we're down *13*–0. And it somehow only gets worse from there.

In the bottom of the third inning, Carla Henderson is due up for the first time—the first of our open-tryout signees to step to the plate. We've had no baserunners, with our first six batters swinging and missing at a lot of bad pitches. In fact, the Hammers pitcher has thrown only five pitches inside the strike zone. And I suspect there's no chance he'll give Carla anything to hit either.

She still looks like she's on the verge of throwing up. More than anything, I don't want her to fail in her first plate appearance the same way I'm failing in my first game as manager.

"Carla." I wave her over from the on-deck circle. She leans in to hear me over the crowd booing a "strike three" call on Amdor at the plate. "Take every pitch. This guy has been all over the place. He won't throw strikes. More than anything now, we just need a base runner."

Carla nods as Amdor steps down into the dugout, grumbling something about the strike zone. She heads toward home as her name is announced over the PA. The crowd gives her a thunderous round of applause.

The first pitch is low and away, clearly off the plate, and for the first time all night, I breathe a sigh of relief.

"Strike!"

My head whips toward the ump. There was no way that was a strike. Someone in the crowd behind home plate agrees, and, to be specific, he calls the ump sexist, along with a few other words I'm not allowed to repeat.

Carla shakes her head, clearly frustrated.

I give her the signal to take another pitch.

The second pitch is below her knees, but the ump once again shouts obnoxiously, "Steeerrriiiiiike!"

Now the count is 0–2. There's *no way* the pitcher will throw anything near the plate, not when he's getting calls from the ump on stuff out of the zone. The only shot she's got is to take another pitch and hope it's not close enough for the ump to give it to the pitcher.

"Let her swing away."

It's our best player, Big Fish, standing behind me. I freeze up, but only for a moment.

"Yeah, but, um, there's—there's no way he's going to throw a strike."

Big Fish shrugs. "He's going to do what he wants. This joke of an ump is going to call what he wants. Can't do anything about that. Let Carla decide."

A vision flashes through my head, of Carla swinging and missing at something way off the plate. I can't let one of our newest players try and swing at something that I know is going to be out of the strike zone. It'll look ridiculous. The *team* will look ridiculous.

I give her the sign to take.

Big Fish shakes his head and heads back to the bench, while Carla frowns, then turns to face the pitcher.

She watches a fastball go right down the middle.

Strike three.

Carla walks back to the dugout with her head down. The crowd is booing the ump. But he's not the one I'm mad at right now. *I've* just ruined Carla's first professional at bat, by taking it out of her hands. Something she'll never get to do again.

Unfortunately, her at bats later in the game don't go any better. I let her swing away each time, since I don't want to interfere again. But she strikes out both times. All of her swings are ill-timed and messy, the kind of hacks she took during the first half of batting practice earlier today—not the raw, powerful swings she took later. I don't know what happened to her. But I'm pretty sure it's my fault.

We go on to lose 19–0.

It's even worse than the score indicates. We get two base runners all night: our third baseman, Chewy Cavanaugh, bunts for a single in the sixth, and Big Fish is intentionally walked later that inning. Our batters strike out a Mabel-record twenty-three times. Add nine fielding errors, another league record, and me using seven pitchers to get through one game, and you've got the ingredients for a total disaster.

The worst part is, I know nobody would be more disappointed in me than Ira.

Chapter 20

OUR SECOND GAME, THE VERY NEXT DAY, GOES ABOUT THE SAME.

Starting with the fact that Slips once again handles the pregame speech, all the way to the embarrassing final score.

And once again, I can't seem to do anything right as manager.

After our leadoff man gets on base in the bottom of the third inning, I take a chance and pinch-run Steven Yu, only to see him get picked off the next pitch. I miss an obvious safety squeeze the other team runs in the fifth inning; I don't bring in our third baseman, and it gives them an easy run. And I pinch-hit Carla in the seventh, only for the other team to bring in their side-armed lefty specialist, who easily strikes her out on three pitches—when we didn't see him in the previous game, I should have known he'd be fresh for tonight's game. There's more, but the point is, I'm not even seeing the obvious.

If I were still sitting in the stands, I'd have made all the right moves. I'd have missed nothing. Were the fate of the team not resting on me, perhaps I'd be seeing things more clearly. Flumpo never got in the way of *baseball* when I was up there, like it does down here, with everyone looking at me.

But it doesn't matter. Knowing I could be better at this doesn't change the results that day: a 13–0 loss. This puts us on pace to finish the season 19–61 with a *negative* 3,109 run scoring differential.

After the game, tensions flare in the locker room.

"Thanks for all the *help* out there, new guys," says Chewy Cavanaugh, one of the veteran Hurricanes.

"We're trying our best," Carla shoots back, defending the new players. "We haven't had the whole year to prepare for this season like you guys. What's *your* excuse?"

The Law suddenly steps between them, pointing a finger at her.

"*You* don't get to call us out!" he says. "We're still here. The rest of the team quit, and they were probably the smart ones. But we're still here! We're here, in spite of all of you!"

Having no idea how to diffuse an actual argument between grown-ups, I slither away to my office, close the door, and cram myself into my chair. But it doesn't fully block out the sounds of the argument. It goes back and forth for a few more minutes, then I finally hear Slips's voice cutting through.

"Hey!" he shouts. "Listen up! I know things are bad. We're all embarrassed. But things will get better. I mean, they have to, right? They certainly can't get worse. But we have to stick together! As a team!" Guilt rips through me as I know *I* should be the one out there saying this, instead of hiding in my office. "We will figure this out. If you guys promise to stop arguing, and have each other's backs like a real team, then I will *guarantee* at least one win during the upcoming road trip. If we don't win a game, then you can all quit with full pay!"

What's he *doing*!?

If I weren't so immobilized by Flumpo, I'd be out

there stopping him. But instead, I continue to cower in my office and listen to the murmurs of the players reluctantly agree to his deal.

"Slips!" I yell when he and Aliyah step into my office a few moments later. "What are you doing? How are we supposed to actually win a game next week?"

"At least he's doing *something*, Weakerman!" Aliyah says. "If you're *so convinced* we can't win a game, then why did you even agree to manage the team at all?"

"I just don't think I'm good enough to do this," I say softly.

"Oh, *come on*!" she shouts. "Now you're just making excuses."

Her words sting, but I can't deny they're true.

"Hey, let's just take a breath now," Slips says, stepping between us. "Don't worry, Alex. Aliyah and I actually have a plan."

"You do?"

"Of course!" Slips says with his signature grin. "Cheese'N Stuff!"

"Your plan is . . . *pizza*?"

I must admit that while it doesn't sound like a very promising plan to help us win, it does sound delicious at the very least.

"Well, that's only part of it," Slips says. "Let's start a new tradition. Let's go to Cheese'N Stuff after every home game. To, like, strategize. And talk about the team. *With pizza.* In our mouths. Doesn't that sound better than just sitting around here sulking? Plus, that way, even when things get depressing, we'll at least have pepperoni to kind of cheer us up!"

I laugh, which surprises me since I've barely been capable of smiling the past few days. "So, your plan is to go eat pizza and . . . make a plan?"

"Better than no plan *and* no pizza, am I right?"

"You're right," I agree. "Let's go."

"Great!" Slips says. "I can't wait to show Aliyah that trick I can do. You know, the one where I eat a whole slice of pizza through my straw." He turns to her. "I bet you've never seen a kid do that before."

She laughs and shakes her head.

Fifteen minutes later, the three of us are at Cheese'N Stuff, and I'm having more fun than I expected. Or deserve to be having, considering how badly I'm failing Ira and the team. But it's hard *not* to have a good time with Slips. Plus, Aliyah can eat more pizza in a single sitting than anyone I've ever met. Which is pretty entertaining.

She inhales slice after slice, eating half an entire large pepperoni pie *by herself* in like fifteen minutes.

Frankly, I'm just shocked she's actually here, willing to hang out with Slips and me for fun. Well, Slips I can understand, as he's basically friends with everyone at school. But I never in a million years thought I'd be casually having pizza with our school's biggest celebrity. Especially not with my well-documented Flumpo condition.

Either way, for the first hour we simply devour pizza and talk about everything but baseball.

"I can't wait to get into some shenanigans with the team on the road!" Slips says. "You know, tomfooleries, hijinks, pranks, mischievous deeds, larks, carryings-on, and such. . . ."

"Jeez, Slips," Aliyah jokes. "How is your vocabulary so much better than mine? Isn't English your second language?"

"Heh, yeah," he says. "Don't you ever wonder where my nickname came from?"

"Actually, yeah," Aliyah says with a grin. "My friend Ellie told me it's because you once slipped and fell in the lunchroom in third grade, but somehow managed to *catch* your tumbling tray of Hot Turkey Surprise, while sprawled on the ground, without spilling a single drop of the brown gravy."

"Ha ha!" Slips nearly shouts, clearly remembering the moment fondly.

And it *was* memorable—the sort of stuff that turns kids without Flumpo into school legends. All four of the times I've slipped and fallen in the lunchroom, I not only did not catch my lunch tray but somehow defied the laws of physics and managed to get the food both all over myself *and* the cafeteria ceiling. Slips has even since given names to all four of those ceiling food stains: Billiam, William, Gilliam, and, of course, Little Roe Poe, the Old Bay Fish Fillet. Slips is so popular that most of the kids at school refer to those stains by name now and have mercifully mostly forgotten how they even got there in the first place.

"That incident *did* actually happen," Slips says. "But I was being called Slips well before that. It actually goes way back to my first year. I had a difficult time learning English when I first moved to America. So, I used to write the English word for everything on little slips of paper—sticky notes—and put them all over everything like labels. My clothes, books at school, my backpack, shoes. It didn't take long for kids at school to start calling me That Weird Paper Slips Kid. Which, by third grade, just became Slips."

"That's pretty cool," Aliyah says. "I guess it's a way better nickname than Sticky. Or Notes McGoats."

Slips and I are silent for a second—then we both burst out laughing.

"Or Posty Posterman," Slips agrees. "Or Rabbit, which is what my last name translates to in Polish. I thought for sure kids here would nickname me Rabbit."

"But no nickname can top Prairie Blaze," I say, referring to Aliyah's infamous nickname from the Little League World Series.

She rolls her eyes and shakes her head.

"That was just for TV," she says. "It's *not* my real nickname."

My cheeks and forehead are suddenly on fire.

"Okay, so what's your *real* nickname?" Slips asks.

"Who says everyone needs a nickname?" she shoots back.

"Fair enough, Miss Aliyah Carolyn Perkins," Slips says all formally.

Aliyah laughs. "Fine, because you're my friends now, I'll tell you. But it's sort of embarrassing, so you can't tell anyone else. . . ."

Wait, did she just call me her *friend*? My stomach flutters, not just at having Aliyah Perkins as an actual friend, but at simply having another friend besides Slips at all.

"Nope. *Harcerze* honor," Slips says, holding a finger to his lips while his other hand is raised like he's taking an oath.

"Same," I say, raising my hand like Slips, worried that if I try to say anything more, I might say something so stupid she'll change her mind and unfriend me in real life.

"What's Har-sayer-sah?" Aliyah asks.

"*Harcerze* is like a Polish version of Boy Scouts," Slips explains. "But it's just way more terrifying—and better—than the American version, since adult supervision and general precautions are minimal at best. During my last *Harcerze* canoe trip, one kid almost cut off his own leg with an ax, and real arrows were fired at one another no fewer than three times, plus— hey!" He cuts off the story abruptly. "Stop distracting me. I believe you were about to disclose your *real*, top secret nickname!"

"Okay, fine," Aliyah says. "My nickname at home with my family and brothers and oldest friends is . . ." She stops for a second. I can tell she's embarrassed, which is something I never thought I'd see. "My nickname is: Crabby."

Slips immediately explodes with laughter and pounds the table with a fist, while she starts slugging his arm, even though she's laughing too.

"Come on, I told you it was embarrassing!"

"I have to hear the story behind *that,*" Slips says.

"Ask me again sometime, *Rabbit.*"

"No, come on!" Slips pleads.

"A person's gotta keep some secrets," Aliyah says, turning toward me. "Right, Weakerman?"

"Uh, sure?" I say, my stomach in ropes. I'm terrified she somehow knows about my deal with Tex, until I realize that's not possible.

"Like, how did the two of you become friends, anyway?" she asks. "You guys seem so . . . *different.*"

"Um, *understatement,*" I say, and both Slips and Aliyah burst out laughing.

"See?" Slips says to her. "I told you he was Undercover Funny."

I'm not sure whether to be thrilled that Slips is telling Aliyah good things about me when I'm not around or embarrassed that they talk about me at all when I'm not around.

"Well, we became friends because . . ." Slips says slowly. "I mean, at first it was just because Alex was the only kid who was nice to me when I moved here. Alex, you know, he never judges. He's never *mean* to anyone. Which, if you know Ira, is not a surprise. But, anyway, Alex didn't care that I had a Polish accent or didn't know what *being cool* was supposed to look like. Then, once I finally got through his shyness, I found out he's super funny. And weird, in a good way. The way he gets so nerdy about baseball and stuff is hilarious. He's just so darn lovable . . . right?"

He ruffles my hair and all three of us laugh again.

"Is that why you gave up your summer to coach a game you *hate*?" Aliyah asks.

It's actually something I haven't considered before. Perhaps I've been taking for granted how much Slips has given up for this? Which only compounds my guilt for dragging him into this sinking hole with me.

"I took this job for Alex," Slips says. "He needed me. And this team means everything to him, so how could I *not* help? I mean, I really do hate this confusing and boring game, and it's not like I know what to say when I have to fill in for Alex as team pep talker . . . but if I ever get the opportunity to achieve my own lifelong dream, well,

I know Alex would help."

"So, what is your lifelong dream?" Aliyah asks.

"To do the moonwalk on the actual moon, of course."

She laughs.

"Anyway, what *can* we do to turn this team around?" Slips asks, finally bringing us back to the matter at hand.

"We have to change something up," Aliyah says. "What we're doing clearly isn't working."

"I agree," I say. "But what if, like, the team, and myself, just aren't good enough to win?"

"That's the sort of thing people who are *okay with losing* say," Aliyah shoots back.

I try not to be too offended.

"I may not know much about baseball," Slips says, "but I actually think this team can win games. We just need a spark of some sort, so we don't get stuck in a self-defeating spiral. Maybe let me heckle the opposing hitters? That's what I do best from the seats, right?"

"No way," I say. "It's bush-league to heckle when you're one of the coaches."

And so we sit there, trying to come up with any sort of idea.

"Well," Aliyah finally says, "my Little League coach last year always said 'one game at a time.' So, I think we start there. We need to figure out exactly how many games we need to win to make the playoffs. And from there, just take it one game, one inning, one batter at a time. Every little thing we need to do right to make the playoffs."

"I agree." Slips nods. "That sounds all sportsy and stuff."

"Luckily," I say, cracking open one of my binders, "'every little thing' is my specialty."

We spend the next twenty minutes going over our remaining schedule and the past few years of the Mabel.

We come up with this:

1. The last-seeded playoff team in the Mabel finishes with an average record of 47–43.
2. With us currently sitting at 19–32, that means we need go 28–11 over our remaining thirty-nine games to have a shot.
3. However, the final two-game series of the regular season is versus the Duluth Harbor Pirates. Easily the best team in the Mabel. A team we've gone an abysmal 4–96 against over the last ten seasons.
4. So, realistically, that means we need to go 28–9 in the games leading up to that final series.

"Ooookay . . ." Slips says slowly. "We can basically only

lose nine more games all season to keep our hopes alive?"

I nod. "If we even lose two more games than that, we'd be stuck having to sweep the Harbor Pirates at the end of the season."

"When was the last time that happened?" Slips asks.

I check my notes.

"Twenty-nine years ago."

"Those were the Dream Team years," Aliyah says. "The Big Four. Early Eights Foster."

"We didn't lose a single game to the Harbor Pirates when Early Eights was on the team," I say. "A perfect thirty-seven and oh, including the playoffs."

"Wow," Aliyah says. "Now *that's* some Baseball Zazzle right there."

"Baseball *Zazzle*?" I say.

"Yeah, I'm also lost," Slips agrees.

"You know what I'm talking about, Weakerman," Aliyah says. "It's that undefinable magic that makes baseball *baseball*. That energy that encompasses all the stuff numbers can't explain. Like how a guy who has ten career home runs suddenly smashes forty in one season. Or how the Minnesota Twins have an astonishing twenty-six-game playoff losing streak, spanning decades, no matter how well they've played during the regular season. Or how Mariano Rivera had a 0.70 ERA in the postseason, less than a third of his career regular-season 2.22 ERA. It's what makes clutch players clutch, and the chokers choke. It's what's behind most curses and hot streaks. It's the *It* in It Factor. It explains how teams with very little talent can sometimes win championships. Baseball Zazzle is the governing law behind the whole game. Most players agree that it's what *really* decides who wins and who loses. The numbers are just window dressing."

I definitely know what she's talking about, I've just never heard it called *Baseball Zazzle* before. Some people call it Baseball Juju, some Baseball Magic; others have their own made-up words for it, like Aliyah. But everyone who knows baseball knows exactly what she's talking about.

The problem is: it isn't real.

"Come on." I laugh. "You don't actually believe in that stuff, do you?"

"Of course I do!" Aliyah says. "Sometimes it's the *only* thing you can believe in."

"But it's basically a total dismissal of logic," I say. "Plus, numbers are not just 'window dressing.' They might not always be right, but that only reinforces how often they are."

"Whatever," Aliyah says, but she's still smiling. "Personally, if I really believed everything was predetermined, baseball would be pretty boring."

I shrug, not really wanting to keep arguing with only the second friend I've ever made.

So instead, I ask: "How did you come up with calling it *Zazzle* anyway?"

"Because Baseball Magic or the Essence of Baseball or whatever people call it is too boring!" she says. "You know? It's like Baseball Razzle Dazzle, but only with more *Zazz*!"

Slips and I both laugh. Aliyah can often be so intense, especially during competition, that's weird to see her being kind of silly.

"I, for one, love it!" Slips declares.

"Thanks, Rabbit," Aliyah says.

Slips grins at her new nickname for him.

"Well, uh, anyway . . ." I say to Slips. "A lot of people would say Baseball Magic or 'Zazzle' is why the Harbor Pirates couldn't beat Early Eights Foster. Rather than recognizing he was part of a legit Dream Team loaded with talent. I mean, the Big Four are a *part* of that undefeated record."

"But the other three guys in the Big Four don't have

undefeated records versus the Pirates," Aliyah counters. "In fact, the Hurricanes got swept by the Harbor Pirates the season after Eights left, in spite of still having three of the Big Four on the team and going an incredible seventy-nine and twenty-one overall."

"So, what did Eights have that was so special?" Slips asks. "I mean, Alex, you always tell me that one great player doesn't make a great team when it comes to baseball."

"What was really special about him, according to Ira," I say, "is that he made everyone else around him play better. To a player, their career statistics when playing with Eights were better across the board than when Eights wasn't playing with them."

"Right: Baseball Zazzle was strong with him," Aliyah says. "Like I've been saying."

"Well, that's what we need, then," Slips says. "If Eights can find a way to get the most out of mediocre players, then I know you can too, Alex." He points at my stomach. "I bet you've got some Baseball Zazzle deep down in there somewhere."

"No, this is mostly just pizza," I say without thinking.

Slips and Aliyah burst out laughing.

"I told you: joke ninja," Slips says to Aliyah between guffaws.

Either way, I know he's right—about the first part, anyway: we need to find *something*, call it Baseball Zazzle or Magic or whatever, to spark the team.

"I think it all starts with us *trusting* them," Aliyah says. "It's not a coach's job to tell players what to do. It's a coach's job to help them do what they already know how to do, but better. We have to talk to them, see how they're feeling—on the mound, at the plate, in the field. And, well, Alex . . ." She looks away, as if afraid to go on.

"I know," I finish for her. "I'm not good at talking to people."

"It's not that," Aliyah says. "Not everyone can be like Slips. But that's what I'm saying: a coach doesn't just talk, they also listen. We need to find ways to unlock the best in each of them. And that means talking *with* them, not just *to* them."

"That's easy for you to say." I just sort of shake my head. "You're you, and I'm . . . me."

"You're not doing this by yourself, though," Slips says. "You've got us behind you. But you need to be confident. Tomorrow at practice, we need to show the players that we know what they're about, and that we're here to help them. But that means you gotta talk to them, Alex. Aliyah's got the pitchers covered, but as far as the rest of them go, I don't know enough about baseball to do this for you."

I finally nod, knowing they're both right.

"Nine games?" I say.

"Nine games," Slips says.

"We can't lose more than nine games," Aliyah says. "And we won't."

Chapter 21

AT THE START OF PRACTICE THE NEXT DAY, I'M LOOKING AT MY TO-DO list.

Flumpo is already at work: sweaty back, damp brow, reddened cheeks, stomach in knots, trouble swallowing and breathing, shaky knees, hollow brain cavity, and most of all, an inability to speak to anyone but Slips.

"You gotta do it, buddy," Slips says, standing next to me. "For the team. For Ira."

"I know," I say, more to myself than anyone else. "Can't let Ira down. Can't lose the team."

We're about to go on the road for the first time. Nine straight away games spanning eleven days. I've never even taken a trip that long with my family, let alone a bunch of professional athletes. And we already know we pretty much need to win at least four of those games to keep our playoff hopes alive. This practice might be my one shot to get them playing better before the road trip. To get the team in the right mindset.

I look down at my list again.

It's eleven names. Eleven players with specific sets of drills to work on. Areas I know they need to improve to better help us win. In rewatching videos of my first two games several times the day before, I identified the eleven biggest causes for concern. More specifically, eleven players I needed to talk to.

I take a deep breath.

"You got this," Slips says. "If things get hairy, just whistle. Anne of Green Gables will be there lickety-split to bash some snakes."

I give him a look, sweat already pouring down my cheeks.

Slips just grins and shrugs, before giving me a light shove in Carla Henderson's direction.

She's sprawled on the grass, stretching near the visitors' dugout.

"Um, hi," I say.

Carla smiles, which somehow makes this worse. Here she is being nice to me when I've pretty much ruined her first two games as a ballplayer, and all I have for her are my observations on why she stunk at the plate.

"What's going on, coach?"

In my head, it goes like this:

Hey, Carla. I think you're doing a great job so far. I'm impressed with the way you're hanging in the box, not stepping out when pitchers come inside. But there are a few things we need to work on, that I think will help the team. First, we need to focus on getting your hands through the zone, and not worrying so much about "swinging." Don't worry about outcomes at the plate, just on staying loose.

But the Flumpo makes it come out like this:

"Um, it's—it's good you're box hanging," I stammer. "*Not* hanging, I mean. Er, hang zone. Uh, swing low hands. And, like, it's the team wants to win. . . ."

"What are you trying to say?" she asks.

"I mean, it's . . . your nerves." I skip ahead. "You, uh, look nervous. Not like batting practice, um, the second half. But your swinging isn't, like, going the way it can. . . ."

"Well, you're not wrong about that," Carla says. "I've got some big shoes to fill. Big expectations."

She must be talking about Pat McGroarty, the Hurricanes' former power-hitting DH who quit last week.

"Well, forget about everyone else," I say, finally catching my breath and forcing myself to calm down. "I know the fans must be adding pressure. . . . I mean, players like Early Eights thrived on extra attention and pressure, but that's not the case for everyone."

Carla is on her feet now, a look on her face that I've never seen before.

"What do you mean by that?" she snaps. "You really don't understand the pressure I'm under right now?"

"Because you're a, the, uh, first woman player in league history?"

"Um, no. It's got nothing to do with that. But now that you bring it up, I'm sure I'm going to get lots more wonderfully intelligent, original questions about being a *female baseball player* from reporters later, so I kinda don't feel like I need to talk about it with a kid right now. No offense."

I try to tell her I didn't mean anything by it, that I was trying to be understanding. But all that happens when I try to talk is my mouth opens and closes silently like a dying fish's.

"Look, thanks for trying, but I think my issues are something I need to work through on my own."

Before I can say another word, Carla heads for the dugout to get her bat.

I don't follow her. I wish I knew how to do this. Talk to people like a normal person, I mean.

Maybe the next one will go better? It can't go any worse.

I check my list: the Law.

This time, I'm at least relatively sure I know what his issues are. He's simply not commanding the zone like a pitcher needs to. Aliyah and I think it's time for him to hit the reset button. Move to the bullpen while he works out a new approach or develops a better secondary pitch. His current arsenal hasn't worked his whole career—you can't get by with *only* a fastball as a starter, no matter how fast it is. Aliyah will be doing most of the specific coaching, but I'm going to talk to him about what I'm seeing first.

I approach him as he's warming up with some long toss.

"What do you want, Alan?" he asks.

His greeting kicks Flumpo into action immediately.

"I don't think your career is going well at all," I blurt out. "I mean, uh, you're going to the bullpen so you can, um, change pitching and help the team and—"

"What?" he demands, catching a long throw from Mayhem. But instead of throwing it back, he keeps the ball in his glove and turns toward me. "You're demoting me to the bullpen?"

"Well, just until you figure out, uh, stuff and things. . . ." I trail off.

If the Law's eyes were actual weapons, I don't think I'd have a face anymore.

"Stuff and things?"

"Um, yeah?"

"Look, Alan," he says, jabbing his glove at me. "I'll do it, because I *am* a team player, and you're the manager, whether I like it or not. But it ain't easy, having to make up for the fact I'm playing alongside retail employees, high school kids, and a manager who can barely speak coherent English half the time!"

He turns and jogs toward the bullpen, not even giving

me a chance to respond. But what would I have said anyway?

I search the field for the next person on my list: Big Fish.

Aliyah is over by the left field foul pole, working on something with the pitching staff. And Slips is near the batting cages, waving around Anne of Green Gables, making a group of players laugh. How is this so easy for them?

I finally spot Big Fish walking toward the dugout. I assume he's heading to the team weight room, where he spends most of his time when not in the batting cage. I hurry over, wanting to catch him before he leaves the field. I don't have a lot of notes, being that he's still our best player by light-years. His fix should be simple but could potentially have a big impact. He's just trying too hard. He's taking home-run swings on every pitch. What we really need right now are base runners. He can help the team most by simply getting on base, not by hitting home runs once every sixth at bat and striking out the other five. A lot of opposing teams are going to pitch around him, which means he can rack up lots of walks, if only he'll stop swinging at bad pitches.

"Hey, Big Fish!" I call out.

I know he hears me, but he takes his time slowing down and turning around.

"Oliver," he says.

"Oliver?"

"Yeah. That's my name. Only *fans* call me Big Fish."

"Oh, um, right," I say, looking down, my face red and sweaty. "Uh, well, anyway, I just, have some, uh, notes for you."

I try to explain my plan. But all that comes out is:

"Stop swinging at pitches."

"Excuse me?" he asks aggressively.

"Uh, what I mean is, um, well, not *every* pitch, but, or, yeah, every pitch, and—"

"Look, kid," he says, pointing a finger the size of my whole forearm. "I'll do what I need to do to get to the next level. I don't care what you say. I got to worry about what I got to worry about. Okay?"

"Um, okay."

"Okay."

He continues into the dugout tunnel toward the weight room.

So, that makes me a solid 0–3 to start my day. And the next two meetings don't go any better.

My notes for Mayhem come out as, "Batton your hatches to protect the gold."

To which he replies, while laughing: "Argh! Ye matey!"

Really, I swear I had an actual analogy that worked to sort out his short stride issues—at least in my head.

And Joe Hoff, who everyone apparently just calls Jof, says, "You want me to lick what?" after I mistakenly tell him to lick his own armpits while merely trying to help him keep his elbows in, so his hands pass through the zone quicker.

I'm feeling so discouraged halfway through practice that I eventually give up and head toward the dugout so I can get back to my office and look at some pitching matchups for our upcoming series. Alone. That's where my real strength lies. Everyone knows that. Whose bright idea was this, anyway? Me, having coherent conversations with players? "Helping" them?

"Hey, where are you going, Alex?" Slips calls out.

"Practice is only half over!" Aliyah adds. "It's the last one before the road trip; you can't leave yet!"

I spin around as I reach the dugout steps to find them jogging toward me.

"Why did you make me do this?" I yell, pointing at my

clipboard. "It only made everything worse!"

They exchange a quick glance, but I don't even give them a chance to respond. I storm down the stairs and through the tunnel toward my office.

They don't try to stop me.

Chapter 22

LATER THAT NIGHT, I'M IN MY BEDROOM PACKING A SUITCASE FOR MY first road trip as manager of the Hurricanes.

It'll be nine games against three teams we *need* to beat. In fact, if we don't win at least four of these nine games, it drops our playoff odds from an already abysmally low 1.02 percent to a basically impossible 0.081 percent. To take my mind off my inevitable failure, I take a quick break from packing to page through a few more of Ira's notebooks. I've been reading a few of them every day. It's sometimes the only thing that can cheer me up.

I start with a newer scorecard from four or five years ago. The very first note is pretty much Grandpa summed up.

—Man, that hot dog might've been the best I ever had!!!

The next game has this gem:

—How DO the seagulls in Chicago know when a Cubs game is ending? Can they really comprehend the passing of innings?

That same game also contains a slightly more puzzling note. It references someone with the initials "A.M.," who I'd seen mentioned in his notes before:

—Still convinced A.M. is key. Ticket sales hit a new low and probably will get worse. Convince him to come back! His Magic could make all the difference. Keeps acting like he hardly knows me though. Imagine that! We were basically family and now he can't even look at me.

I earmark the page with a sticky note, wondering if it might be worth looking into further at some point. Even if just to figure out who Ira could have known so well that he apparently never mentioned to me before.

I'm still pondering A.M. when I catch my name on the next page.

—Wish the other kids at Alex's school knew how smart and sweet he is. He's the best grandson a guy could want. He'll—

I close the notebook and toss it aside before finishing the sentence. I cannot be reading things like that right now.

Instead, I reach for one of the oldest notebooks I can find, one where I *know* I won't be mentioned, because I didn't exist yet. The pages are so yellow, they almost look coffee stained, and the ink so faded that some of the words are illegible. It's from fifty-six years ago, when Grandpa Ira was just thirty. That season, the Hurricanes went 67–31, eventually losing to the Williston Wingnuts in the championship. Like the newer ones, this notebook contains a lot of extraneous details about people and just the bare minimum game stats:

—Great to see our league's first Japanese player in person! A special guy!

—REMINDER: Speak to dad again about using original farmland for a new stadium. Pitch: call it Mustard Yards. He'll love it!

*—Guy in section 102 has a great hat! *Find him after game to see where he got it*

But at times, younger Ira is, well . . . a bit more like me. For instance, from a game three weeks into the season:

—Boots Poffenberger strikes out three times—again! Former big leaguer or not, he stinks! Tell dad we GOTTA cut him! Even if he does bring in the crowds . . .

I turn the page slowly and scan the next game. My eyes stop on a single word scrawled on the bottom:

PoTTY.

No, he wasn't writing about urine. As I look closer at the faded ink, I realize I've stumbled across something unexpected.

—Grandpa Magnum is here tonight. A rare visit. (I hope I never get too sick to take care of myself!) He never cared much about baseball.

Then, later down in the scorecard, at the very bottom, there's tiny writing that clearly *isn't* my grandpa's:

—Hello Ira, Magnum here. You went to get a hot dog and I figured I'd use this time to write you a note. Your great-great-grandpa Powell didn't take his secret recipe for PoTTY sauce to the grave like we always said. Maybe try to make it someday? Either way, take care of yourself—don't get too wrapped up in this team.—PAPPY MAGNUM

Powell's Tasty Tangy Yellow Sauce:

1 cup homegrown Weakerman farm mustard seed

½ cup water

¾ cup apple cider vinegar

1 tsp fresh ground nutmeg

¼ tsp fresh ground smoked paprika

¼ tsp dried lavender

1 tsp Weakerman farm honey

1 clove dried black garlic

1 tbsp pork sauce

Grind mustard seed and all dry ingredients to fine powder and mix together. Boil water and vinegar. Add mustard mix and pork sauce and stir. Reduce heat and simmer for 3.4 hours precisely, stirring every 279 seconds. Remove from heat and stir in honey. Enjoy.

I blink a few times, not comprehending what I'm reading. Ira must have never seen this note. He'd definitely have told me about it if he had. Knowing he never saw this note from his grandpa that was meant for him is painful. It feels like my chest is being tightened in a vise. I wish more than anything Ira were here, so I could show him this. He's the only other person I know who would care. As it is, I'm looking at the long-lost recipe to Great-Great-Great-Great-Grandpa Powell's bestselling, legendary mustard, and there's *nobody* to share it with.

"What's wrong?" my dad asks, poking his head into my room.

"What?" I say. "Nothing."

"Then why are your eyes red?"

"It's . . . I was just thinking about mustard."

"Mustard?"

"Never mind."

"Okay, well, listen: I know you're packing but I need some help with this turkey I'm brining. Just real quick. Meet me out back?"

"Okay, sure."

"Great." He spins and heads down the hallway like he's got a brisket on fire or something. Which actually happened once. You ever seen a grown adult on his hands and knees crying over a charred and smoking hunk of brisket?

I glance back down at the PoTTY Sauce recipe, still thinking it's a shame there's no one to share it with, especially Ira. It's been believed extinct by the Weakerman family for decades.

"You coming?" my dad calls out from the living room.

"Yeah, hang on!" I yell, taking a quick photo of the old notebook page. If there's anyone who might care, it's my dad.

I head out to the patio, where he's stirring the ingredients in his huge brining Tupperware with a massive wooden spoon.

"I need you to slowly pour this into the brine," he says, motioning toward a pitcher filled with a strange brown liquid.

I grab the pitcher and pour, while he stirs. It smells

like moldy socks soaked in bacon fat, but I don't complain. Whatever it is, I know it will taste delicious in the end. It always does.

"I've got something for you," I say as I help him lift the turkey rack into the finished brine.

"Oh yeah, what's that?"

"I just texted it to you," I say as we secure the Tupperware lid in place.

He quickly writes the date and time on a piece of masking tape on the Tupperware lid, and then pulls out his phone. He reads my message, squinting to see the faded ink on the photo of the old page.

"PoT-TY Sauce?" my dad asks, looking confused. "Is this some kind of joke I'm missing out on?"

"No, Dad, it's Powell Weakerman's mustard recipe!" I say. "The one that put Weakerville on the map? That he supposedly took to his grave? You know the family story; Ira told it a bunch of times."

"Oh yeah," he says, as if I just reminded him he has a dentist appointment tomorrow. "I remember now. Huh."

"I know it's not a big deal," I say. "I just thought it was cool that I found it and I couldn't think of anyone else besides Ira who might be interested. Since you're, like, the barbecue guy and make sauces all the time . . ."

"Yeah, I guess it's pretty neat," he says, taking a final look at his phone before putting it back in his pocket. "I usually make barbecue sauce, not mustard, but it might be interesting to try someday."

But he sounds about as interested as if I'd texted a photo of a small rock lying on the ground.

"Well, anyway, am I all done?"

"Not just yet," he says. "I need to talk to you about . . . well, I'm worried, Alex."

"Worried? About the team?"

"No," my dad says, scratching his head uncomfortably. "It's just, this whole thing with the Hurricanes, and being their manager. Ira probably thought this would be fun for you. But if it's not, there's no shame in quitting. It's not your fault, you know; the team has been failing for years, and . . . I just want you to know that you won't be letting him down. He just wanted you to be happy, Alex."

"Yeah, well, the *team* makes me happy," I say, unsure of where he's going with this. "And if they go away, *then* what will I do?"

"Alex, I'm just saying that you're not—"

"Look, I gotta go finish packing, okay?" I interrupt. "Say hi to mom for me. I'll probably be gone by the time she's home from her night shift. See you in a week or two, I guess."

I turn and head back to my room.

"Alex!" my dad calls after me, but I ignore him.

I shut my bedroom door and then plop down on the bed. *Nobody* thinks I have any chance to do this. How can I believe it myself when my own father doesn't think I can do this?

I wonder what Ira would do in my place. Sure, he'd maybe handle this all with a lot more grace and dignity, but the team had been languishing for years, even when he *was* here. So clearly Ira didn't know how to fix this either. I mean, his ultimate solution was apparently *me*.

Where does that leave us now?

Chapter 23

IT'S A LOT QUIETER THAN I EXPECT.

Thirty people—twenty-two players, two equipment managers, a team trainer, a travel coordinator, one grizzled driver with the thickest mustache I've ever seen, plus Slips, Aliyah, and me—are crammed onto a small, aging charter bus. I expect it to be rowdy and loud the whole drive to Joliet, Illinois. But barely anybody talks. The hiss of every soda being opened and the crinkling of every bag of chips can be heard with shocking clarity as open prairie scrolls past our windows for hours on end.

Most of the team is spread out in the middle and back of the bus, wearing hats pulled down low, their faces glued to glowing screens. A few are reading, the rest are sleeping. Aliyah's dad is in a blue Toyota Corolla behind the bus. He'll be staying with Aliyah at the team hotel each night.

Slips, Aliyah, and I are sitting near the front. We went over lineups for a minute after boarding that morning, but for most of the drive we either sleep, read, or play games on our phones with earbuds in.

At the hotel, we barely have time to unpack and get to the field for pregame practice. Once there, it's all business. Even Slips is pretty quiet most of the day, except to excitedly point out how much nicer the visiting locker rooms are than our own back at Mustard Park.

The whole team has another rough night.

Our offense is abysmal, getting just five base runners all game. Carla goes 0–3 again, making her 0–9 on the season with eight strikeouts. I suppose the fact that she actually makes contact tonight, popping out in one at bat, is progress. Plus, she does seem a lot less nervous, perhaps bolstered by the rousing ovation she gets from the away crowd when announced. But it's odd she'd be more at ease on the road than at Mustard Park, so maybe

I'm just seeing things that aren't really there.

Either way, it's a team effort, losing the first of our three-game series versus the Joliet AirHogs by the score 9–0. The AirHogs are a team we should beat in normal circumstances. Their two best players just signed minor league deals in the MLB system, taking away a combined 17.8 WAR (wins above replacement). But then, these aren't normal circumstances.

The mood is somber on the bus ride back to our hotel that night. And why shouldn't it be? We're now 0–3 under my "leadership," putting us at 19–33 on the season. We still haven't scored a single run.

Slips, Aliyah, and I haven't spoken much since I snapped at them after practice yesterday. Which is why I'm surprised when they ask to sit next to me on the bus ride back to the hotel.

"Sure," I say, scooting over so they can cram into the seat.

"So, what now?" Slips asks.

"I don't know, I was hoping you were here to tell *me*," I say.

"Losing this game isn't the end," Aliyah says, keeping her voice low so the players don't overhear us. "But it feels like it with the way we played. We're down to an eight-game margin of error, based on your models, Alex."

"I know, it . . . well, it feels *impossible*," I admit. "I don't know, maybe it is. The models I've worked up give us under one percent chance of making the playoffs at this point, and if we lose the next game—"

My words are cut short by the bus's air brakes as we pull under the awning of the La Quinta Inn. As the team stands up to pile off the bus, someone up front shouts for our attention.

"Hey, I was going to wait until our first win, but . . . whatever," the voice says. This is met with some bitter laughs. "As some of you know, I love to bake and am trying out for the next season of *America's Great Bake-Off.* I stayed up all night last night making these cupcakes for you to try and tell me what you think. All feedback is welcome!"

"Wow, you made the frosting into sparkly unicorn heads!" someone yells, and everyone laughs.

"They look pretty good!"

I still can't see who it is, and I can't imagine who on the team loves to bake unicorn cupcakes as a hobby. I assume it's one of the new guys. But then we finally get to the front of the bus, and I see who it is.

My jaw drops.

Big Fish holds an open Tupperware toward me. It's filled with cupcakes frosted to look like unicorn faces, and they are pretty incredible.

"Adorable!" Aliyah says, plucking one from the container.

"The horn is made from marzipan," Big Fish says. "Enjoy."

Slips and I each take one and then file off the bus.

"See, *this* is why we can't give up!" Slips whispers as we head into the hotel lobby. "What statistical model could have predicted *that*?"

"Okay, fine," I admit as I unwrap my cupcake. "But we still need to *do something* to turn the tide. It won't just happen on its own."

"Yeah," Aliyah says through a mouthful of frosting.

Once in the lobby, the players and other team personnel head off to their rooms or to the lounge next door. As for me and my fellow coaches, though, I get the sense that none of us will get any sleep until we come up with something. Slips and Aliyah must be thinking the same thing because we all silently plop down on the empty lobby couch instead of heading to our own rooms. For a few seconds, the only sound is us smacking on Big Fish's delicious cupcakes while we brainstorm.

"What we really need is some Baseball ZaZa," Slips says. "If I'm understanding correctly how it works."

"It's Zazzle," I remind him.

"And Baseball Zazzle isn't something you can just pull from your pocket like a simple pack of gum," Aliyah says. "It's hard to come by."

"I feel like all I've been hearing lately is Baseball Zazzle talk," I say. "You guys and Ira. He called it 'the Magic of Baseball,' but it's the same deal—"

"Ira?" Slips and Aliyah ask in near perfect unison; their teeth are stained blue from the unicorns' frosting hair.

"You've been, uh, *talking* to him?" Slips adds. "Have you?"

"No, not like that," I say. "Just from all the scorecards he left me in his will. They're filled with all kinds of notes. They're more like journals, I guess."

I tell them about Ira's notebooks—the funny and caring and random things he'd write, the recipe for my family's famous mustard, even the mysterious A.M. person who Ira had speculated might possess enough Baseball Magic to help turn the team around.

There's a moment of silence, and then they both grin.

"Weakerman, that's it!" Aliyah says. "We gotta find this A.M. guy."

"Yeah," Slips says. "If he knew Ira as well as Ira seems to know him, maybe he could help to inspire the team!"

I shake my head. "These notes were from a while ago. If he was Ira's age, I'm not even sure he's still alive."

"But what if he is?" Slips counters.

"And what if Ira was right about him?" Aliyah adds.

"But how can we even find out who it is?" I say.

"Well, can we think of anyone with those initials?" she asks.

"My dad's name is Andrew Meachum," I say. "But there's no way my dad would be the key to saving the team. He *hates* the Hurricanes. Plus, Ira and my dad were definitely not pals."

"There's Anderson Mikkeller from school?" Aliyah suggests.

"He's not old enough," I say. "Besides, Anderson just moved here two years ago."

"It's entirely possible A.M. is someone we don't even know," Slips says.

"Maybe it's a former player?" Aliyah suggests.

"Yeah!" says Slips. "What about those Big Four you

guys are always talking about? Could it have been one of them? Ira would have known those guys for a while, wouldn't he?"

"Maybe . . ." I say.

We go through them one by one. Early Eights Foster and Seven Fingers Bowman are both dead, so it can't be them, since Ira mentioned seeing A.M. as recently as two years ago. Which leaves Luis "Dirty Ball" Mendez and Bernie "BAM" Morgan. Both have last names that start with *M*, which is promising. But according to Google, Dirty Ball presently resides in California, where he coaches a local college team, and BAM Morgan has basically no online presence at all. So, it's possible it's him, if we're willing to overlook the fact that Bernie does not start with an *A*.

It's a good lead, but without any way to find out where BAM is now, we're at a bit of a dead end.

"Hey, here's an idea," Aliyah finally says, exhausted. "Let's just find a time machine and go back and get Early Eights Foster in his prime."

"That's it!" Slips says.

We laugh sadly.

"No, I'm serious."

"You really know where we can find a time machine?" I ask.

"No, that's not what I'm saying. What I mean is, we don't actually need A.M. or this Eights Bananas Foster guy. We just need to recapture what it was *about him* that made the Hurricanes unbeatable. *Why* everyone played so well around him. Alex, you're always telling me how good some of the current players are. Like master cupcake baker Big Fish. All last year you kept saying he had the raw talent to maybe make it to the majors someday, right?"

I nod, surprised he'd actually been paying attention.

"Okay, so it's not just talent that made Frosty Morning Bananas so special. What *else* was it?"

"I never actually saw him play," Aliyah admits. "I only know the stories my dad told me."

"I've seen him play," I say. "My grandpa and I used to watch his old games on these DVD things all the time."

"And that was enough for him to be your favorite player?" Slips prods.

"Yeah," I say, seeing what he's getting at, even if he doesn't know the specifics himself. "And you're right: it was more than talent. He played with relentless passion. Like every play, every pitch, was the defining moment in a World Series game. He *hated* losing. But it went even deeper than winning and losing. Ira said it wasn't pride or pure competitiveness that made him that way—it was that he didn't want to let down the people of Weakerville. Eights once told Ira that at the start of every game, he looked up into the stands, reminded himself that every fan there had spent their hard-earned money and time to be there and watch him play. And he owed it to them to make it worth it, every time. Every play. Every moment, he dedicated to the town and fans. And you can *totally* see that when you watch Eights play, even on video. He was easy to love, because it felt like he loved you right back, if that makes sense. He loved the crowd, the stadium, the game. And so, everyone around him did too."

A strangely tense moment follows.

"Yeah," Slips finally says. "*That's* what we're missing."

"I know, but who else loves the Hurricanes that much?" I say.

"Maybe not any of the players . . ." Aliyah agrees, looking to Slips to let him explain what I'm apparently missing.

"It's *you*," Slips says, breathless. "No one loves this team as much as you do. Believe me, I've been dealing with it for years. The Hurricanes are in your blood."

"The problem is, no one on the team would know it!" Aliyah adds.

"She's right," Slips says. "That's *why* Ira made you manager. Not because of your knowledge about baseball, or any of that statistical garbage you're always going on about. It's because no one cares about the Hurricanes the way you do! I mean, look at me: I hate baseball, but I still go to most of the games every summer because *you make it fun* for me."

"I don't have any doubt he's telling the truth, Weakerman," Aliyah adds. "The problem is, nobody can feel that right now. In fact, ever since you took this job, it almost seems like you *hate* baseball."

I open my mouth to argue with them, but I realize something in that moment.

They're right.

When I'm silent, Slips continues. "You can't worry about losing games so much that you forget what makes baseball fun in the first place."

"It's nearly impossible to be successful at this game if you're afraid of losing," Aliyah adds. "Just focus on the game itself, not the outcome. That's where the joy comes from."

"Is that something your Little League coach told you?" I ask.

"No," Aliyah says with a smile. "It's something your

grandpa Ira told me after my first, and *only,* loss."

My throat clenches as my chest swells with pride. But then it fades as I realize just how poorly I've been handling the task Ira gave me. They are right: there hasn't been a single fun moment so far.

"The point is," Slips adds, "we're three kids managing our hometown baseball team, one that has been here for over a hundred and fifty years. This is supposed to be the best summer ever, *especially* for you! And think about the players—they're just as afraid as you are, if not more so. If *you* loosen up, maybe the team will too. And even if that doesn't help us win games, at least we'll be having fun while we lose, right?"

I nod.

If this is the team's last season, do I really want to waste it being miserable, stressed, and afraid every game? The metrics say we're a 12–78 team. So maybe it's time to ignore the numbers for once and get a bit more creative? That is, after all, part of the joy of baseball—it can be, and has been, reinvented again and again and again.

"Okay," I finally say with a smile. "I can do this. I've been going to Hurricanes games my whole life and loving every minute of it. This is the same thing, except now I'm sitting in the dugout, not in the stands."

"*Yes,* that's the Alex I know!" Slips says, clapping me on the shoulder. "Tomorrow is the start of a new season for us. Bring the fun, Alex. Do what you were born to do. You really think Ira gave you this job to sulk? To play it safe? To be miserable? He wanted you to *have fun*!"

"Let's try new things," says Aliyah. "Mix it up. And most of all, stop coaching scared."

They're right. I've let Flumpo invade the one place it never used to get me: baseball. And it made me miss the most important fact of all: We can't keep playing baseball in the normal way with an anything-but-normal roster of players. We need to figure out the best each player has to offer and find a creative way to bring that out in our games.

Tomorrow, we'll play the game like none of us have before.

At this point, what else do we have to lose?

Chapter 24

IT ALL STARTS BEFORE THE GAME THE NEXT DAY, IN THE LOCKER ROOM, when I make Slips tell Eldridge Zimmer he won't be the starting pitcher as planned.

"What do you mean?" he says, practically jumping out of his uniform. "Who's going to start, then?"

"*Nobody,*" Slips says with a smile.

Everyone is stunned. The whole team freezes—Mayhem stops mid-shoe-tie; Big Fish is mid-belt-buckling—and stares at us. Which of course makes the Flumpo kick into action. Sweat oozes down my lower back, my hands shake, my brain feels numb. But I swallow, and breathe. We've got a plan to unveil.

"Are we forfeiting?" Carla asks, poking her head out from behind her partition.

There are murmurs of disappointment at this suggestion, even as poorly as things have been going.

I close my eyes and take another deep breath, knowing that if I don't concentrate and try and explain the first of our many new strategies, Flumpo is going to make me say something like, *Don't you think chicken nuggets would, like, taste pretty good dipped in Elmer's glue?* Which, I kid you not, is something that actually came out of my mouth once during a class presentation in second grade.

But this time, it's not a class presentation. I'm talking *baseball*. It's the one thing I actually know. The one thing in my life about which I can ever use the words *I* and *confident* in the same sentence.

"We're not forfeiting," I finally say through an exhale. "Hurricanes don't quit. Instead . . . well, I guess by definition hurricanes do *have to* quit shortly after reaching land. Um, but, uh, where was I?"

The Law sighs dramatically and I can see I'm in danger of losing them again. I know Slips is probably moments from stepping in to save me again, but I can't let that happen. I can't. I need to be the leader. I need—

"I got it from here," Aliyah says. I breathe out in equal parts shame and relief. "I'm the pitching coach after all, and this was a joint decision. What's happening is this: Nobody is starting, because we don't have a starting rotation anymore. It's gone. Done. Over. Instead, we're matching up our pitchers with the other team's batters, *all game, every game.*"

Some players look skeptical, but others, mostly the bullpen guys, actually look excited to be part of something new and different. This strategy isn't totally unheard of—it has some history of working in the minors, other independent leagues, and even the MLB in recent years, where some teams have gone with "openers" in place of a traditional starter, to be replaced by a long reliever after an inning or two. And it should work even better here, with me possessing more data on Mabel players than probably all the other teams have on each other combined.

"If it doesn't work," Slips adds, "then we'll throw it out and try something else. We'll keep changing things up. But it's time we start paying attention to you all, instead of you paying attention to us."

"Plus, now every pitcher may be playing a meaningful role in nearly every game," Aliyah says. "We're doing this as a *team*."

Several players are nodding, which is more than I expected.

"So who's 'opening,' then?" Eldridge asks.

"The AirHogs' first three hitters have, uh, struggled against lefties throughout their careers," I manage to say. "Especially sidewinders."

Everyone turns and looks at the one lefty on our team who throws sidearm: forty-six-year-old Farmer John, one of the tryout signees.

"Me?" he says, pointing at himself.

"Yep," I say. Though he has a fastball that tops out in the low eighties and only two pitches—a slow fastball and slightly slower slider—he also has a funky delivery that stumped one of the Mabel's better lefties when Farmer John faced him during his lone appearance two games ago. "You're, um, opening the game . . . I guess."

"You guess?" the Law says.

"He *is* the opener," Aliyah says with authority. "And he *will* get us through the first inning without giving up a run. Now . . . let's go have some fun."

* * *

Farmer John pitches a perfect first inning.

He gets a round of high fives as he heads back into our dugout, but the best part is looking across the diamond and seeing the AirHogs manager flipping through a binder with a red face and furrowed brow. He hadn't expected a forty-six-year-old farmer to start the game. His gears are already spinning in all the ways I'd hoped.

Even though we didn't get a baserunner in the top of the first ourselves, our three batters did make some nice contact, and I'm already having more fun than I have since taking this job.

The new approach extends to our offense as well. Which is why Carla becomes the rare hitter batting .000 to hit cleanup, which means she's leading off the top of the second.

"Carla," I say in the dugout as our fielders jog off the diamond after the bottom of the first inning. She's putting on her helmet. "Why did you try out for this team?"

She seems surprised by the question.

"Because . . . I love baseball."

"That's what I thought," I say. "So, like, forget everything I've ever said to you before and just go out there and *enjoy this.* Don't worry whether you get on base or you strike out. The *results* don't matter. The only thoughts going through your head up there should be: stay loose and look for *your* pitch. Don't swing at anything that isn't where you want it, but if he does throw something in your spot, you jump on it. The outcome will be what it will be, the rest will take care of itself. As long as you're playing the game you love the way you want to, I'll be happy. And you should be too. Forget everyone else."

A thin smile appears at the corners of her mouth. She takes a few deep breaths, nods, and steps past me toward home plate. After three practice swings, she steps into the batter's box.

And on the very first pitch, Carla Henderson crushes a fastball down the left field line. The left fielder is able to get over to it and get it in quickly, but not before Carla has her first major-league hit.

Our players explode off the bench in celebration, high-fiving and jumping around like we just won the whole game in one pitch. Carla smiles from first base as she looks back into the dugout and points at us.

While I'm as thrilled as everyone else, I still have a game plan to execute, so I motion to the ump that we're making a lineup change.

"We're taking out our DH in the second inning?" Big Fish says.

I nod, consulting my notes.

"We've got a chance at our first run. I think it would be pretty great to finally have a lead in a game, don't you?"

He doesn't respond, but he also doesn't protest as Steven Yu trots out of the dugout to pinch-run.

As Carla walks off the field, I give Steven a few instructions. He grins and nods as I talk, then runs to first as the next batter steps to the plate. Everyone in the stadium expects Steven to steal second at some point, especially the AirHogs—why else would I pinch-run him so early? But he actually has just one job, and it's *not* to steal a base.

It's simply to annoy the heck out of the pitcher.

Steven does a lot of dancing around and takes massive leads on almost every windup. He draws seven pickoff attempts during the at bat. The pitcher is visibly flustered and after five pitches ends up walking Jof, who's playing short today.

We now have runners on first and second with no outs.

More important, our dugout is filled with smiles and cheering as Big Fish steps to the plate with a runner in scoring position. Moving him from third in the batting order to sixth had been another unusual move, but it was all a part of a larger plan I'd devised the night before in my hotel room, after dissecting all the numbers with a clear head for once.

I give Steven the signal to steal third on the first pitch of Big Fish's at bat.

He takes a small lead, but the pitcher is so focused on what he's going to throw to Big Fish that he's not paying any attention to Steven. His jump is legendary, reminding everyone why we signed him off the streets despite his having next to no fielding or hitting skills. It catches the AirHogs so off guard that the catcher doesn't even attempt a throw.

The team goes berserk as Steven slides safely into third.

Even after that wild play, no one expects what happens next, when I give the signal for a double steal.

Both Steven on third and Jof on first barely hide their excited smiles. They know as well as I do the AirHogs won't see this coming.

As the pitcher begins his windup, Jof takes off for second base.

The pitch is a sinker in the dirt, which Big Fish lays off.

Steven stays near third, waiting for just the right moment.

The catcher scoops up the ball and hops to his feet. Once Steven sees he's committed to throwing to second, he breaks for home like a flash of lightning. His speed is shocking as he streaks toward the plate, just as the catcher releases the ball.

Jof is called out at second, but the damage is done.

Steven Yu slides safely into home, giving the "new" Hurricanes our first run.

No matter what happens from here, the cheers that go up through the dugout are worth it.

We end up losing 4–3.

It's yet another setback on a road trip in which we can't afford to lose more than five games. But you wouldn't know it from the attitude around the locker room after the game. For the first time, it actually feels like we're a *real* team capable of competing. Playoffs are still a long way off, but winning a game or, heck, maybe even a few games no longer seems impossible.

In fact, it feels inevitable.

Chapter 25

"BAAAAAAAATTEEEEERRRRRRRRR!" THE VOICE ECHOES THROUGH THE stadium. "Baaaaaaaaaaaatter! BAAAATTERRRR! Swing BATTER-batter! SWING!"

The AirHogs shortstop swings and misses for strike three. The home crowd groans. The ump raises his mask.

"That's the second time!" he says, pointing at our dugout. "Knock it off!"

The heckler is none other than one Szymon "Slips" Zajac.

Slips grins and shrugs like he didn't know any better.

Our bench is in stitches, and even I can't help but crack a smile. It *is* pretty bush-league for a coach to try to distract a batter from the other team.

Then again, if I'm expecting my players to be themselves, why should I expect anything else from one of my coaches?

It's the final game of our series versus the Joliet AirHogs. After getting whooped by them in game one, then holding our own in game two, our new strategy is truly being put to the test.

And it's *working.*

The game is tied 1–1 after four innings. Having our closer, Mayhem, open the game put the opposing manager on tilt right from the beginning. And then I finally agreed to let Slips do a bit of the heckling that was one of his only joys when he would accompany me to Hurricanes games, which I have to admit is totally energizing the team and bothering at least a few of the AirHogs batters.

It's now the top of the fifth and Carla Henderson is at the plate. Once again, she's looked much more comfortable than she did at our first few home games. Her first at bat, she crushed a line drive right at the third baseman for an unlucky out. That's baseball, though. Sometimes there are outs that shouldn't be outs, and hits that shouldn't be hits.

She takes the first pitch for ball one. And she must be remembering what I told her yesterday, because on the second pitch, she doesn't hesitate, and puts another smooth and confident swing on a fastball up and inside.

It's not the hardest hit ball, but the grounder manages to squeak past the diving AirHog first baseman for a single.

I motion to the ump to sub in Steven Yu again as a pinch runner for Carla.

It's a risk taking out someone as dialed in as Carla in the fifth, but it will be worth it if he scores. He's probably three times as fast as she is, and his mere presence on the bases has already proven to be disruptive.

"Great job," I tell Carla as she passes third on her way to the dugout. "You look like a totally new player."

I don't expect a response, so I'm surprised when she stops.

"I feel like one, being here," she says, lifting her hands. "It's Mustard Park that makes me so nervous."

"Mustard Park?"

"Yeah, it's where he played, after all," she says, heading down the dugout steps.

"He?"

But she's already in the dugout getting a round of high fives from her teammates. I want to know who she's talking about, but I have a game to manage.

Our next batter, Josh Carlson, who will only be a senior in high school next year, surprises me by getting his first career double. Steven looks like he wants to score, but I hold him up at third. With a great start to the inning, I don't want to take any chances of him getting thrown out at home. We find ourselves with runners on second and third with no outs.

Big Fish steps to the plate and a chorus of boos erupts from the crowd. As one of the best hitters in the Mabel, he gets automatically booed by away fans.

I want to give him the signal to take the first pitch. With first base open, and no real threats hitting behind him, they likely won't give Big Fish anything decent to hit. Probably everyone in the stadium knows this.

But he's also *Big Fish.* He's the only one on the team who doesn't need my help. So, I give him the signal to swing away.

The first pitch is a fastball way outside, but Big Fish still takes a huge whack at it, missing badly. The next pitch is high, but Big Fish swings again. This time, he manages to make weak contact and lobs a blooper into shallow right field. It's one of those hits you either love or hate, depending on which side you're on: the soft fly ball lands in the exact spot that's too shallow for the outfielder and just too deep for the second baseman, dropping in for a single.

Steven and Josh read it perfectly, and two runs score, giving us a 3–1 lead.

"Yeah, BAAAATTERRRR! Great SWING, BAAAATTERRRR!" Slips yells from beside me. He looks at me. "What? The ump can't do anything if it's one of our own players, right?"

Once again, I can't help but grin.

By the seventh inning, we're up 4–1.

But the AirHogs have the bases loaded with only one out. The metrics say they have a 64.41 percent chance of scoring at least one run and a 29.73 percent chance that they score more than that. But I can reduce those numbers slightly by playing the individual matchups.

I signal to the ump for a pitching change.

As our new pitcher, Javy Rivera, throws warm-up pitches on the mound, Slips taps me on the shoulder.

"Alex," he whispers, "mind if I do some more heckling? Baseball has never been this fun for me."

A smile spreads across my face.

"Great, so what's the next batter's deal?" he asks. "What gets his goat? When does he struggle?"

"Inside heat," I say as the hitter steps to the plate.

"Call for that, then."

I nod and give our pitcher the signal.

"Hey, number fourteen!" Slips screams. "Watch your head on this next pitch!"

The batter, who definitely heard him, swings defensively and misses the high inside fastball. I try to hide my smirk as the ump glares at our dugout.

"Hey, pitcher! *Pitcher!*" Slips shouts gleefully before the next pitch. "This guy can't hit nothin' inside. Glaze his ribs! Smoke his tenderloin! Baste his chicken! He's scared of the ball!"

The batter fouls off the second pitch as he tries to ignore Slips, who doesn't let up.

"One more time!" Slips yells. "Hope you got a *dental plan*, batter!"

The hitter strikes out looking on the next pitch—a changeup on the outside corner.

He slams his bat into the dirt and makes an obscene gesture at Slips. Our entire bench erupts with laughter and jeers.

"What did I tell you?" the ump shouts at us. "Last warning! Next time, you're outta here!"

"There's no rule against this!" Slips shouts back, then turns toward me. "That's true, right?"

I shrug as the ump wags his finger, warning us not to test him.

"He can technically eject anyone he decides is acting in an unsportsmanlike manner," I say.

The bases are still loaded with two outs. We're potentially one pitch from getting out of this mess with our lead intact. In fact, it's now 68.66 percent likely that happens.

I switch pitchers again, to get our best matchup, boosting the odds even more.

During the entire warm-up, Slips is silently doing something on his phone, seemingly not paying attention to the game at all. The hitter eventually works the count full, and Slips's face is still buried in his phone behind me.

The sixth pitch is fouled off.

The crowd is roaring.

Then, just as our pitcher is about to begin his windup, Slips is on his feet again, leaning over the railing next to me. He has an old-fashioned megaphone he got from somewhere pressed to his lips.

"Hey, number thirty-four!" he screams into it. "Yeah, you! Johnson! Your car is getting towed! No, seriously, the red Ford Bronco with plates U-Y-H-2-2-3!"

This actually causes the player to freeze, and he strikes out looking to end the inning.

I honestly don't even want to know how Slips found out his real car model and plate number.

The ump immediately takes two steps toward us.

"That's it!" he shouts. "You're ejected!"

Slips runs from the dugout and marches right up to the ump, shouting vague obscenities, mostly in Polish. It doesn't matter what they translate to—he has no argument—but he's clearly enjoying this. Then Slips starts kicking dirt onto the ump's feet. The ump shouts a few choice words back and again motions that Slips is tossed.

Our bench loves it. Even the Joliet hometown crowd is cheering and laughing.

I let it go on for another minute, then head out to retrieve Slips, pulling him back toward the dugout by his arm. He continues to scream and throw a fit the whole way back just for the fun of it.

Once in the dugout, he grins.

"Welp, that was fun," he says as he skips toward the

tunnel that leads to the locker room. "Now win us the game!"

And we do.

The game ends 5–3.

Our first win.

The players celebrate as if we just won a World Series. The postgame atmosphere is more like a huge party than what you might expect from a team whose record is 20–34. One of the equipment managers runs out to get ingredients for Big Fish to make a cheesecake. I think someone even smuggles in a live goat. It's borderline out of control.

But I don't want to spoil their fun. That's what this is supposed to be about.

They earned this.

I only wish Ira were here to see it.

Chapter 26

THE BUS RIDE FROM JOLIET, ILLINOIS, TO LINCOLN, NEBRASKA, FOR THE second series of the road trip feels like the start of something special.

Will it be a simple two-game winning streak? An unprecedented mid-season turnaround? The beginning of a playoff run that will become the stuff of legend? All three? These are the insanely optimistic thoughts rolling around in my head as I watch cars crawl past us on the rainy interstate.

But then a simple, one-line email from Tex ends all that.

Congrats on your 1st win son! Just 40 more to go, right? 😂

He knows we only have thirty-six games left. He's messing with me. But if he's trying to tell me that the odds are high he'll be shutting down the Hurricanes and selling the land, he's right. That's the worst part. I'm 1–4 as the manager, and we need to go 27–7 over our next thirty-four games to keep playoff hopes alive, since the last two games versus the dominant Harbor Pirates will certainly be losses.

One victory is no reason to celebrate.

I'm still staring down at my phone, trying to convince myself that the numbers aren't impossible, when a voice interrupts my thoughts.

"Hey, Weakerman, can I sit?"

Aliyah is standing over my bus seat.

"Um, yeah?" I say, struggling to mash by body farther against the window in the tiny charter seat.

I glance out the window at the fields of glistening, golden crops rolling by as she sits next to me.

"What's wrong? You look like your dog just died, not

that we got our first win."

"I know, it's just, I'm worried it won't be enough. Tex is emailing me, trying to psych me out." I lift the phone to show her.

"Tex?" she says. "He seems like a *weirdo.* Making fun of you for winning."

"Yeah, but he's right. Even after this win, making the playoffs still feels impossible."

"Weakerman, I told you. We're not going to worry about the playoffs, just the next game."

"Yeah, but we *need* to make the playoffs because—" I stop myself just short of slipping up.

She doesn't know. I'm so caught up in the team, I forgot that I've been keeping Tex's plans to sell the team if we don't make the playoffs a secret from everyone except Slips.

"I mean, that's what Ira wanted, is all," I say quickly. "The point is, we *need* to keep winning."

"Actually, that's why I'm here," Aliyah says. "I talked to the Law before we got on the bus, and he said seeing how the team responded to the changes we made the last few games convinced him he needs to be more open to changes himself. I'd like to work on a new approach with him. I have a pretty radical change in mind, and he's open to it, but it will mean he won't be available to pitch for at least a week. Maybe two."

"Two *weeks*?" I say, my eyes going wide. It's not like the Law is a great pitcher as is, but he does match up well against a lot of hitters, and he's easily our most experienced player. He's valuable, especially now, when every single game matters. Losing him for even a week might sink the season, no matter how good he is when he's back.

"It'll only be eight games, tops," she insists. "Plus, it'll be good for his career, long-term. I mean, we need to figure out how we're going to win next season too, right, Weakerman?"

I swallow and shift the conversation back to the Law. "He's okay with being out that long?"

"Yeah, he seems willing to try anything. I know how it sounds, but I think he actually still thinks he can make it to the big leagues someday." Her face scrunches up and she launches into a pretty admirable impression of the Law: "'This year is like nothing I've ever experienced, what have I got to lose?'"

I laugh, and she winks and sticks out her tongue.

"Okay, well, if you're both decided, then . . ."

"I promise nothing," she says solemnly. "But we gotta try."

"Okay, well, I suppose I agree," I say. "But on the condition that if there's some sort of emergency, and I need him for a perfect matchup, I can still call on him?"

"Break glass only," she says, holding out her hand. "Deal?"

I stare at it, suddenly realizing how sweaty and gross my own palms feel, even to me. But I reach out and shake her hand anyway. If she notices how moist my palm is, she doesn't let on.

I don't know what to say because I cannot believe Aliyah Perkins is shaking my hand.

"Thanks, Weakerman," she says with a smile. "You know, this whole thing, being a coach, is not at all what I expected. It feels like we get much better results when we're actually asking players what they think, not just telling them what to do. My coaches, my manager . . . I feel like they just see me as this arm, and nothing else. Like how my coach tried to desperately talk me out of taking this job, ignoring the fact that it's what I said *I wanted* to do. All he could think about was what it would mean for *him*. Even half my teammates were mad at me, which I guess I understand, but shouldn't what I want matter? To at least one person other than me?"

"Definitely." I nod. I don't think I've talked with

anyone besides Slips about something this personal, but now that I'm doing it, it's not nearly as hard as I would have expected. "What about your dad, though? Was he okay with it?"

"Ugh, my dad. Do you know what he said to me?"

I shake my head, even though I know it's a rhetorical question.

"He wasn't upset at all. He was just like 'probably a good idea.' When I asked him what he meant he said, 'Crabby, honey, no college is going to give a girl a baseball scholarship. After this summer, I was going to tell you to switch to softball anyway.' Can you *believe* that?"

I shake my head again as she continues.

"And I said, 'What are you talking about?' And then he says to me, 'You're old enough now to start thinking like an adult, Crabby. You need to go to college. You can't *eat* baseballs, after all. And the only way we're going to afford college is if you get a scholarship. That means softball.' This whole time, him telling me I should follow my dreams and play baseball, it was all a lie."

That sounds awful. And at the same time, my stomach is flooded with guilt. I've been lying to her too, about the future of the team. Just to get her help. The same way her dad was lying to her, not caring about what she wanted. But I swallow it back down and try to convince myself that if she ever learns the truth, she'll understand.

Probably the same thing her dad told himself.

"Anyway," she says, "sorry, I didn't mean to get into all that."

I shake my head. "No, it's okay. I'm really sorry that, uh, all happened. It's just . . ."

"Yeah?"

I swallow.

"I . . . Are you ever going to tell us how you got that nickname?" I ask, trying to change the subject.

"Yeah, I've been wondering the same thing," Slips says, popping up over the back of the seat in front of us.

"Were you listening this whole time?" Aliyah asks.

"Nah, I just woke up," he says. "Now, c'mon, tell us about being Crabby, Crabby."

Aliyah scowls at him but is smiling again by the time she finally nods and says, "Okay, fine, *Rabbit*," even though she says it like we just asked her to deadlift a pickup truck. "When I was little, me and my brothers and some neighborhood kids used to sneak into this one backyard filled with crab apple trees. We'd have these epic crab apple fights back there. But eventually nobody would play with me anymore because they said I threw too hard. So, when I'd complain about them being quitters, they started calling me Crabby 'cause they knew it'd drive me nuts. And then, well, it just sorta stuck. Now even my parents call me that. I sorta hate it but sorta don't."

"Well, at least I know now to never follow you into an orchard," Slips says.

Aliyah grins and rolls her eyes.

"At least it's definitely better than that stupid nickname they gave me at the Little League World Series."

"Do you regret that you're not still playing?" I ask, not able to get my guilt to go away. "That you won't get back to the World Series this year?"

"I miss my teammates," she says. "And I miss pitching too. I've been thinking about what my dad said a lot. . . . I can dominate kids my own age, but unless I find a way to get my fastball above eighty miles an hour, my dreams of playing professional baseball probably are a long shot."

"You never know," I say sheepishly. "I mean, who at school would have guessed *I* would become the manager of a professional sports team this summer?"

Aliyah smiles politely, but I know what she's thinking: *Nobody*. Probably because they never think about me at all. I'm less like a classmate and more like something that's just there, like a cafeteria table.

"I don't have as much fun coaching as I do pitching," she continues. "But I wouldn't trade this summer for anything. All I've ever wanted since I was little was to play professional baseball. To be in the majors, just like all my other teammates dream about. But who knows if that could ever even happen? There's never been a woman in the major leagues. And I have no idea if I'll ever be able to pitch at that level. One of the reasons I said yes to you is that if I can't *be* a Cy Young winner, maybe I could one day *coach* one? I want baseball to be my life, one way or another. I don't want to just use baseball, or softball, whatever, to pay for college and then pursue another career. I want *baseball* to be my future. My dad's wrong; I *can* eat baseballs." Slips shoots her a weird look and so she quickly adds, "Metaphorically speaking, of course. Anyway, I would have regretted not taking this opportunity to learn about the game from another perspective. Plus, this could be a great summer job for the next few years, right?"

I nod, the pent-up guilt making sweat drip down my face like I just ran through a sprinkler. I try to think of something else to say. Something like: *That's incredible that you're not letting anything stop you.* Or: *Never say never. You'll find a way to make it as a pitcher. You've already been in a Nike commercial!*

But instead, I stammer Flumpisms:

"Um, well, I'm, uh, glad there's no *regerts*," I say, waiting for a laugh that doesn't come. "You know, *regerts* from that commercial? With the tattoo and stuff?"

She's just staring at me blankly, as if waiting for me to say something more. Something better. But she should know me well enough by now to know this is the best response I got.

"I remember that commercial." Slips tries to save me, still hanging over the back of the seat. "It was pretty funny. Hey, Alex, is the next team we're playing really called the Lincoln T-Bones?"

"Yup," I say with a grin, relieved to be moving on. "Their mascot is a huge steak with two skinny white legs. Which is another reason I love independent baseball: we have team mascots that are literally giant slabs of meat."

"Just thinking about that is already making me hungry," Slips says.

Aliyah and I laugh.

I quickly glance out the window as we pass a sign that says: *NEBRASKA . . . the good life.*

* * *

It's a few hours later when I get up and sit down next to Slips as the bus is exiting the interstate into Lincoln, Nebraska.

"Can't wait to get to the hotel," he says, rubbing his eyes. "What is it, like midnight?"

"One."

"Even better," he says, sitting up. "What's up?"

"I need your help," I say. "Talking to Carla. She's looked like a totally different player on the road than she did in home games. I know it has something to do with Mustard Park. She's basically been trying to tell me that for a while. But my . . . I mean, I haven't . . ."

"I think you got this, Alex," he says, understanding what I'm trying to say. "You have way more in common with her than I do."

"Yeah, but . . . I mean, I don't even know what to say."

"It's not that hard, man," Slips says, and there's a bit of annoyance in his voice that I don't think I've ever heard from him before. "Remember that time at Family General, when you bought that shirt? You both love the Hurricanes Dream Team, right? Maybe start there. Bond over that. Jeez-Louise."

It's a good suggestion. Though I can't help but be hung up on the frustration in his voice. All I say, though, is, "Okay, yeah."

"Good, you got this," he says, patting my shoulder as we pull into the hotel parking lot.

As we're piling off the team bus, I ask Carla if I can talk to her for a moment. I take Slips's advice. At the very least, I can probably speak coherently about baseball long enough to ease my own nerves.

"Remember the Dream Team?" I start.

Carla quickly looks down for some reason, and I'm already tilted. But I press on.

"I'm asking because I see some of BAM Morgan's natural power in your own swing, you know?"

She actually bursts out laughing, and now I'm completely confused.

"What? What did I say?"

She's shaking her head, covering her mouth. "Nothing, nothing."

"Um, okay?" I'm not sure where to go from here. "Well, I guess the point is, I think you've got some real talent, and it's hard to not see your struggles in our first few games as something possibly psychological. You seem so much more relaxed these last few games than you did at Mustard Park. What did you mean earlier by 'it's where *he* played'?"

"It's . . . complicated," she says, watching for her bag as the equipment manager and bus driver unload the cargo hold.

I wait for her to say more.

When she doesn't, I say, "Who is *he*?"

"Alex, I don't . . . I mean, I can't talk about this now. I'll be fine. I'll figure it out."

I want to tell her we don't have time for that. That we have to make the playoffs or the team is toast. That every single game matters. But that would also mean telling her I lied to everyone about this season likely being the team's last. "I can't . . ." I start, staring at the floor for courage. "Help me understand. I want you to be able to play this way at home too. The team needs you."

Carla sighs as she grabs her bag from the pavement and then steps aside, under the hotel awning. She looks up at the lights.

"It's just, Mustard Park has a lot of meaning for me," she finally says. "I grew up there. Spent nearly every day of my childhood there. It's like a second home. Or was, anyway. And now, being back as a player, it's hard. It reminds me of my dad. What he was and what I've lost. It makes me wonder if I can actually do what he did. Every time I step up to that plate and hear the crowd, something that he used to love so much, it has the opposite effect on me, I guess. I start thinking about the past. And I guess, without, I don't know . . . You wait long enough for something, well, you can sometimes forget if what you're waiting for is even worth it."

Now I'm more confused than ever. She had a dad who played baseball at Mustard Park?

"I don't . . . your dad . . . I mean . . . was he a Hurricane?"

Carla looks at me like I've got a small creature growing out of my neck that can talk and has a filthy mouth.

"If you're not going to take this seriously . . ."

"No, I am," I insist. "I just, I don't know who you're talking about."

"You don't?"

I shake my head as earnestly as I can.

"I thought that was half the reason I got this job," she says.

"You got this job because you crushed the ball that

day at tryouts," I say. "Because you have one of the best natural swings I've ever seen. And I sure wish we could see more of that in games."

Carla is silent for a moment, her huge eyes seeming to bore holes into me.

"Alex," she says quietly and slowly. "My dad was on the Dream Team."

My jaw makes a thud as it lands on the asphalt of the La Quinta Inn parking lot. Or at least that's how it feels. "Who . . . *who* was it?"

"It doesn't matter anymore," she says. "Honestly, I don't want people to know, because I don't want to be compared to him all the time."

I silently go through my mental roster of past players, and I'm nearly certain we've never had a Henderson on the team before—definitely not the Dream Team. So who could it be?

"Still, I wish I had what he had," Carla continues as we watch the last of the bags get unloaded. Just about all the players have their luggage and have gone inside. "He just had that special thing . . . that baseball *energy* that separates the great from the good. I'm worried no matter how talented I am, I'll never have that."

Right away I know she's talking about Baseball Zazzle.

Not everyone calls it the same thing, but anyone who knows baseball, knows what it is—and also whether they believe in it or not.

Could her dad have been one of the Big Four? If there was anyone on the Dream Team who had that *energy*, or magic, or Zazzle, it was them. Was that why she laughed when I compared her to Bernie "BAM" Morgan? He and Luis "Dirty Ball" Mendez are the only two who are still alive.

"I get that," I finally say. "About Baseball Energy, as you call it. But to be honest, I don't really believe in that stuff too much. No matter how much people want to talk about players being great performers in the 'clutch,' the numbers usually average out. People just remember the times that feel extraordinary more than the times that don't. My point is, you've got more than enough talent to live up to your dad's reputation, whoever he was. I'm sure he'd tell you that too, if you asked him."

"We don't really talk anymore," she says. "Not for a few years now. It would probably help if I could talk to him again, but I don't even know where to find him anymore. I've tried."

She leaves it at that, and I don't press further. Whatever is going on between them is between them.

"Well, at least I finally know why home games are so tough for you," I say. I don't know how to help her, so all I say next is, "Thanks for telling me."

"Thanks for listening," she says. "I'm sorry I didn't say more sooner. I didn't want it to seem like I'm making excuses. Still don't. I'll work it out, I'm sure."

I nod, hoping she's right. But I can tell she doesn't quite believe it herself.

"Hey, maybe you can use Anne of Green Gables in the next home game?" I suggest, trying to lighten the mood. "I mean, your best batting practice to date was with that old bat."

"Yeah, well, Slips's rental prices have gone up dramatically."

It's true Slips has gotten really attached to that old bat.

"I think he even sleeps with it next to him in his bed now," I say.

Carla and I look at one another for a second and then burst out laughing.

And I just have this feeling, that some of that cloud that has been hovering over her has parted, even if only for the moment.

Chapter 27

"HEY, ALEX, WANT TO TRY SOME OF THAT SMOKED TURKEY YOU MISSED out on?" my dad says as I'm unpacking my duffel bag in my room.

I follow him to the kitchen, where he already has a turkey sandwich sitting out. I plop down and take a bite, still exhausted from the long road trip.

"So, I saw you won some games," my dad says as I chew.

"Yeah," I say through a mouthful of turkey. "We won five games and lost four."

"That must feel like a weight off your shoulders," he says. "Maybe I was wrong to suggest you should quit."

Knowing my dad, this is as close to an apology as I'm going to get.

But I still have a long way to go, in spite of how well the road trip ended. We went 1–2 versus the T-Bones, one of the best teams in the Mabel. Then we swept the Rapid City Explorers 3–0 to close out the trip, mostly on the back of a monster series by Big Fish. Which means we got back to Weakerville with a 24–36 record. I'm 5–6 as manager, and the simple facts are: 5–6 isn't good enough. We need to go at least 23–7 the rest of the way, against much better teams. Not to mention the unwinnable two-game series against the 52–8 Duluth Harbor Pirates to close out the season.

But I don't want to burden my dad with this, so I change the subject.

"This is pretty good," I say, holding up the sandwich.

My dad smiles.

"*I* thought so," he says. "After the brine, I tried a new rub. Then it was double smoked in and out of foil."

"It was worth the work," I say, taking another bite.

"So, what's next for the team?"

I finish chewing.

"We have twelve games here at home over the next two weeks, then back on the road for another nine. Our final home stand is after that."

He nods.

"Well, I'm impressed that you're sticking with this. It seems like a real challenge."

I shrug and take another bite, not sure what else to say. My dad doesn't say anything else while I sit there and chew the dry turkey sandwich. It's plenty good, really smoky, with lots of flavor, but it sure could use some mustard.

"Are you coming to any of the games?" I finally ask.

"Oh, well, you know," he says, looking around, as if trying to find an emergency exit in his own house. "I hadn't thought about it."

Yeah, I noticed, is what I want to say. But instead, I just kind of stare over his shoulder at the kitchen window. The truth is, I'm too worried about what else I can do to improve the team to worry about whether my dad is going to come see a game.

"You know, with my work schedule," he says, "it's tough. Plus, I've got a new side project at the moment. . . ."

"It's fine, Dad."

"I'll take a look at what I can do with my schedule," he quickly adds.

"Dad, really, don't worry about it," I say, and I actually mean it.

"The Hurricanes were always you and Ira's thing, anyway," he says. "Maybe it'd be more special to keep it that way? It was like your Baseball Magic or something, right?"

"What did you just say?"

"I don't know what it means—I figured you did," my dad says. "I heard Ira say that once: that you had Baseball Magic like he hadn't seen since the Big Four, whatever that means."

"Yeah, yeah," I say absently. What my dad just said reminds me that the team is still missing something, and I have more work to do. I stand up to take the rest of the sandwich to my room. "Thanks for this, it was really good. But I got to go get ready for our series versus the Winnipeg Yetis on Tuesday. Lots to do!"

"Okay, good luck," he says.

I smile and nod as I pass him. The truth is: we won't need luck if we can actually get some more Baseball

Zazzle on our side. Whether I believe in it or not, everyone else does, and that's what matters. If the players think we've got someone with real Baseball Zazzle on our side, even as a coach or consultant or whatever, then it might actually work. A self-fulfilling prophecy or whatever.

And I know where to keep looking for it: the answer has always been in Ira's journals.

We *need* to figure out who A.M. is.

I stay up the whole night with my reading light on the lowest setting, skimming through Ira's scorecards for any mention of A.M. And it's funny what happens: my biggest break doesn't even come from a note about A.M. at all.

It's from a scorecard dating back to the very start of the Dream Team era, the season right before Early Eights joined the team:

> *—Remember: the new kid, Bernie Morgan, prefers to go by his middle name, Arlon. The team calls him BAM because they think it's funny his initials match his power. But he told me today: 'Arlon, boss. Just Arlon. Arlon Morgan.'*

ALSO: remember to tell him his little girl is always welcome at Mustard Park.

This is *it*, exactly what I was looking for. The key to unlocking this whole thing.

Chapter 28

I CAN'T WAIT TO UNVEIL MY PLAN TO SLIPS AND ALIYAH.

But I wait until after our home series against the Winnipeg Yetis. Prepping for games takes a lot of time—we have to switch up our lineup every day in order to have a shot. Fortunately, the series goes about as well as we could have hoped: we win three of four games, mostly by piecing together favorable pitching matchups, lots of small ball, and some clutch contributions from Big Fish, whose hot streak shows no signs of ending. Since we're back at Mustard Park, though, Carla is once again a black hole in the lineup, managing just one bloop single in ten plate appearances.

If we're going to get her going again, and keep this progress up, we need something special. We need some Baseball Zazzle. Or, at least, the belief we have it.

Which is why I'm going to pitch my plan to Slips and Aliyah at Cheese'N Stuff Pizza after our final game versus the Yetis.

Gloves grabs my arm as we pass him near the front entrance of Cheese'N Stuff. It's normal for him to call us names, but he's never grabbed anyone like this. I'm startled silent.

"Hey," he says, his hot breath smelling like something vaguely medicinal. "Gimme some money, you Donkey-Faced Puss Welt!"

I pull my arm away.

"Want some free Hurricanes tickets instead?" I suggest.

"*Baseball* tickets!" he sneers like I offered him a wad of boogers. "What would I do with those? Wipe my butt?" He stumbles past me, toward the alley, stopping at the corner of the building just long enough to turn back and add: "You Trout-Faced Handle Knob!"

"Trout-Faced Handle Knob?" Slips says.

"The insults just keep getting weirder," Aliyah says, shaking her head.

"I think they're fun," Slips says as we head back toward our booth.

We order the usual: one large pepperoni. Nothing too fancy. You really can't go wrong with pepperoni. There's no need to sully things with gross green peppers and other garbage like that.

Normally, we spend the first half hour joking around and focusing on the greasy pizza. We don't usually get down to business until the pie is gone. But tonight, there's too much work to be done.

"I think I figured it out," I announce before anyone has even taken a bite.

"Figured what out?" Slips asks as he prepares his first slice for consumption. "My secret to eating whole slices of pizza in one bite without choking to death?"

"Ha, I wish," I say. "No, this."

I throw down the journal containing Ira's note about Bernie "BAM" Morgan. They both read it a few times.

"I don't get it," Aliyah says, then finally takes a bite of pizza.

"Yeah, so he liked to go by Arlon," Slips says. "How is that relevant?"

"*Because*," I say, not even able to think about pizza for perhaps the first time ever. "We all agreed that figuring out who A.M. is might help us add some much-needed Baseball Zazzle, right?"

"Right," Slips mumbles, his mouth now full of whole slice of pizza.

Aliyah looks thoughtfully at the note again, and then it must click for her.

"A.M. is BAM Morgan!"

"Exactly," I say. "Has to be. He was one of the Big Four. And his initials fit, now that we know he went by Arlon. It all makes sense." I don't tell them about the Carla connection, that she's almost certainly the little girl mentioned in the note, because she didn't want anyone to know. "If we can find a way to bring him back to the team, it'll be exactly what we need down the stretch—a reminder to the players and the fans that the Hurricanes were great once, and that we can be again."

"I love it," Slips says. "So how do we find him?"

"Well, that's the problem," I say. "Still can't find anything online."

"Really?"

"Really. The Great All-Knowing Wizard of Google does not know where Bernie Morgan resides today. Or seemingly anything about him at all, in fact. But I have reasons to suspect he's still in or near Weakerville."

"How can you know that?" Aliyah asks.

"From these." I dig into my backpack, haul out a huge stack of old notebooks, and plop them down with a table-shaking *THUD*. "The most recent mention I could find of Ira seeing A.M. was from eight months ago. But there might be more. These are all of Ira's old scorecards from the past four years. We need to go through these. Page by page. Word by word. There *has* to be a clue somewhere in here about how we can find BAM Morgan."

They gape at the pile of notebooks.

"Of course," I go on, "even if we do find him, there's no guarantee he will, or even can, help. But if Ira was so convinced A.M. had real Magic that could help the Hurricanes, I feel like we have to try."

"I thought you didn't *believe* in Baseball Zazzle," Aliyah says with a smirk.

"Well, the numbers say we shouldn't be winning," I say. "Yet we *are*. And besides, it doesn't matter whether or not it's real. We're seeing what happens when our players start to believe in themselves. If enough players believe we can win, and we do, isn't that its own form of Baseball Magic or Zazzle or whatever you want to call it?"

“Ugh, this is a lot,” Slips says, pulling the top notebook toward him.

“I know,” I say, handing another to Aliyah. “But it’ll be fun. Ira’s margin notes can be pretty entertaining sometimes.”

Our late night at Cheese’N Stuff, fueled by bottomless Pepsis, ends up being worth the work. After two hours skimming through his old notebooks, Aliyah guffaws so loudly she turns the heads of several teens in a nearby booth.

“What is it?” Slips asks. “Another reference to that scouting trip Ira took to the Dominican? Man, that was a wild trip. Wish I could have gone with.”

“You were two at the time,” I remind him. “And living in Poland.”

“Hey, two-year-old me was a relentless party animal.”

“It’s probably more funny than useful,” Aliyah continues, “but, anyway, here it goes.” She starts reading aloud, using her finger to follow along with my grandpa’s cramped cursive: “‘Went to see A.M. again. Asked to buy him dinner. Said he’d rather be dead! Then called me an Antler-Licking Spleen Butler. Had a good laugh over it, but still sad he said no.’”

Slips and I chuckle. It’s not the first reference to A.M.

we've found that evening, but it's easily the funniest.

"Hah," Slips says. "That sort of sounds like something Gloves would . . ."

As soon as the words leave his mouth, our eyes widen as we stare at one another in near disbelief.

"No," I say quietly.

"But, maybe . . ." Slips says in a near whisper.

"It can't be."

"But what if it *is*?" Aliyah says.

"Nobody knows Gloves's real name," Slips reasons. "He could easily be this BAM guy. Plus, your grandpa knew everyone in town. You really think he never *once* talked to Gloves? I mean, you haven't found a single reference to Gloves in all his notes, right? Maybe that's because he knew him by a *different name*? Arlon Morgan, perhaps?"

"But Gloves looks way too old to be BAM Morgan," I say. "BAM would be around fifty today, and Gloves looks like he's pushing eighty. . . ."

"Welp, there's really only one way to find out for sure," Slips says.

It's nearly 11:00 p.m. in a quiet, dead, dark corner of downtown Weakerville.

"Remind me," Slips says as he and I creep through a dark alley, while Aliyah holds down our table inside Cheese'N Stuff. "What are we doing again? There's easier ways to go missing, you know."

"We're *trying* to get the Hurricanes to the playoffs," I say.

Slips looks dubiously at the dark shape digging through a dumpster up ahead, in the alley behind Cheese'N Stuff Pizza.

"Aaaand getting stabbed by the town vagrant accomplishes that *how*?" he whispers.

"It was *your* idea come back here and talk to him, remember?"

"Oh, right," Slips says.

Then he marches right up to Gloves, who appears to be searching through the dumpster for unscathed slices of pizza.

I follow cautiously.

"What do you want, Butt Professor?" Gloves says.

"We just want to talk," Slips says.

"I got nothing to say to Porky Piper and Dipstick Pirate Shiner."

We were ready for this. Slips holds out a five-dollar bill.

"I don't want or need your charity, you Eyeless Scrum Pile Collector," Gloves sneers, but he grabs the five and stuffs it into his pocket anyway.

Then Slips takes out a ten and holds it front of him just out of Gloves's reach. "For just ten minutes of your time."

"Fine," Gloves says, snatching the bill. "But I'm only doing it to get you Reedy Fart Maggots to go away."

"Ira!" I blurt out. Classic Flumpo moment.

Gloves glares at me.

"I don't know nothin' about nobody named Ira." He scowls through clenched teeth.

"But the, A.M., and, uh, the, uh." I'm huffing, struggling to breathe, as my throats seizes. "You know? The letters and, um, stuff . . ."

"Don't worry, I got this," Slips whispers sharply, then turns back toward Gloves. "We don't believe you."

"I don't care what you believe, you Wagon Droppings Sniffer."

Gloves starts to walk away, but Slips doesn't give up easily.

"We know who you are," he calls out.

Gloves stops but doesn't turn around to face us. There's a long silence and then he finally sighs.

"And who do you think I am?"

"Bernie Arlon Morgan," Slips says.

Gloves doesn't react at first, but then when he finally turns around, we're shocked to see a smirk on his face.

"Oh yeah?" Gloves says. "That's real funny. Like I'm really someone named Kaboom. Go on believing whatever you want, Colon Whales. I got things to do."

"Either way, we know you still care about Ira," Slips presses on. "That's why you came into Cheese'N Stuff to talk to us after he died. You came to pay your respects, didn't you? You just chickened out first."

Gloves's smirk disappears and the scowl is back.

"You don't know anything about me."

"You're right," Slips says. "And it doesn't matter. All we care about is saving the Hurricanes. The future of the whole team is in peril, did you know that?"

"So what?" Gloves sneers.

"The team is going to be dissolved if we don't make the playoffs," Slips presses on. "And *you* can help us do that."

"How am I supposed to do anything to help a *baseball team*? Huh? Look at me! I'm literally rooting around in garbage for old pizza."

"We're pretty sure Ira believed you could."

"Well, I don't know anything about that," Gloves says. "Now leave me alone, you Soiled Biscuit Filchers."

"We'll pay you a salary," Slips says, trying a new tactic.

"You think I beg and eat garbage because I need money?" Gloves asks.

"Um . . . yes?" Slips looks at me. I shrug. I can't think of any other reason someone would live this way, digging through the trash for pizza leftovers, calling everyone names while asking them for money.

But Gloves doesn't respond and instead just starts to walk away.

"You'll turn your back on your old team, then?" Slips says. "On Ira?"

"Stop saying that name!" He scowls, spinning back around. "He's dead, ain't he? Which means there's nothing I can do for him even if I did know him. Which I don't! I got nothing to do with that team and never did! Now stop mocking me and leave me alone before I huck this bottle at your head!"

He brandishes a half-full bottle of something, then opens it and takes several long swigs.

I stand there and wonder if we might be wrong after all. Maybe this isn't A.M. from Ira's scorecards? Maybe it's not Bernie Morgan or *any* former player? Which makes us just some kids harassing a sad, confused old bum in an alley.

In the long silence, Gloves has begun hastily digging through another sack of garbage. His movements are jerky and rapid.

There's only one last thing I can try. I take a deep breath—which I immediately regret in the garbage-strewn alley—and try to focus through the Flumpo.

"It could help your daughter," I say. "Coming back to the Hurricanes, I mean."

"Leave her out of this, you Pig-Faced Fart Slapper!" he shouts, then rears back the bottle to throw at me.

Slips and I take off running back down the alley. My lumbering steps shoot needles of pain into my feet. The bottle hits the wall next to us and glass sprays everywhere as we turn the corner.

My huffing turns to wheezing, and a concerned family leaving Cheese'N Stuff stares at me, likely deciding between calling 911 or offering me a slice of their leftover pizza.

"We're fine," Slips calls out to them, while patting my heaving back.

I'm more sure than ever that Gloves *is* Bernie Morgan and is also Carla's dad. But I'm also more skeptical than ever that he could actually help the Hurricanes. Seems as if there'd be no convincing him either way.

If Ira couldn't talk his old friend into helping, why on earth did I think he might listen to some random kids?

Chapter 29

"THE LAW IS READY, AND I THINK HE SHOULD START TONIGHT."

Aliyah is standing in my office doorway a few days after the Gloves debacle. She looks like she's expecting the announcement to take the sting out of losing our most recent game against the Joplin Railcats, but it would take a lot more than that. Sure, we're now 9–5 since we changed up our game plan, and yeah, that's almost impossibly good. But it's *still* not good enough. We have to go 19–5 our final twenty-four games.

That's probably why my response is so underwhelming:

"Okay."

"That's it?" she says. "That's all you have to say?"

"Well, it's just I already have a perfect opener in mind for tonight, if the Blasters bat their shortstop leadoff again, and—"

"I know, I know, Weakerman," Aliyah says, sitting down across from me. "But I think you'll want to make an exception tonight. You'll agree once you see the new and improved Law in action."

"Okay, sure." I give in. "The Law will start tonight."

Aliyah grins excitedly. "You won't be disappointed."

"I hope not. Have you told him he's pitching tonight?"

She shakes her head. "I think *you* should."

"Do you really think so? I mean, he kinda hates me, and . . . I'm not all that great at talking when . . . well—"

"Look at us right now, *you and me*," she continues. "You're talking to me now like you talk to Slips. Back in gym class, and right after you offered me this job, you could barely even form real words."

I hadn't stopped to consider until now that I was actually talking *talking* to Aliyah Perkins. Like, in a normal way, without mumbling things about strange hamburger toppings or whatever. The same Aliyah Perkins who used to make cold sweat pool in my shoes and my knees weak with panic and Flumpo seep out of my ears like noxious gas. But over the past few weeks, it has become something I don't think about anymore.

"Okay, you're right." I stand up. "I'll go tell him right now: *the Law is back in session*!"

I pause so she can laugh at my clever pun. But she just smiles politely. "Perhaps, um, use a different line?"

"Yeah?"

"Definitely," she says with an encouraging smile.

When I'm approaching him later in the locker room, my plan is to take her advice. Of course, at least some Flumpo will always be there, and so in my determination not to say anything dumb, I just blurt out:

"Start the game tonight, do you want to?"

It's too loud, and more like a Yoda quote than exactly how a normal manager would say it. But it's still perhaps the most direct and coherent thought I've ever spoken to him.

And it apparently doesn't matter how I say it, because a thin smile spreads across the Law's face. It's the best reaction I could have asked for. And I realize this was part of Aliyah's genius plan. Even me, a kid born with so much Flumpo my parents might has well have named me Flumpo Flumpy Flumperman the Flumpth, can't mess up when the news is good.

And that little act of generosity from Aliyah only makes the guilt of lying to her all season sting that much worse.

"Strike three!" the ump shouts, making a punching motion with his fists.

The home crowd goes berserk as the Law strikes out the third straight batter to start the game. But to simply call it another strikeout wouldn't do the inning justice. He struck out all three batters in just ten pitches!

The final strike is a perfect display of what he and Aliyah spent the past several weeks working on: a *wicked* knuckleball that floats and dances like a flower petal in the wind, a frozen particle drifting through space, or something else equally poetic and stuff.

It makes so much sense I can't believe nobody thought of it before. The Law's biggest problem has always been command of his secondary pitches. With a knuckleball, control and velocity aren't nearly as important as unpredictable movement. And a good knuckleball paired with a plus fastball is a combination that can fool nearly any batter, when it's working.

And it's working.

The results speak for themselves. The swinging strikes he elicits the first inning make the batters look like medieval peasants trying to fend off dragons with twigs. Knuckleballers aren't common anymore—many of these players have likely never seen a legitimate knuckler before.

I can see Aliyah high-fiving the other pitchers in the bullpen as the Law struts triumphantly off the field. He grins as he comes down the steps, and the team is all over him with congratulations. Nobody is more thrilled at his successful return to the mound than his teammates.

By the fifth inning, the Law has thrown sixty-six pitches and struck out eleven batters.

But he's also just walked two in a row, and I suspect the fatigue of having not pitched in a few weeks is setting in.

I signal to Aliyah to get up a righty and lefty in the pen.

She signals back for a mound visit.

"I got this, Alan," the Law says to me as I get to the mound.

"He's good, Weakerman," Aliyah agrees, meeting us there. "Three of those balls were terrible calls. This ump is probably as thrown by his knuckler as the batters are."

I look at the Law and Aliyah, then past them at the

cheering fans. I see several jerseys bearing his number behind our dugout—the fans must have rushed to the merchandise stand between innings to buy them. The hometown crowd loves the new, improved Phil "the Law" Sherriff.

But we're only up 1–0. One bad pitch could turn this whole game around.

"You're good?" I finally ask.

"Are you kidding?" he says with a grin that makes him look sixteen instead of thirty-six. "I'm having a blast!"

I take a deep breath.

Every metric in the book says that it's time to make a pitching change. It's how we've been winning these past few weeks. But I realize in that moment that there's more at stake than just getting this next batter out. Deep inside, I know that if I take the Law out now, he's going to carry that disappointment into the next game. And if I leave him in, and he manages to get out of this inning, the confidence he'd take with him and transfer to the rest of the team, well . . .

"Okay, then, strike this guy out!" I say and head back to our dugout.

Mustard Park's unusually large crowd goes nuts when I leave the mound and the Law stays in session. Our last four home games had more people in attendance than I've ever seen—it's nearly full tonight.

I get back to my stoop atop the dugout stairs and spin around to watch him face the next batter. My stomach is in knots over ignoring the baseball metrics that have gotten us this far—we don't have enough games left this season for *any* mistakes.

The Law gets the signal from the catcher and then gets into his short stride stance. He glances back at the runners on first and second and then delivers a dancing knuckler that still looks plenty fast up close.

"Ball," the ump calmly calls out.

"That was right down the plate, you Festering Glob of Knuckle Goo!" Slips shouts next to me as he makes a move to go argue with the ump.

It *was* right down the plate, but I hold him back. The last thing the Law needs is a five-minute distraction watching Slips get ejected.

The Law looks annoyed as he shakes his head and leans in for the next signal.

I'm really regretting my decision now. This ump clearly has no feel for the knuckler and the opposing team has figured that out. They are simply laying off the pitch, meaning they can sit back and look for fastballs exclusively.

The second pitch is another knuckleball, this one low and away.

"Ball two," the ump says.

I'm ready to head back out to the mound, but the Law glances at me and actually smirks, which freezes me in place.

His next pitch is a 96-mile-per-hour fastball at the shoulders. The hitter, who'd been sitting on a fastball the entire at bat, takes the bait and swings. He fouls it off behind home plate and into the stands.

Next, the Law delivers the exact same pitch, and once again the hitter can't resist swinging at his expected pitch at eye level.

Another foul ball.

It's clear now that the Law knows exactly what he's doing. He has pitched over 2,500 professional innings of baseball in his career, after all.

The Law gets the next signal from the catcher, nods, steps back, doesn't even bother checking the runners, and then delivers another fastball—this time right down the middle of the plate.

The hitter watches it zip right past him, frozen like a statue.

"Steeerrrriiiike three!" the ump shouts as the hitter slams his bat into dirt.

The Law somehow only gets more effective as the game progresses.

The new two-pitch combination is, quite simply, *devastating.* The Law almost single-handedly wins us the game, finishing with an astounding stat line:

9 Innings, 1 Hit, 0 Runs, 5 Walks, 19 Strikeouts

Even better than the victory itself, though, is what I see happen that night. The whole team rises up to match Phil's performance. Guys who have been averaging nearly an error a series make diving stops and jaw-dropping throws. We rally in a way I've never witnessed before, and the whole stadium feels like it's on another plane of existence.

This is it.

I realize it the moment the Law gets that final strikeout, and the entire team runs from the dugout to mob him on the mound. I'm seeing actual Baseball Zazzle in action. Nothing else can explain a transformation like this, or the way our players play behind him. This sort of event can't be defined or explained by numbers.

We've finally found some *real* Baseball Magic to take us to the next level.

Chapter 30

“YOU’VE DONE IT, SON!” TEX SHOUTS HOARSELY AS I STEP INTO HIS office for our first meeting since he arrived back in town.

So much has happened since he left, I hardly know where to start. But it appears he’s heard about our turnaround.

“Done what?” I say, sitting down across from him, unable to keep the smile off my face. “We’re not in the playoffs just yet.”

I’m a little surprised he’s so happy that we might actually do it. Make the playoffs, I mean. It’s been just over three weeks since the Law made his return to the team, and the difference has been dramatic. Not only have I been able to pitch him on four days' rest, getting him five more dominant starts—all wins—over that span, but the whole team, even Big Fish, is playing way better than their stats could have predicted. We've won fifteen of our last twenty games—even the best teams in the league don't often have a run like that.

In fact, pretty much the only person who hasn't improved is Carla. She's hitting .274 with 8 RBI on the road, and just .094 with an abysmal strikeout rate at home. But even though we have just three games left, all home games, I'm optimistic. We're currently 45–41. We still need to win one of our final three games to clinch a playoff spot, but if we can do it tonight against the St. Paul Saints, we won't even have to win either of our last two games against a stacked Duluth Harbor Pirates team. Plus, the Law is starting tonight, which gives us as great a shot as we could hope for. Even if Carla can't work out her issues, we can still—and I *can't believe* I'm actually thinking this—make the playoffs.

"No, son, I ain't talking about no playoffs!" Tex says. "I'm talking about how we've sold enough tickets to actually turn a profit this season! Lucy as my witness!"

My mouth opens and closes a few times. Is it possible he's finally seeing things the way Ira did? Maybe he'll want to keep the team even if we don't make the playoffs. Maybe this is why he scheduled this meeting with me. To tell me he's decided not to sell the team either way, now that they're profitable!

I nearly start shaking from pure relief. I won't ever have to tell anyone how close the team was to being shut down forever. Aliyah and the players will never know.

I let out a giant breath I didn't know I'd been holding. "That's good! Because I—"

"*Good?!*" he screams, then cough-laughs so violently I expect to see blood droplets all over his yellow suit. "*Good?* Boy, this is much better than *good*. I'll tell you straight, I expected to lose five figures on this darn team's last season. And now, because of you, I'm gonna *make money*. You're like my very own gold claim from 1849! I should be firing shiny pistols wildly at all who step near, is what should be happening. *Good*, ha! Good, he says. *Good*."

It's hard to follow what he's saying, but that's Tex for you.

"So, we're keeping the team, then?"

Tex explodes in another round of hoarse laughter.

"You got yourself quite an imagination, son! Lucy *dearest*."

"Huh?" is all I can manage to say before he continues.

"This is a lot like what happened to my great-grandpappy," Tex says. "Arcane Cohaagen was his name. A Dutch immigrant. Barely spoke any English. But, then again, he didn't really *need* to. His Colts did most of his talkin'. And I ain't referrin' to his horses."

I've never wanted more to interrupt one of Tex's stories to find out what the heck he's thinking. But I know at this point that there's no way around a Tex story, only a way through it. So I try to settle my breathing and lean back in my chair.

"Arcane was sitting on this oil claim once. This would have been back in . . ." Tex looks at the ceiling as if it will help him get the facts straight. "*Eighteen* eighty-six. His claim was in a dry riverbed somewhere in eastern Texas. It had been a mighty hot summer. The middle of a drought, so it were. People starving to death all over the state, reportedly. But worse than all them folks dying was that my grandpappy Arcane is sitting on this oil claim and the ground is too hard and dry for him to properly drill. Not with the gravity-powered drills of that day, which weren't so good as hydraulic drills are now. Anyway, in order to get the ground right for drilling, Arcane needed himself some rain. He was desperate for rain. You ever been desperate for rain, son?"

"Uh, I don't think so. . . ."

"But suppose you were," Tex says thoughtfully. "Suppose you needed rain in the worst way. What do you do?"

"Well . . . nothing, I guess," I say. "You can't *make* it rain."

"See, that's what most folks would think," Tex says. "But not Arcane. *No,* he was as stubborn as an old hog. He lived by old Dutch principles, which meant he would make it happen or die trying—and maybe even keep on trying as a ghost if that's what it took. And so, he gathered up hisself all the hired guns he could find: friends, the stable boy, his bartender, anyone and everyone. He promised whole towns of men a stake in his oil claim, if only they would help him. Well, turns out, stakes in oil claims can motivate many a hired gun or rancher or banker. Arcane rallies himself well over a thousand people to come on out to his oil claim with all the guns they had. He amassed an entire *army* of a mercenary posse."

"I don't get it," I say. "How is assembling an armed posse going to help it rain?"

Tex answers with bellows of laughter.

"That's the best part!" he says. "Well, actually, no. It ain't. But it's *one* of the good parts, anyway. So Arcane has himself this idea that he can threaten the sky with violence. Then, if she don't listen, they can all fire up into the heavens and open her up like a pig in a slaughterhouse. The way Arcane figures it, the sky ain't nothing but a big container of weather—like a huge grain bin full of precipitation or something. And if they fire enough holes into its belly, then all that built-up rain will come pouring out like innards. So that's what they do. After he threatens the sky, shouting up at her like she's a stubborn old cow, and she don't listen, all thousand of his hired guns open up with everything they got. They empty every last round up into the air. By the end, the gunpowder smoke is so thick nobody can even see the person standing next to 'em."

My eyes are wide, and I'm not sure if I can allow myself to believe this story. But, somehow, and for some reason I'll likely never understand, I *want* to believe it.

"Now *here's* the best part . . ." Tex says, before pausing again. "Well, actually, no, it still ain't the best part. But, anyway, as sure as I'm standing here before you, and swear to Lucy and all her honor, the sky done opened up just a few minutes later and began pouring out all her blood and guts in the form of fresh, clean rain."

"That's impossible," I say, frozen. "Or else it was just an incredible coincidence."

"Well, see, that's what many folks thought for a long time," Tex says. "But it ain't the case. Nor was it any sort of magical hoo-ha, like many believed at the time. The Army Corps of Engineers eventually did a study and experiment right there on the same land some ten years later, after a ranking general had heard about what Arcane done. And they found out there's a way to produce rain clouds using gunpowder. They weren't quite so successful getting it to actually *rain*, but they got as close as being able to *smell* the rain in the air. What Arcane Cohaagen done is so widely accepted around those parts that Texas even made a law against changing the weather, I kid you not. That law is still in place today. It is *illegal* in Texas to attempt to change the weather without prior written notification."

Tex grins, and I know that whether the story is true or not, he, at least, believes it wholeheartedly.

"So, what's the best part, then?"

"Beg your pardon, son?"

"You said two parts were and then weren't the best part of the story," I say. "So, what was?"

Tex laughs as if just remembering the best punch line he ever heard.

"Ah right, well, the *best* part is what happened with the oil well. Old Arcane did get his rain, and so eventually got the drilling done, and got hisself a mighty fine well that spat out a *fortune* over the next decade. But Arcane didn't get a penny of it! He died broke and alone somewhere near Tulsa. They say he was shot in the back while urinating on another man's horse. Anyhow, turns out he gave away too much stock in his claim gathering up that posse to shoot guns at the sky. By the time the well was pumping, and everyone got their shares, there wasn't nothing left for him!"

Tex laughs as if such a terrible misfortune befalling his father's father's father is the most hilarious thing in the world. And while it is ironically, darkly funny, I'm left feeling a little disappointed at coming so close to finding out how Tex's family might have made their fortune, only to end up empty-handed.

"Okay, but how does our current situation remind you of that story?" I finally ask.

Tex chomps on his unlit cigarette thoughtfully.

"What are you talking about, son?"

I resist the urge to scream in frustration.

"I asked if you were going to keep the Hurricanes, now that they're turning a profit?"

"Oh yeah, that!" he says and laughs. "Oh, *no.* Dear Lucy, no, no. No, we're getting rid of the team and selling this land. See, what you got yourself here is a classic Arcane situation. He thought he made it rain the way *he* envisioned, but it turned out he did it a whole other way on accident. A way that weren't *sustainable.* You get what I'm saying, son?"

"But . . . but . . . we're winning!" I plead. "And you just said yourself we're now making a profit!"

"Son, that measly profit ain't nothing compared to what I'll make sellin' everything off!" Tex says. "You don't get rich and stay that way by makin' bad business decisions. A contract is a contract. If you don't make those playoffs, this team is finished, my boy."

"Okay," I say, nervous all over again.

But I try to tell myself that the situation isn't any different than it was before I walked into this office. We just need to keep winning.

We can still save the team.

"But, furthermore, the *real* point of the story is that your current situation here reminds me of what happened to Arcane. He oversold hisself. Got too successful for his own good."

"What . . . what do you mean?"

"Sometimes you get what you want, just like Arcane," Tex says, his eyes glinting under the wide brim of his pure-white Stetson. "And then it *backfires* on you."

"I still don't . . . ?"

"Well, son, thing is . . ." Tex stops for a few seconds. "You done such a good job with this here team that some big-league scouts took notice. You see, that knuckleball pitcher, Policeman Dan or whatever—"

"The Law."

"Sure, okay. Well, he and that other guy, Giant Tuna—"

"Big Fish."

"Son, quit interrupting," Tex says, leaning forward, putting his elbows on his desk. "Delivering bad news to a youngin is hard enough as is without interruptions. *Now,* they been playing so well that a couple big-league teams bought out their contracts this morning. They're no longer members of the Hurricanes, effective immediately."

"But . . . that's not possible," I say weakly. "We can't let them . . . *What?*"

"Unfortunately, son, that's what's happening," Tex says. "Mabel rules dictate that any player signed to a higher league must be released from their contracts. This league is about developing players, not holding them back."

I knew the rule; I hadn't needed him to tell me. It happens to a few players in the Mabel every year. But it usually doesn't happen this late in the season.

We just have three games left, including two against the Mabel's best team. And now we've lost our two best players.

"I'm sorry, son," Tex says.

The weird thing is, I can tell he *is* sorry. Even though he wants to sell the team, it's obvious he's getting no joy from this.

"What are we going to do?" I say, not realizing I'm saying it out loud. "We were so close. . . ."

"Hey, don't be so hard on yourself, son," Tex says gently—as gently as a man like him is capable of, anyway. "It's a testament to the job you done here, if anything. Keep your head up. Your family will make out all right in this. All these extra ticket sales are just more gravy for your chicken."

But I don't care about *more gravy on my chicken*. Money is as meaningless to me as it was to Ira. All I want is to make the playoffs. I can't let this team go. It's all that's left of him. . . .

Not to mention that failing to make the playoffs will mean I'm letting down Aliyah, Slips, and all the players who stuck with us through the rough beginning. And Ira most of all.

"It was a valiant effort, son," Tex says. "I mean, it would be tragic if your own success ends up being your undoing, but them's the breaks, so they say. . . ."

"No," I say.

When the word leaves my mouth, I honestly don't know where it comes from. But apparently, there's more.

"We're not done yet," I hear myself saying. "We'll make the playoffs. I'll find a way."

Tex, for once, doesn't say anything. He just smiles, pulls the unlit cigarette from his lips, and tips his hat at me.

Chapter 31

"YOU CAN'T SIGN THAT CONTRACT!" I SAY.

The Law looks up at me from the bench in front of his locker. He's in the middle of packing up his things. A quick glance at Big Fish's empty locker tells me he's already long gone. That's fine—he was great, yes, but the Law is the one who brought us the Zazzle.

"Hey, Alan," he says with a smile. "I was going to find you before I left, to thank you for—"

"But you *can't* leave," I say. "We're a team. We need you. Your Baseball Zazzle."

"Baseball *Zazzle*?"

"I just, we're doing something special here—"

"You are, I know," the Law says, stuffing some undershirts into his sports bag. "It's hard to leave now, but I have to. This is my dream, Alan. Not many players get a second chance like this. I mean, I really ought to be thanking you. Without what happened this year . . ."

"Don't thank the team you're quitting on!" I snap.

I expect him to get angry, but he doesn't. Instead, he goes quiet. He just seems more hurt and confused than anything else.

I'm about to keep yelling. Now that I've found my voice, I want to tell him how much we need him and what he brought to the team. That same thing that guys like Early Eights and BAM Morgan did back in the day. This is what Ira always wanted for the team, and we finally got it back.

But before I can, someone grabs my arm and stops me.

"Weakerman, come *here*."

It's Aliyah, and she's angrily pulling me away toward my office.

"Thanks again, Alan," the Law calls out, waving goodbye as Aliyah drags me into my office.

"It's *Alex*, by the way!" I shout back, but I don't think he hears me.

Slips is already there, sitting in the corner with Anne of Green Gables resting in his lap.

"What are you doing?" Aliyah demands once we're inside with the door closed.

"What do you mean?" I say "Trying to save . . . I mean, we're so close to making the playoffs, and . . ."

"You should be *happy* for him," Aliyah insists. "The Law is finally going to get a shot at playing in the big leagues! This is his dream. What this whole thing is about."

"Not if it means quitting on the Hurricanes!"

She lets out a hollow laugh and throws her hands in the air like a frustrated mom dealing with a toddler in the middle of a tantrum.

"Nobody is quitting the team, Weakerman," Aliyah says. "Nobody but *you* thinks that. The *whole team* is happy for Phil, and for Oliver. Rabbit, back me up."

"It's true, buddy," Slips says, though he doesn't meet my eyes. And I know why: he's the only other person who knows the truth.

"It was bound to happen, the way they were playing," Aliyah continues. "I mean, the Law has over a *hundred strikeouts* in his last fifty innings! And Big Fish, in case you didn't realize it, is on pace to lead the league in home runs by double digits!"

"I know, you're right," I say. "I just need to . . . I want to make the playoffs so much, for Ira."

I can tell Aliyah is still frustrated, but her face softens a bit.

"Missing the playoffs won't take away from what we've accomplished. Nobody thought we'd get even this close. What we did with this team, Weakerman, it's amazing. And think of it this way: we're totally primed to come back better than ever next year, with the hometown fans behind us from game one!"

Of course, Aliyah has no idea there won't *be* a next year if we don't make it this year. I exchange a look with Slips.

"Hey, let's not be so negative," Slips says desperately. "We still got a chance, right?"

"Sure, we have a chance," Aliyah says. "We still only need to win *one* of these last three games."

"So . . . that sounds doable?" Slips says.

"Without our two best players?" I say.

"Weakerman, you're thinking like a loser again!" Aliyah says. "You're looking for reasons we will lose rather than focusing on reasons we can still *win*. For one thing, we're at home these final games, and for once, that actually means something. I just heard that we sold out tonight, with a chance to clinch the playoffs on the line! When's the last time Mustard Park sold out?"

"Let me guess," Slips says, cutting in. "Thirty-some years ago, back when the Big Four played?"

"Exactly," Aliyah says with a heartbreakingly determined stare. "We can do this! Baseball Zazzle is about more than just one or two players. We still have the momentum. We can find a way to win *one* game, right?"

For the second time today, I find hope creeping in, even when every instinct I have tells me we're in real trouble. Maybe Aliyah's right? If Carla can finally get her swing going the way she does on the road, and all the players keep feeding off the energy we've developed, then why can't we still make the playoffs?

It's just one game out of three, after we've gone 29–9 since I took over. The numbers *and* Zazzle are both on our side.

One game.

We can do this. Can't we?

The sold-out crowd of 4,884 gets to their feet and roars

when Carla Henderson steps to the plate.

We're down 3–1, and it's the bottom of the ninth inning.

But the bases are loaded. And no one is out.

We still have a chance to win this game, the last of our penultimate home series against the St. John Saints. It would mean clinching a playoff spot and saving the Hurricanes for at least one more year. If we can win tonight, we won't need to rely on a miracle victory versus the Harbor Pirates for our final two games.

And now's our chance—if Carla Henderson can come through in the clutch. She's gone hitless in her last twelve at bats here at Mustard Park.

"Carla." I wave her over from the on-deck circle.

She hurries over, and I can tell she's thinking about her dad. About how well he would play in this spot—and it's true, BAM Morgan was incredible in big situations like this. The Big Four had a combined .512 average with runners in scoring position after the seventh inning during the Dream Team's three-year run.

"Hey," I say. "You're just another Hurricane. A part of *this* team, here, now. Stay loose and aggressive, right?"

Carla nods, but her mind is obviously still on her dad.

As she settles into the batter's box, digging her cleats

into the dirt, the sold-out home crowd explodes. They don't care that she's 0–13 with runners in scoring position at Mustard Park. Heck, they probably don't even know that. She's a fan favorite, and the fans cheer for her no matter what.

It's no secret that Carla's a free swinger. But she's been working hard in practice at taking more pitches. That's always the first thing to work on if you're struggling at the plate. Make the pitcher work. And it shows, because she takes two very close pitches on the corner to start the at bat. The third pitch is way outside, and it's suddenly a 3–0 count. The Saints pitcher is one pitch away from walking in one of the two runs we need to tie the ball game.

All I can think is: perhaps we *do* still have some Baseball Zazzle on our side.

It's an obvious time to take a pitch. For once, my faith in the numbers, the metrics, the baseball probabilities are all in line with what I want Carla to do, deep down. What she really needs is to finally be the hero. Walking in one of the last two runs we need wouldn't win the game, but given how Carla's been swinging the bat, it's likely the best we can hope for.

I give her the sign to take the next pitch. She turns to

face the pitcher, getting into her stance.

He winds up and deals an 88-mile-per-hour fastball on the inside corner of the plate.

It might be that Carla is surprised by the pitch, coming inside like it does. It doesn't look like she means to swing. But instead of stepping out to avoid the inside pitch, she turns slightly and drops her hands, bringing her bat over the plate in a limp check-swing.

To her horror, and mine, it makes contact, sending a weak dribbler back to the mound.

The pitcher scoops it up and underhands it to the catcher, who's already standing on home, for one out.

The catcher should look immediately at first for a second out. But he must know that Carla is one of the slowest players in the league, because he fires the ball to third for a second out—

Then the third basemen whips it over to first a moment before Carla reaches the bag.

It's a game-ending triple play.

The odds of that happening were literally 11,355 to 1. And it suddenly feels like we now very much have whatever the *opposite* of Baseball Zazzle is on our side.

A cheer goes up from the Saints dugout as the crowd falls silent. Carla is hanging her head as she walks back to the dugout, where the rest of the players are lining up to pat her on the back and give her some encouragement.

"It's not your fault . . ." I begin as Carla walks past me on the dugout steps.

But either she doesn't believe me or she doesn't hear me, because she walks straight into the tunnel and back toward the locker room without lifting her head.

In that moment, a voice comes from deep inside my brain. Maybe it's me from a couple months ago, right after Ira died.

Nice job, Weakerman! You've now engineered the End of the Mighty Hurricanes of Weakerville, Iowa.

Chapter 32

BY THE TIME THE FIRST GAME OF OUR FINAL SERIES VERSUS THE Duluth Harbor Pirates rolls around, I know what must be done.

After Carla's game-ending triple play versus the St. John Saints, we're left having to win one of these last two games against the Harbor Pirates, a team we can't beat even with our best players.

Which means it's time to come clean.

The season will be over soon, and my secret will have to come out. I already made the mistake of lying once;

I'm not going to make things worse by waiting any longer to tell the team the truth. I owe them better than that.

The worst part, as I head to the locker room before the game, is that I know I was wrong from the start. Slips, Aliyah, and all the players have giving everything they have to a team that was probably doomed the moment Ira died. And I never told them. Everything they've worked so hard for will be gone at season's end and everyone will hate me for lying about it.

And I will deserve it.

As I turn the corner into the locker room, it feels like I'm walking into my own funeral.

Nobody notices, because they're having too much fun preparing for the final series of the season. One in which two players got their contracts picked up by big-league clubs, one in which we will finish with a winning record for the first time in a decade, regardless of the outcome of these final two games. And those *are* remarkable accomplishments.

Or at least they would be if it weren't for the fact that this will be the Hurricanes' last season ever.

As I enter, Slips slings an arm around my shoulder. Aliyah is already under his other arm.

"You kids want to go get pizza after the game?" he asks.

Both Aliyah and I pull away from him simultaneously, but she's grinning.

"Don't you ever get tired of eating pizza?" she asks.

"Pfft, no!" Slips says as if this is the most ridiculous question he's ever been asked. *"Do you?"*

"Well, I guess not," Aliyah admits. "I just like to eat other stuff . . . sometimes."

"Ugh, *okay,* fine." Slips relents. "Let's go to Homesteaders Family Restaurant instead? The Thursday-night special is liver and onions. Almost as good as pizza, right, Alex?" He nudges my arm, raising his eyebrows.

"No, I, uh. Well . . . I have to, um, something to say . . ."

"What's wrong?" Aliyah asks.

"To the, uh, whole team."

Slips must know what's about to happen, because his smile disappears. He doesn't say anything; he just pounds Anne of Green Gables on an empty locker. The players know this is their cue to gather around for a classic Slips pregame speech.

"Um . . ." I start, and the team's attention hesitantly shifts over to me. "I need to tell you all something. . . ."

Everyone's still smiling, but I can tell from their eyes that they know this isn't good news.

"I've been lying. . . ." I start. "I . . . I mean . . . I can't—I can't do this."

So many eyes on me. I can't go through with it. I still have never addressed the whole team like this.

"Slips, can you . . . ?"

He glares at me, looking as angry as I've ever seen him. But I think he knows if he doesn't take over, then this won't happen. And we both know it needs to.

"What Alex is trying to say is . . ."

Slips goes on to explain everything. About how Tex will sell the team unless we can win one of these last two games against the Harbor Pirates and make the playoffs. About how I've known all along but couldn't bear to tell anyone. About how it basically means the team will be finished forever after this season.

"I'm sorry," I say as he finishes. "I'm so sorry. . . ."

Mayhem is the first to speak.

"Kid, we even asked you that at the start . . ." he says, but he seems more disappointed than mad, which confuses me.

"I know," I say. "I know, I messed up. . . ."

"I can't believe it," Aliyah says, slumping down onto the bench next to Slips.

"I know, I can't believe it's all over either . . ." I say.

"What!" she says, standing back up. "That's not what I meant! I was about to say that I can't believe you lied to all of us. We're *definitely* going to have words about that later. But let me be clear, to you and everyone else: this is *not* over!" Her fists are balled up at her sides like she wants to throw one at my face like a fastball. "We can't just give up! We have two games left! We can still make the playoffs! This weird deal with Tex doesn't change anything about these last two games."

To my surprise, this gets a few nods of approval from the players.

"We at least need to go out there and give it our best," Carla says. "We owe it to each other and to the history of this team."

This is met with a few murmurs of agreement.

"Plus, if this team really is getting folded," Mayhem says, "then we at least need to make a good showing if we want jobs on another team next season."

This gets a few louder responses.

I figured they'd be equal parts mad at me and

depressed, but if anything, they just seem determined. Which somehow makes this feel even worse.

Just like that, what I thought was going to be a soul-crushing speech has somehow turned into exactly what it seems like the Hurricanes needed to hear. By the time they're leaving the locker room, they're actually smiling and patting each other on the back, trying to get pepped up for the game. My team charges out toward the field seemingly ready to take on the 1927 New York Yankees, even in spite of everything else.

And I couldn't prouder of them.

And more ashamed of myself.

Of course, we get crushed that night.

I mean, it's the Duluth Harbor Pirates. Yeah, our players give it everything they have. But talent is talent, and the Pirates are loaded with it. It's a 12–2 drubbing.

The Hurricanes' only hope is to win our very last game of the season against that very same loaded Pirates team.

The locker room after the game is somber. The players are telling one another, "There's still one game left," and, "It's not over until it's over."

But by now I think we all know it's over.

For my part, I hide out in my office like a coward, studying my binders on the Pirates, trying to find more matchups to exploit, some angle we can use to maybe squeeze out a win. I've already been over the numbers a dozen times now, and I find nothing new. Even the Harbor Pirates' worst player is statically better than everyone left on our team.

It's a pointless exercise, but it's all I know to do.

Sometime later, after all the players have left, Slips and Aliyah show up at the door.

"Oh, hey guys," I say. "I guess I figured you'd already left for Cheese'N Stuff."

Slips opens his mouth to say something, but Aliyah cuts him off.

"I said we were going to talk about this later, and I meant it," Aliyah says. "I'm not mad that we lost, or that the team might be finished; I'm not even mad that I'm missing my final Little League season. I'm mad that *you* lied to everyone. To *me*. And then didn't even have the courage to tell us yourself! Here I thought you were this genuine, honest kid. Awkward as a giraffe on ice skates, sure, but I *liked* that about you. I thought that nothing was more important to you than baseball. But, honestly, it kinda seems like you're just the same as everyone else. The same as my dad, keeping me in the dark, like you know what's best and I don't deserve to know the truth. You know what, Weakerman? You're just a coward."

I know her words are true, and they hit me where it hurts most. My brain goes fuzzy with something that's like Flumpo but that I've never felt before. And then I'm suddenly speaking before I even know what I'm going to say.

"It was his idea!" I say, pointing at Slips.

"Dude!" Slips says.

"Wait, you *knew*?" Aliyah says, turning on Slips. "This whole time?"

"I . . ." Slips says, but then closes his mouth.

For perhaps the first time ever, he has nothing to say.

"Forget both of you," Aliyah says. "I'll be back for the final game. For the team, and for Ira. But not for you guys."

She spins and storms out of the room, leaving Slips and me gaping at each other.

"What the heck, Alex?" Slips says, looking more hurt than I've ever seen.

"I'm sorry," I say. "I don't know why I did that. But you *did* tell me to lie to her!"

"Whatever, man," he says. "I guess you're just being you. Blaming me to shift the attention off yourself. As usual."

"What's that supposed to mean?"

"Come on. Don't you think I sometimes get tired of being your spokesperson? Of having to do all the talking for you? I do it because we're friends, but you rely on me too much. You take advantage of me. I'm tired of taking care of everything just so you can avoid your own problems. So yeah, I feel terrible I told you to lie to her. Of course I do. But I didn't *make you* lie to her. Don't try to pretend this is my fault. This was all you."

"I know," I say. "And I'm . . . I'm sorry that I take advantage of you or whatever. It's not fair, though. I just, you know, it's the Flumpo, it makes me—"

"*Stop!*" Slips says, and my stomach drops. "Stop making excuses. Talking to people, connecting to them . . . it's not always easy for *anyone*, Alex. And there are probably some people who just can't do it. But you're not one of those people. I *know* you're capable of it, because I've seen you do it. There's no such thing as Flumpo, dude.

You know what I think? I think Ira did all this to help you figure that out. To help you realize you have something to offer besides baseball stats. And for a second, it felt like it was working. But now here you are, when things get tough, blaming it all on some made-up word again. If you truly believed you had what it took to lead the Hurricanes to victory tomorrow, I think we actually could win. Ira would agree. Some people *do* believe in you that much."

He's shaking his head, looking at the ground. After a few uncomfortable moments he finally looks up. He's been the most loyal, supportive friend anyone could ask for.

I have to look away.

"You really messed up," he finally says, before turning and leaving.

Just like that, I'm alone in the belly of Mustard Park. The place my grandpa built on the very ground his grandpa's grandpa first settled nearly two centuries ago. And I'm the one who's ruined it all because I can't figure out how to believe in myself. Instead of even trying, I just bury myself in cold, static numbers. So much so that I don't even know how to trust anyone else when they say they actually believe in me.

There's no way I'm going to figure out how to do that myself tonight. So there's only one thing left to do.

It's not something I want to do, but I'm out of other options.

Chapter 33

THERE'S ONLY ONE WAY TO SAVE THIS TEAM NOW.

And no, it isn't to win our last game against the Harbor Pirates. That's just not happening. They are 78–11 and a better team than us by every conceivable metric. So that really leaves me with just one option.

I have to beg Tex for mercy.

"Better make this quick, son," Tex says. "I've got appointments with a *lot* of developers today."

I'm sitting in his office. His chair is turned around so his back is to me, but I can still see the sides and top of his huge white Stetson. And I can almost *hear* his smile.

"Fine," I say. "I'm here to ask you: please don't sell the land and dismantle the team."

He sighs as he spins around in his chair, the unlit cigarette hanging from his lips like always.

"Son, we've been *over* this. Why make us go through all the unpleasantries again and again?"

"Please," I say, knowing that groveling is about as appealing as a carton of chunky spoiled milk. But this is all I have left. I don't even have friends left to talk me out of it. "*Please* don't sell. Please?"

"I already told you, I'm here to make money. And there's more money in the land than there is in the team, son, that's just a fact. I've got several offers worth *millions* on the table already. It's all quite complicated, but it's much more reliable than banking on a *baseball* team. Baseball is unpredictable—whether a team is going to win, whether people are going to buy tickets—and when you're in the money-making business, what you prize above all is *predictability*. I'm sure you know what I mean, my boy."

The sad part of all of this is that I do. So I can't even argue with him.

And so instead I say: "P-Please, Mr. Cohaagen?" I feel tears stinging the backs of my eyes. It would be the ultimate indignity to start bawling now, here in his office, and to be honest, even I'm not sure where all the emotion is coming from. "Please don't sell them. I can't lose the team. *Pleeeease.*"

"Now, don't cry, son," Tex says, shifting in his seat like it's covered in cactus needles.

"Please, please," I say, feeling a few tears actually streaming down my cheeks now. "I *need* this team. They can't go away."

"Son, get *ahold* of yourself, it's just a dadgum baseball team."

"It's not *just a team*!" I cry. The words are out before I can even think over what I'm saying. "It's not just a team. It's what my grandpa and I . . . It's *our* thing. It's what we have left. All I have left. When he died, I thought I was . . . but . . . You just wouldn't understand. Nobody else but me and him would."

Saying it aloud only makes the reality of his absence worse. It feels like my stomach is on fire, and all I can do to keep from sobbing uncontrollably is to grip the arms on the chair and stare down at my sneakers.

Tex sighs again and I hear his chair creak as he leans back in it. There's a long silence while I keep staring down at my shoes, trying to keep a grip. Begging for mercy is one thing. Throwing a grief-laden tantrum is another.

Whatever important meetings Tex had to rush off to, he doesn't seem concerned about them now, as he's just sitting here with me, letting the minutes pass by.

"You know," Tex finally says. "I had something like that once. Ain't no replacing a bond like that. Believe me. She made me a better person, same as Ira done for you, I'm sure. Lucy was as fine as they come."

I rub my eyes and lift my head, trying to avoid direct eye contact. But Tex isn't even looking my way. He's turned slightly to the side and is staring at a painting on the wall—of a lone man fishing on a dock. For the first time, he actually lights the unlit cigarette that's always clamped between his teeth. He takes a huge, deep drag, smoking almost a third of it in one deep inhale. Then he looks at the burning ember as he exhales enough smoke to make me cough.

"She actually got me to quit these," he says somberly. "That ain't no small feat. But that's gone and by now, I guess. She was right. Lucy was always right. . . ." Tex trails off and stares vacantly at the floor behind me. For a second, it's as if he's forgotten I'm even there. "Right about this team. Right about this town. Right about . . . *everything*."

I'm not sure how long to sit there, waiting for Tex to snap out of it.

"Lucy?" I finally ask.

He looks at me sharply, almost startled to see I'm still there.

"You know who that is, don't you?" he asks.

I shake my head.

"You mean to tell me you don't even know your own *aunt Lucy*, son?"

I shake my head again, slowly this time.

"Figures," Tex says, looking up at the ceiling as he mashes the cigarette into the clean ashtray on his desk. "She died long before you were born, I suppose. Lucy was Ira's twin sister."

I knew Ira had a sister who died before I was born, but I never knew they were twins. He didn't talk about her much.

"She was also my wife of fifty-seven years. Well, would be fifty-seven, if she was still alive today, of course. She and your grandpa were the same, in so many ways. She loved this here town. She was always wanting to come back here, see Ira, watch a Hurricanes game. And I was as stubborn back then as I am now. I was always busy in places that felt like they mattered much more than a place like *Weakerville, Iowa*. So, I never did come with her. And over the years, as I realized that nothing I was doing mattered to her nearly as much as what was here in this sad little town, I started resenting your grandpappy. We never did get along much, Ira and me. He's a fine man, but we just got different values.

"Well, anyway, once Lucy passed on, there wasn't much reason for us to speak anymore. Her death broke both our hearts. Shattered us, in a way. And I think even lookin' at one another got to be too painful 'cause it just reminded us of Lucy. But I kept this team alive and funded Ira's failures here because I always thought she would have wanted me to help him. I convinced my business partners it would eventually prove to be a good investment, and after I sell this land, that will be true. But that wasn't the reason I gave Ira what he needed to keep the team afloat. I did it for *Lucy*."

Tex looks down at his hands, and then one of them quickly wipes at his eyes.

"But over time, I've come to realize that it's not the things we associate with lost loved ones that matter," he continues. "Keeping this team around won't bring her back or make me feel any closer to her than I already do, every day. And you'll eventually feel the same about Ira, son, trust me. You're still young, and I know it don't feel like it right now, but once this team is gone, you'll still have everything left of Ira you ever did."

I sort of get what Tex is trying to tell me, but he doesn't understand. This wasn't just a *thing* between Ira and me. It was who we were. The only thing we both cared about, and that nobody else did. The hours we spent discussing players, games, moments. That's not even mentioning how he *expected* me to get this team to the playoffs. He told me so directly in that letter.

"But wouldn't it honor Lucy to keep the team around, like she wanted?" I finally say.

"You don't get to tell me what she would or wouldn't want," he snaps in a tone that's as close to anger as I've ever heard from him. "That ain't fair, and I won't tolerate it. Understand?"

I nod slowly.

"Okay," he says. "Sorry for getting cross, but the same as you and Ira shared a bond nobody understood, it's the same for me and Lucy as well. Now, I feel bad for you, I really do. But I ain't changing my mind. That's that."

Right here is where I should be rallying, formulating a plan to find a way to win our last game. This is where I should be telling Tex he's wrong and it's not over until it's over. But instead, all I can think about is losing the last part of my grandpa I had left. It's like feeling him die, all over again.

I have no defiance left. Just sorrow for what I've lost: my best friend, my new friend, my favorite baseball team, and most of all, my grandpa and the one thing we shared that nobody else did.

So instead of saying something bold and brave like, *Excuse me, then, I've got a game to go win,* what I say is:

"Okay."

Tex nods and picks up his phone as I stand to leave. He's already talking to someone else on the line as I'm walking out of the room.

His hoarse laughter follows me the whole way back home.

My dad has a serious expression on his face when I get home, almost the same one he wore the day Ira died.

"What is it?" I ask.

"I need to show you something."

I follow him to the patio, my gut already twisting. How can this day get worse?

Both grills and his smoker are lit and working, which isn't too unusual if he's having a barbecue this weekend or something.

"Remember how I told you I was too busy to come to your games because I was working on a side project?"

"I guess," I say.

"Well, here it is," he says, motioning toward a plate of food on the patio table.

On closer inspection, it's not even a plate of food. It's just a single hot dog in a bun on a paper plate. So why is he treating it like a dish on *Top Chef*?

"Um."

"Go on," he prods. "Try it."

I sit down and look at the sad, lonely hot dog. It's dressed only with mustard. I usually like my hot dogs loaded with everything, and my dad knows this. Then again, I'm not one to pass up a free hot dog, no matter what's on it.

I pick it up—the bun is still warm—and take a huge bite.

My mouth erupts with a tangy, sweet, and slightly spicy flavor. It's mustard-like yet also tastes totally new. Almost as if it's unlocking a sixth taste-bud profile that I never knew I had. It takes me just three bites to devour the rest of the hot dog. And once I'm done, I'm filled with a devastating sadness that it's gone.

"Did you like it?" my dad asks as if he prepared this hot dog for an audience of one.

"Like it? Dad, that was . . . I mean, I've never . . . What I'm trying to say is . . . I . . . MORE! I want more! What is that sauce?"

My dad grins.

"That, my boy," he says, wearing his *I know I just done good barbecue* smile, "was my version of Great-Great-Great-Great-Grandpa Powell's PoTTY Sauce."

"*That* was Powell's Tangy Tasty Yellow Sauce?"

I'd completely forgotten I gave him the old recipe I found in Ira's notebooks over a month ago. He hadn't seemed all that excited in the moment.

"I thought it turned out pretty okay," he says.

"It's way better than 'pretty okay,'" I say. "I wish Ira could have tried it before . . . well . . ."

I can't really think about Ira right now. Not with probably the Hurricanes' final game ever coming up tomorrow night.

"I'm hoping to maybe sell it, along with my smoked brisket and ribs, at Mustard Park during Hurricanes home games next season."

"Dad, I don't think there will be a next season," I say.

"What? Why not?" he asks. "From what I hear, if you win tomorrow night, you're in the playoffs. Isn't that all you need to do?"

"Yeah, but we *won't* win tomorrow night."

"Alex, why would you say that?" my dad says, sitting down next to me. He puts a hand on my shoulder. "You're doing great. Everyone I've talked to seems to think you guys will find a way to win, like you have been doing all season."

"Everyone you've talked to?" I mumble. I'm so confused now. "I thought you didn't even like baseball."

"Well, I still don't, to be honest," my dad says with a grin. "But it's hard not to be hearing about the Hurricanes. Everyone at work talks about them all the time. I mean, the whole town is into the team right now."

"They are?" I ask.

"Alex, Weakerville only has ten thousand people," my dad says. "Which means that literally *half the town* has been at the home games the past few weeks. They've become a pretty big deal. My buddies at work are excited for next year too. It was actually their idea for me to sell barbecue at the stadium next summer."

I don't even know what to say. I'd been so focused on winning that I hadn't really noticed just how much the town was getting into the Hurricanes. I know it sounds dumb now, but I hadn't really been thinking about the fact that the people in the stands at Mustard Park were my neighbors, people I know from around town, even kids from my school.

While I listen, my dad tells me more:

—Half of his buddies from work are wearing Hurricanes caps and shirts around town, and they aren't the only ones. Before this season, pretty much no one but me and Ira did that.

—Family General signed an advertisement deal with the Hurricanes. Billboards for the store showing Carla Henderson in her Hurricanes gear have shown up all over town.

—Cheese'N Stuff signed a deal to start selling their pizza at the stadium. Which probably explains why Slips has been frequently disappearing between innings the last few weeks, only to return with grease all over his shirt, a bulging stomach, and a huge grin on his face.

—Local businesses have painted Hurricanes logos in their store windows.

For the first time in my life, the whole town of Weakerville knows who the Hurricanes are. I'd never considered before that this team might mean something more than just a way to spend a summer afternoon to anyone else but me and Ira.

It hurts, because this is possibly why Ira wanted me to make the playoffs and help keep the team alive in the first place. Nobody would have loved to see what's happening in Weakerville more than Ira.

Which is why I now know I can't just give up. It's not just the team and my friends and Ira I'd be letting down. It's all of Weakerville.

If everyone believes we can win this last game, then there must be a way to pull it off. And I think I know what that is. I always have, or at least have for a few weeks now, but I've just been too afraid to do it on my own.

But now I have no choice.

Because we *have to* win this last game.

Chapter 34

IT'S NEARLY 11:00 P.M. IN A DARK CORNER OF DOWNTOWN WEAKERVILLE, and I'm pounding on a sturdy wooden door on an old brick building.

Not just any building. It's the old defunct movie theater—and rumored residence of Gloves. A.k.a. Bernie BAM Morgan. A.k.a. A.M. A.k.a. Carla's dad. I've been standing here for several minutes already, but I know he's home. He wasn't at any of his usual spots, and I saw the curtains in the window move the first time I knocked.

I knock again.

He must realize I'm not giving up, because the door finally opens a sliver.

"What?" says a gravelly voice from the crack in the doorway.

"I want you to tell me why you won't help your old friend Ira," I start.

"Ira's dead," Gloves shoots back.

"But the Hurricanes, Ira's Hurricanes, need you," I say. "We're one game away from the playoffs, and—"

Gloves cuts me off. "No."

"Fine. But you at least owe me an explanation as to why you would turn your back on him and the team."

Gloves stares at me, his face cut off at the sides behind his door.

"I don't owe you nothing," he says. "You Soggy Water Trash."

"Look, Gloves—" I start, but he cuts me off again.

"That ain't my name, kid," he says sharply. "And it never was."

"So what should I call you, then?" I ask. "BAM? Bernie? Arlon?"

He just stands there glaring at me.

Instead of trying to get an answer out of him, I move on, opening up one of Ira's journals to a marked page, and begin reading a note from three years ago:

"'Got a call today with nobody on the other end. I know it was A.M., calling to apologize, then changing his mind. I wish he knew I don't want an apology. Just my friend back.'"

Gloves growls at me like a dog.

I pull a different notebook from my backpack and quickly start reading another earmarked passage.

"'A.M. was like a brother,'" I read. "'The closest thing to a sibling since I lost my sister. I just wish he could forgive himself like we all do.'"

And one last one:

"'Spoke to A.M.'s daughter again. Breaks my heart he stopped talking to her too. She misses him so much. I saw him near Family General, and—'"

"Enough!" Gloves cuts me off with a raspy growl.

Then he disappears inside the darkness of his apartment, leaving the door open behind him. I'm not sure if he meant to leave the door open for me, and I'm terrified of going inside Gloves's home. But this is one of many little moments tonight when I need to be bold and believe in what I'm doing for once. So, I take a breath, and then push my way into the apartment.

My heart is pounding, and I can't see anything but

darkness at first. Then my eyes adjust to a faint light coming from a room near the back of the apartment. I'm standing in a small, surprisingly clean, living room. The only furniture is a weathered couch in the center and a wooden chair in the corner. There are no photos on the walls, no TVs, no houseplants. Just a couch and a chair. The place smells musty, but not as bad as I expected given how much time Gloves spends rooting around in old garbage. I pull the front door closed behind me.

Gloves motions for me to follow him as he heads toward a short hallway to the right. It leads to a small kitchen, dimly lit by a blinking fluorescent bulb on the low ceiling. There is a brown mini-fridge, a toaster oven, a small sink, a two-burner stove, and a chipped wooden table with a single chair beside it.

Gloves is standing by the sink, fiddling with a small coffee maker.

"Wasn't sure Hippopotamus Brain Goop like you would know an invite when you saw one," he says, not turning around yet. "Want some coffee?"

"Um, no thanks."

"Wise decision," Gloves says, finally getting the machine going. He turns around to face me and I'm surprised to see a faint, wry smile touching the corners of his mouth. "I make miserable coffee."

The traces of the smile disappear, and he sighs, leaning back against the counter. Seeing him inside his apartment, under an actual light, he doesn't quite look as old as he usually does. There's something about seeing someone outside, digging around in garbage, that ages them a bit. Not that he looks young; his face is wrinkled and haggard with sunken cheeks. It almost looks like his face would just plain break if he ever allowed himself to smile for real.

"Look," Gloves finally says. "I want to help Ira—he was one of my dearest friends. But I can't."

"Why not?"

"Because of *who I am*," he says. "The town hates me. The team, the fans, they don't want me around. I always told Ira that, but that hopelessly optimistic dreamer would never listen to me."

"People in this town may not like getting called names all the time," I say, trying as best I can to keep my voice even. "But they hardly *hate* you. I mean, I think most people find you . . . weirdly charming?"

"I'm not talking about me *now*," Gloves says. "I'm referring to my past. Who I was. Before this."

I try to remember how Bernie BAM Morgan's career

ended. As far as I know, he was nothing but beloved by all Hurricanes fans, even though he did move on to the Korean leagues himself a few seasons after Eights left.

"Does this have anything to do with why Ira calls you A.M.?" I ask.

Gloves actually lets out a single, breathless laugh, almost as if it escaped involuntarily.

"That came after I stopped playing," he says. "It was an alias Ira made up to help keep his promise to me, I suppose. He swore to never divulge my identity or whereabouts to anyone. When we were together, he always just called me by my real name."

"Using your initials, even if it's your middle and last name, isn't exactly the best alias," I say.

"A.M. aren't my initials, kid," he says. "My name is Early. Early Foster."

Chapter 35

IT TAKES A WHILE FOR HIS WORDS TO SINK IN.

Early Foster. *The* legendary Early Eights Foster.

Grandpa Ira calling him "A.M." makes more sense now—"Early," "morning," "A.M." Clever. And it also makes sense why my grandpa thought "A.M." could have a huge impact on the team. There's literally no other Hurricane, past or present, as popular as Eights was in his prime. Even after the scandal that got him banned from the majors, his mere presence at Mustard Park would surely create a stir—and definitely bring some much-needed Baseball Zazzle to the Hurricanes locker room. After all, nobody had more Baseball Zazzle than Eights Foster. In fact, he had more Zazzle in one pinkie finger than half the league combined.

Still, as the reality of what he's saying sets in, I realize there's no way Gloves is Early Eights Foster. He's too old, for one. They don't even look like the same person. Plus, there's that little, teensy detail about how Early Eights Foster is, well, *dead.*

"I don't believe it," I finally say.

"You're telling me I don't know my own name, Mange Collector?" Gloves says.

"You *can't* be Eights Foster."

"Why not?"

"Because he's dead."

"Since when is being missing the same as being dead?" he asks.

"Since Eights was legally declared dead by a judge!"

He merely lifts his arms and looks down at himself.

"Fine, let's say Early Eights Foster isn't dead," I say, not really sure how to delicately put this. "You're still too . . . *old.*"

Gloves just laughs—he even has a way of laughing without smiling.

"Come on," he says, moving back toward the living room.

He leads me to a tiny closet, not much bigger than a school locker. Inside is pretty much a shrine to Early Eights Foster. Photos, baseball cards, and even several jerseys on hangers. Two of Early Eights Foster's trademarked royal-blue bats are stacked next to each other in the corner. And though it's true that the collection is impressive and would have been very hard to compile if he wasn't Early Eights himself, it's still not definitive proof. And even now, seeing old photos of Early side by side with Gloves, there's not much of a resemblance.

"It's a nice collection," I say. "But you look *fifty* years older than the guy on that baseball card!"

"You're right," Gloves says sadly. "Years of drinking and such have taken their toll. But it's my penance."

"Penance for what?"

"For disgracing the game, for disgracing Weakerville, for what I did to . . ." He doesn't finish that last thought. "I don't deserve anything better than this life."

I stand there and watch this defeated old man switch off the closet light and close the door. He faces me again, somehow looking even older than he did a second ago—he looks nearly as old as Ira, which is remarkable if he really is Early Eights Foster, since it would mean he's only fifty-four.

"If you're still not convinced . . ." he says.

Gloves lifts up the left sleeve of his shirt. There it is, definitive proof: Early Eights Foster's signature 88 tattoo. It's wrinkled and faded and has clearly been there for decades. Either this person was an Early Eights Foster superfan way before Eights went big-time, or . . .

This really is him, *the* Early Eights Foster.

My heart thumps wildly. I'm struggling to swallow.

Flumpo has made a comeback.

My favorite baseball player in the world is standing right there in front of me. The guy who was once—and still is, depending on who you ask—a legend. The guy who shattered almost all of the Mabel's records. The guy who was the greatest hometown hero Weakerville ever had. The guy who went on to cheat in the majors and eventually got banned from baseball for life.

The guy who went missing and has been presumed dead for over a decade.

It all makes sense now. Why Ira thought he could reignite the team, and why Eights never did. Why Ira never said anything to anyone about the person he called "A.M." Why Eights Foster chose to come back here to hide in plain sight.

I'm so stunned it's actually *him,* I can barely move. I'm afraid if I try to speak, Flumpo will cause me to puke all over his surprisingly clean apartment. But I have to rise above myself in this moment. Not just for Ira. Or the team. Or the town. But for myself.

I channel my inner Slips and try to make a joke.

"Wow, if you really are fifty-four, you should probably go see a doctor."

"I don't deserve medical care, you Filthy Nugget Cleanser," Eights shoots back, but it's less of a snarl than usual—it sounds more sad than anything else.

"You can come see the team doctor for free."

"It's not about money," Eights says. "I still got plenty of that from my playing days. Made some good investments. All the money people give me around here, I donate to the food bank, you know. The reason I can't see your team doctor, or *any* doctor, is because this is my—"

"Penance, yeah," I finish for him. "You've said that."

"And it's not just the sport or the town," he says. "It's also what I did to . . ."

Once more, he doesn't finish his thought. But this time, I know who he's talking about.

"You know, we have a new player on the team. I think

she could actually be the Hurricanes' leader, that glue, that clutch player whose Baseball Magic elevates a whole team. But she struggles at Mustard Park . . . partly because she has some unresolved issues with her dad. A former player. Someone she told me she needs to see again. Do you know who this player is?"

"Carla," he whispers.

I nod.

"Does she . . . does she know you're alive?"

"Yeah," he says. "But I haven't spoken to her in years. That's why I can't come back. The way I left things with her, there isn't enough forgiveness in the world for that."

After that, he says nothing.

It's now or never. Time to do what I came here for. I know it's an idea so insane that I should probably be committed. Or given a healthy bump on the head to knock some loose gears back into place. But it's also our only hope. And, I realize, what Eights has been searching for all this time.

"I want you to come back to the Hurricanes," I say. "Your lifetime ban can't affect you here; the Mabel has no official ties to the majors."

"And do what? Be your mascot? Come out in an old-timey Hurricanes uniform and wave at the crowds, tell the kids on the team today to keep their eyes on the ball?" He scoffs, takes a sip of his coffee and grimaces. "You've got it all wrong. I'd be a curse. The town hates me. My daughter hates me. I'm a disgrace to them, and the game."

I shake my head. "I'm not talking about a clubhouse visit, or even a coaching position. I want you to *play* for the Hurricanes."

Now he looks at me like I'm the one in need of a doctor's visit.

"Have you lost your mind, you Scum-Sucking Garbage Leak? I'm hardly in any condition to play professional sports."

"Hey, if Bartolo Colon could pitch in the majors at forty-six, then I think you can manage a few at bats for *one game* in a small independent league. Besides, it's not just about your talent. It's about the Zazzle, the Magic, you brought to the team. You're *not* a curse. You're the opposite. You have an undefeated record against the first-place Harbor Pirates. I don't think that streak's going to break anytime soon. That's not how Zazzle works."

"You believe in that codswallop?"

"I didn't used to," I say. "Not until my team this season proved me wrong. I used to just think baseball was a game of numbers. That statistical anomalies, unpredictable occurrences, were just exceptions that proved the rule. It was all just percentages and data—and that no one, all things being equal, could play beyond their skill for any significant stretch of time. But now I know there's more to it than that. Baseball is a game of moments. One little moment after another that can't be replicated. Every inning, every at bat, every single pitch could amount to nothing or mean everything. And when there are no limits to *possibility*, every moment becomes a vital part of the game. This is our moment, right now. Your moment. Help me beat the Harbor Pirates one last time."

He doesn't say anything for several seconds. His dark eyes search mine, and I will myself to *not* look down at my shoes again.

"Ugh." He finally shudders. "I *do* hate those Welted Scrum Scab Harbor Pirates. Always have."

"So, you'll come back?"

"You're forgetting one thing," he says. "The town hates me. I'm not going to put myself or anyone else through the uncomfortable experience of seeing me back on the field in a Hurricanes uniform. Especially my daughter."

"I think you need to give Carla and everyone in this town—and yourself—a chance. Carla told me she wants to see you again—I don't even think she knows you're still in town. As for the rest of the folks in Weakerville, they don't even know you're still *alive*. This is the only way to undo whatever damage you think you've done. The team needs you or it will go under, just like you did. But you can save it, and yourself. It's not too late."

A weird look lights up his wrinkled eyes.

"So, you *really* think I can still play?"

"Does it matter? You don't need to hit a home run every at bat. You don't even need to get a hit at all. It's a team sport. All the Hurricanes need right now is a teammate like you."

He doesn't say anything, but he smiles, just a little bit.

"Practice is at three p.m. tomorrow," I finally say. "We play our final game against the Harbor Pirates tomorrow night. A must-win game." I hand him Rick Larsen's business card. "Call this number. He'll take care of the contract details."

Early Eights Foster shakes his head but takes the card anyway.

"Well, I guess it's finally time for Early Eights Foster to come back from the dead," he says.

Chapter 36

EARLY EIGHTS FOSTER ISN'T THERE AT THE START OF PRACTICE THE next day.

Despite being on our way to our first winning season in a decade, the mood at batting practice is somber. Because of me. Nobody will even look at me, let alone talk to me. Especially not Slips and Aliyah. We're back to looking like the team who couldn't win a game only a few weeks ago.

By the time four o'clock rolls around and Eights hasn't shown, I figure he changed his mind. It was a long shot anyway, I guess. I send the pitchers back to the bullpen to start their warm-up routine and tell Aliyah and Slips to get the position players going on some last-minute fielding drills.

"Mind if I head down to the batting cages?" Carla asks me. "I want to get some extra swings in before the game, just in case . . ."

She trails off. I nod, and she leaves through the dugout tunnel to head back to the cages underneath the stadium.

But five minutes later, everything changes.

Everyone on the field stops what they're doing when a man walks out from the dugout with the team's part-time athletic trainer. It's Gloves, but he's barely recognizable, freshly showered and shaved. He already looks much closer to his actual age—and more like the Early Eights Foster we used to see on the huge billboard outside of town.

He's suddenly the guy from my old baseball cards again.

The murmurs of shock are plain. Here is a local legend who everyone assumed to be dead. Who *is,* in fact, *legally* dead.

Halfway to home plate, Eights twirls around with shocking grace and barfs all over the field. A stunned *silence follows* as he wipes his mouth like he's done it a thousand times before. The team's athletic trainer, an energetic, smiley guy named Mike, leans over Eights and asks questions.

Eventually they keep moving and walk over to me.

"Sorry about that," Eights says.

"He should be fine . . ." Mike says with a smile. "Maybe?"

The whole team whispers excitedly around us. I can tell they're struggling to wrap their heads around this. Can this old guy really be who they think it is?

"Um . . . want to start with some batting practice?" I suggest.

Eights nods and drops his glove right there in the grass. It's old and faded and gray, and so loose and worn that it sits flat in the grass like a leather pancake.

Early Eights Foster steps into a batter's box for the first time in two decades.

Everyone is watching. All other practice activities are on hold. Some of these guys might not know who Early Eights Foster is—but it's clear from the looks on their faces that most of them do. Either way, the field is buzzing with energy.

The rust of not having played in a quarter century is

painfully evident the first few pitches. Early Eights Foster's swing is awkward and slow. He misses everything. In some ways, it's hard to watch. But that ends by the eleventh or twelfth pitch, when his swing starts coming back to him, more quickly than seemed possible moments before, and in that way it only can for someone with all the natural talent in the world who spent over half his life playing the game, day in and day out, every waking hour.

Don't get me wrong, his swing is absolutely slower than it used to be. But it's still the effortless, smooth stroke that Early Eights Foster always had. The same one Carla has, at least at away games. And while he probably wouldn't be able to hit upper-nineties fastballs the way he did back in his twenties, his swing is still more than enough to handle batting practice meatballs.

We watch in awe as Early Eights Foster blasts four consecutive pitches over the left field fence. Two are foul balls, technically, but the dazzling display of raw power is still as clear as the blue sky on this glorious afternoon.

The entire team cheers as they watch a former MLB All-Star, and local legend, hit bombs, live, in a stadium empty except for the Hurricanes. The ball explodes off his bat. He hits close to fifty pitches, and by the end of practice, the whole team is beaming. We have a legend among us now. It doesn't matter that batting practice is far from competitive professional pitching, or that he barfed no fewer than three times in less than an hour of practice. He's brought just what we need, just when we need it: the belief that we can win, even if the odds are against us.

Practice is winding down when I look around and realize someone is missing.

Carla.

I don't know if she's even aware her dad is here. As practice breaks up so the team can get some rest in before warm-ups, I head for the dugout tunnel. Before I can make it to the batting cages, though, I pass the locker room and glance inside.

Carla is sitting in front of her locker, picking at the loose stitching on her mitt.

"Hey," I say. I'm about to ask if she knows, but it's clear, even to me, that she does. "You knew he was alive, right?"

"Yes," she says softly. "I just can't believe he's *here*."

"I'm . . . I'm really sorry," I say. "I should have warned you. . . . It's just that, I didn't know if he'd show up, and—"

"It's okay, Alex." She shakes her head as I sit down on the bench across from her. "I'm not mad. At least, not at you. And not at . . . I don't know . . . I *did* tell you I wanted to see him again."

"When's the last time you talked to him?"

"It was . . ." She sighs. "A few years ago. He came into the store. We'd spoken on the phone and exchanged a few emails before that—I'd known he hadn't died in the plane crash, and when he came back to town, I wanted him to come live with me. But he just wanted to disappear—wouldn't return my calls, wouldn't acknowledge me on the street. He clearly hated himself, and after a while, well, I just stopped trying. I could have forgiven him for anything—cheating, faking his own death, anything. But it didn't seem like he was interested. Not until he came into the store that day. But then, when he saw me, he chickened out and left before I could go talk to him. I guess I thought he left town again after that. I never could have imagined he was here all along. That he was *that guy* digging through the trash. . . ."

"Do you know why he did that?" I ask.

Carla shrugs.

"He called it his *penance*," I continue. "For disgracing the town and the sport. But mostly for what he did to you."

"Well, that's great," she says bitterly. "But I'd rather he

would have just come and talked to me!"

"I . . ." I start before I realize I have no idea what to say.

"I'm here now," a voice says.

Carla and I look up to see Early Eights Foster standing in the doorway of the locker room. Carla doesn't say anything, and I can't tell how happy she actually is to see him.

"Can we, uh, have a moment?" he asks.

I look at Carla. She nods at me.

"Oh, yeah, of course," I say, standing up and heading toward my office.

The last thing I see is him sitting down next to her on the bench. I close my office door, and I don't hear what they say.

Chapter 37

BEFORE THE PREGAME WARM-UPS THAT EVENING, I'M WEAVING THROUGH the locker room, looking frantically for Slips and Aliyah.

Because I know it can't go down like this. We can't head into the final game of the season barely speaking to one another. Even if we win and save the team, it will feel totally empty if we don't do it together.

I find Slips talking to Mayhem. They're both laughing.

"Slips, can you meet me in my office?"

The smile slides off his face, but at least he nods.

Aliyah is talking to Farmer John, our opener that night, discussing the top of the Duluth Harbor Pirates' stacked lineup. She rolls her eyes when I ask her to follow me to my office, but she does it anyway.

When we get there, Slips is already leaning against the wall with his arms folded across his chest. I sit down at my desk as Aliyah sits on the other side from me.

All three of us are spaced about as far apart as possible inside the small office.

"Well," I say. "I have been a Trout-Faced Handle Knob lately. *And* a Donkey-Faced Puss Welt, for that matter . . ."

Slips laughs and shakes his head, but Aliyah keeps her arms folded across her chest and continues to glower.

"Will you let me buy you a pizza after the game tonight, win or lose, so I can say I'm sorry properly?"

"No," Aliyah says. "You can say you're sorry properly now. *Then* we can have pizza later. *If* I decide to forgive you."

"Fair enough. Well, okay, then: I'm sorry. Not just for lying to you and to the team. But for not trusting that you could handle the truth. For not believing we could tackle the problem *together.* But mostly for not treating you as actual friends from the start, and instead only looking at the ways you both could help me. Aliyah, I mean . . . I just didn't think you would ever agree to do it, because I didn't believe I even deserved a friend like you. But that's my problem, it isn't about you at all, and it isn't fair that I made assumptions about you because of my own issues. We wouldn't be in this position as a team without you, and *I* wouldn't be able to say all this coherently without having you as my friend. You trusted me, and I let you down. But I won't let that happen again. Winning this thing, making the playoffs, it won't mean anything if you're still angry with me."

She doesn't say anything; she just listens. I can't decide if that's a good thing or a bad thing.

"And, Slips," I say, turning toward him. "You're right that I've been taking you for granted. Not just this season, but our whole friendship. And you're a good enough friend to help me anyway. You're one of the most generous people I know, and I let my own insecurity take advantage of that for years. The fact is, I still need you. I'm never going to be the most confident or likable kid, I know that. But I won't make excuses anymore. I won't look to you to fix all my problems. I'm gonna start fighting my own fights and, I guess, believe in myself sometimes."

My oldest friend (now that Ira is gone) is still silent. He only moves to rub his eyes, and I can't tell if it's to stifle a tear or out of annoyance. Or maybe he's just tired—it *has* been a long season.

"Anyway, I hope you'll both forgive me. Then we can talk about actually *winning* this game."

"Of course I forgive you," Slips finally says, smiling now. "We all make mistakes. *Przebaczam tobie.* And I want to apologize to you too, Aliyah. I never should have encouraged Alex to lie. I was only looking out for my friend, but that doesn't make it okay."

Aliyah takes more time with it, almost like she's literally dissecting our words to see what's inside them.

"All right," she finally says. "I know you just wanted the same thing I do: to see this team succeed for once in our lives. I mean, we're *one win* away, and there's no way I want to lose another baseball game, not after everything we've been through. So I'm going to forgive you both—*for now.* But I reserve the right to revoke that forgiveness later."

"Okay, fair enough," I say. "But for now: let's get to work."

At first, nobody notices my presence in the locker room.

The team is getting ready for what could be the final Hurricanes game ever, but spirits are high. The sounds of the sold-out crowd arriving in droves can be heard above us like hopeful thunder. My gaze shifts around the room, taking it all in.

Early Eights Foster still looks like he might puke at any moment, but he's in the corner giving some sort of hitting tip to Josh Carlson, the Mabel's youngest player, and Carla. There's Farmer John, the forty-six-year-old actual farmer we signed at the open tryout. He's wearing an ice pack on his shoulder and making some kind of joke about cattle from the look of his hand gestures—he's always making cow jokes nobody else really gets—while Aliyah laughs. Slips is joking around with Mayhem, as he puts the goofball closer's long hair into a man-bun. Earlier this season, Mayhem vowed he would not cut it until the Hurricanes clinched the playoffs. Already past his shoulders at the start of the season, it now hangs nearly to his waist in long stringy tangles, so greasy you could probably cook the whole team breakfast in it.

Slips sees me looking at him, says something that leaves Mayhem laughing, and then hurries over to where I'm standing.

"You look like you're about to give a rousing pregame speech," he says.

"Yeah, but I don't think they need it, I mean, look at them. . . ."

"Well, you should at least apologize to them like you did for me and Aliyah."

I just look at him, not wanting to admit I'm still afraid, even after everything that's happened. The fact is, I have yet to address the whole team before a game this season. It's something I've never thought I could do. Especially now with my favorite player, Early Eights Foster, sitting right there.

"I can, like, wait, uh, maybe, until—" I start.

"Alex, stop making excuses," Slips says. "This is *your* moment. Don't be such a *balwan*."

Balwan is Polish for snowman, and doubles as slang for wimp, wuss, wet noodle, spineless weakling, person who melts under pressure, etc.

Slips is right. This is something I have to do. And it's something Ira apparently knew I could do all along.

I turn and clear my throat, suddenly finding the whole room silent.

"Um, I want to start by saying, uh, well . . ." I stop and take a few deep breaths. I glance at Slips, but he's looking down at Anne of Green Gables as he twists the barrel on the floor like a drill. I know it's his way of making *me* do this. "First, that I'm sorry. I'm sorry I lied to everyone. I was trying to protect you, I mean, uh, not that I think you're weak or anything. Or *need* my protection." I stop, trying to ward off the Flumpo coursing into my brain. I know I just need to open myself up and get this out. "The point is: I'm truly sorry. I lied because *I'm* the one who's weak. Because this team just means so much to me and I was so afraid of losing it like I lost Ira. And I was scared to let you down. So, I'm not lying now when I say: we *can* win this game. I know that because the fact that I'm, like, standing here now saying all of this to you without flumping over my words, or accidently admitting that I like to eat my own toe jam in a nervous panic . . . uh, wait, did I just admit that . . . uh . . ." I stop, hoping they'll figure out that I'm kidding, but no one laughs.

But it's not because they're cringing; it's because they're actually leaning in, listening to me. They actually want to hear that I believe in them. That I don't need to lie anymore, because I really think we can do this. So now, even though they all actually think I eat my own toe jam—which, for the record, is absolutely not true—I still press on, because for the first time ever a group of people are actually listening to me without snickering or rolling their eyes.

"What I'm saying is, if I can do *this,* then anything is possible. This is baseball, a game we all love. Well, except for Slips." This actually does get a few chuckles. "And we all know baseball well enough to know that the beauty of the game comes from its limitless possibilities. Which means there's no reason we can't go win this game. Of course, I can't guarantee a win, but I can promise you this: every pitch, every swing, every little moment *matters.* So let's, um, play like that and stuff, and . . . well, okay, then . . ."

It had been going so well, but I suddenly realize I'm out of things to say. I don't have enough experience doing this to know how it's supposed to end.

Slips steps up onto the bench, Anne of Green Gables slung over his shoulder, and helps me out, like a good friend always does.

"*Kopniemy ich w dupe!*" he shouts in Polish.

The players surely have no idea what this means, but he sells it so well they all figure out the essence of it. The team cheers and moments later is jogging through the tunnel toward the field, determined to win.

Once they're gone, I turn to Slips.

"I thought you wanted me to give the speech?"

He smiles. "You did! That last bit was for me."

"Okay . . . What did you just say?"

"Basically," he says with a grin, "let's go kick their butts!"

Chapter 38

MUSTARD PARK IS ALIVE THAT NIGHT.

The buzz around Eights's return is electric. Shortly after practice, the news that Early Eights Foster was not only *alive* but would be playing that night with the Hurricanes of Weakerville went viral. It even appeared on ESPN several times, including a show called *Important Opinions,* where two blustering hosts pointlessly debated whether Early should be allowed to play in an independent league, considering he has an active lifetime ban from baseball.

But I'm not worried about any of that. All I care about is winning this game.

During the national anthem and starting lineup announcements, we get our first taste of what a playoff atmosphere is like. Because, essentially, this *is* a playoff game. Win, and our season continues. Lose, and we're eliminated. Not just from the playoffs, but from existing as a team forever.

The fans don't know that, but it *feels* like they do.

I've been to almost every home game during the past six seasons of Hurricanes baseball, and nothing has ever come close to this. The stadium feels like it's a whole living organism in itself, and we're just a bunch of bacteria inside trying to survive as it pulsates with energy.

The players can feel it too. The dugout is all smiles and excited high fives as our defense takes the field. One of our outfielders, Javy Rivera, is eating a huge plate of mofongo, like he always does before the first pitch. He offers some to Early Eights Foster, who promptly runs into the tunnel to puke again.

Eights looks terrible—even worse than at practice earlier.

"I'm batting leadoff?" he asks when I post the batting order in the clubhouse.

"We need to start the game with a runner on base."

"And what if I can't get a hit?"

"I don't think you'll have to."

He hesitates, but apparently figures out what I mean, and then nods with grim acceptance. We both know what's going to happen when he steps to that plate for the first time. And we also both know it will only help the team.

"Okay," he finally says. "But I'm doing it for Ira, and the team, and my daughter. Not my Scum-Sucking Leaking-Wound manager."

"Fair enough," I say with a smirk.

He actually smiles back, before taking a seat on the end of the bench.

Farmer John goes on to post a near-perfect first inning, giving up a leadoff walk before logging three straight outs to escape with no damage. It's about as good a start as we could have hoped for.

When Early Eights Foster is announced over the PA in the bottom of the first, the crowd goes berserk. It's almost like he never stopped being their hometown hero. Time really does heal old wounds, especially in sports.

As Eights steps into the batter's box to lead off the

game, he eyes the Harbor Pirates pitcher on the mound, Billy Bob "Buck" Meehan. Buck Meehan is an old-school baseball purist. A guy who grew up eating raw deer hearts and studying the "unwritten rules" of the game. He's notorious in the Mabel for following the old code. And the old code has a way of dealing with guys who are known cheaters.

He throws the first pitch right at Early Eights Foster, beaning him on his bony old thigh.

It almost drops the old man. But to his credit, Eights stays on his feet and limps awkwardly toward first while the crowd boos Buck Meehan so viciously that I almost expect them to start raining down empty soda cups and half-eaten pretzels onto the mound.

Early stands on first grimacing and holding his right leg.

That's all we needed from him. I had no delusions that a fifty-four-year-old freelance bum was going to walk in off the streets and actually contribute in his first professional baseball game in twenty-plus years.

But we don't need him to. He's already done what he was signed to do. The team is energized, electricity is flowing through the crowd, and Carla Henderson seems more confident than I've ever seen her.

If Eights had any Baseball Zazzle left, he's already given it to us.

I signal the ump for a pinch runner.

Steven Yu is our best base runner. In fact, that's pretty much all he's done all season. He has just eleven plate appearances and no hits but has stolen thirty-four bases and scored twenty-seven runs. But I leave him on the bench for now. After all, we are only one batter into the game, and he can't really play in the field.

Instead, our utility infielder, Jes Bradshaw, comes into the game to run for Eights, with Carla coming to the plate.

Carla and Eights share a brief exchange as they pass each other near the dugout steps.

"Carla!" I say, walking out to her a few feet from the dugout.

"You know who you are now?"

She looks confused. I turn and motion to Slips.

He runs out of the dugout and slaps a piece of duct tape over the *HENDERSON* on the back of her jersey. The name *FOSTER* is scrawled on the tape in Sharpie.

"You've got nothing else to live up to," I say. "You're already a Foster, right?"

Carla grins and heads to the batter's box.

She settles in, digging her cleats into the dirt. Her three warm-up swings look so easy, it's like she's taking swings in the backyard instead of the most important professional baseball game of her life.

I don't know if it's nerves, or Eights's Baseball Zazzle, or the raucous home crowd. But Buck Meehan throws three pitches way out of the zone to start the at bat.

Carla is suddenly up 3–0 with a runner on first and no outs.

It's perhaps the most obvious time in all of baseball to take a pitch.

Which is exactly why I give her the sign to swing away.

She suppresses a grin, and taps the tape covering her name on her jersey, before getting into her stance.

Buck winds up and deals an 88-mile-per-hour fastball right down the plate. Carla takes a confident, smooth swing and laces the pitch over the third baseman's head. It slices down the line and lands fair, rolling into the corner.

Carla stops at first as I wave Bradshaw home.

He easily beats the throw from left and we're up 1–0. Mustard Park is practically shaking from all the fans jumping up and down. Eights and Carla make a gesture to one another, some sort of inside thing between them, I'm guessing, as the team pummels Bradshaw with high fives.

The first inning ends 1–0.

We all know it won't be enough. The Harbor Pirates are offensive juggernauts. The only way to beat them is to find a way to outscore them. They average an obscene 6.8 runs per game. But a lead is a lead.

Which is something you will eventually need to win a game.

Chapter 39

I WISH I COULD TELL YOU ABOUT EVERY PITCH, EVERY AT BAT, EVERY moment from our final game.

But those are all just details that lead to the same place: the bottom of the ninth inning. It's the moment that matters most, because it's the moment happening now.

As the last half of the last inning opens, we're down 8–5. And yet, all around me, I can feel that the players know we're still in this. Feeding off the energy of the sold-out crowd and Eights's Zazzle, they have played a valiant game. Every single Hurricane has played their best game of the season, and then some. It's been gutty and gritty and scrappy. And they're not giving up.

In baseball, I've learned, *anything* can happen in any given moment.

As our players come running in from the outfield after the top of the ninth, I know we have to *do* something. A three-run deficit is not easy to overcome. In fact, the odds of scoring three runs in one inning is only about 3.08011 percent. But numbers are just numbers, I know that now. These players don't care what the percentages say.

We're going to change the odds. A combination of Baseball Zazzle and metrics are what got us here, and that's what will get us through.

"Bring it in," I say as the last two outfielders descend the dugout steps.

The team gathers around, sweaty, tired, hopeful.

"Remember: *nobody* thought we'd be here," I say. "I've been managing all season like we have everything to lose, and . . . well, yeah, I guess we do have a lot to lose. But that's what everyone expects will happen. Even them." I point across the field to the opposing dugout. "But here's the thing: *you are going to win this game*."

There are murmurs of agreement around the dugout.

Mayhem says, "We have to win, right? Eights has *never* lost to the Pirates."

"It's true," Eights says. "And I don't want to start now either, you Scrunchy Commode Jockeys."

"What he said," I say.

A few players laugh. Several others are nodding. The whole team seems a little looser. A little more determined, but a little less anxious.

"Okay, you two," I say, pointing at Chewy Cavanaugh and Jof, the first two hitters due up this inning. "A word."

They lean in to hear what I have to say as the rest of the team disperses.

"I want you to take every pitch you see," I say. "I know it sounds crazy, but trust me. Take. *Every. Pitch.* No swings."

"But, Coach . . ." Jof says.

"Trust me."

He finally nods, and then Chewy does too.

The Harbor Pirates closer, Wilson Wilson—yes, that's his real name, and I have to simply assume his parents are *hilarious*—relies on getting swings and misses on his devastating slider. Most pitchers primarily use a fastball, but not Wilson Wilson. He leads with his slider, and it's effective—it has a very late break, which means it looks like it's going to be a strike until suddenly, at the last moment, it dives, usually off the corner of the plate. It's made him one of the best closers in the league; his WHIP is an amazing 0.791. My stats from the past seasons, however, indicate that he's *never* gotten a strikeout during an at bat where the batter didn't swing at least once. He relies on batters chasing that slider.

And so, we won't be swinging. At least, not yet.

Jof steps into the batter's box.

Pitch one is a strike looking, a wicked slider that just catches the corner. The second pitch is nearly identical but breaks just a bit more, and it's called a ball. Another ball and then a strike follow. On the 2–2 pitch, Jof strikes out looking at another slider on the corner, the bat never leaving his shoulder.

It's the first time that's ever happened for Wilson Wilson in hundreds of career batters, yet it only reinforces my belief that we can win this game.

"Good work," I say as Jof passes me into the dugout. "It'll be okay. . . ."

His bat clanks loudly into the rack. It seems like a failure, but right now we need more than a solo home run. We need base runners. And there's only one way to get them against a closer this effective.

I take a deep breath and hope that Chewy has better luck. And he does, taking five straight pitches without lifting a finger, bringing the count full at 3–2.

Wilson Wilson seems agitated at not getting a few close calls. He's sweating now, after ten pitches. The sixth pitch of the at bat is a borderline fastball up and in. The ump calls ball four and Chewy trots to first as the pitcher shouts obscenities into his glove.

I motion to the ump for a substitution. Steven Yu jogs out to first.

Chewy fist-bumps Steven as he comes trotting back toward our dugout to an ovation from the crowd above.

Josh Carlson steps into the box and looks my way.

I give him the signal to take the first two pitches. He does, and they are both strikes, but that's okay—in this case, this is what I was hoping for. At 0–2, the pitcher will throw something off the plate hoping that Josh will chase. It's likely going to be a slider off the plate, since Wilson Wilson throws his slider 92.1 percent of the time when the count is 0–2.

I signal to Josh to take the third pitch, while giving Steven the green light to steal second base. Normally, I wouldn't call for a steal in this situation—we need three runs to tie the game, and it would be foolish to risk making an out on the bases just to get a runner to second. Taking the double play out of the equation isn't a bad idea, but still, it's a base we don't need.

Which is exactly why I call for it. It's unpredictable. And right now I want Wilson Wilson to be thinking that the Hurricanes of Weakerville might do *anything* to win.

Steven dances out to a massive lead and flusters the pitcher enough that he actually draws a couple throws to first, which Steven easily beats back to the bag. His lead is a hair shorter as Wilson Wilson finally delivers a slider low and away, just as predicted. Sure enough, with Steven's great jump, the catcher doesn't even risk making a throw.

The crowd goes berserk.

It would be near insanity to not allow our hitter to finally swing the bat with a runner in scoring position. But I also *know* the Harbor Pirates closer will not throw a strike.

I give the signal to take another pitch.

And I give Steven the green light to steal third.

Wilson Wilson is so frustrated that he doesn't even look back toward second before the pitch. Steven responds by taking a significant lead, then bolts on the pitch, another slider outside. Josh doesn't swing, and

Steven steals third, again without a throw. The crowd is going nuts now, as if someone just hit a walk-off grand slam, even though we still haven't even brought the tying run to the plate. Steven's steals don't put us in a much better position to win, statistically, but it feels like the momentum is building behind us, and the Harbor Pirates feel it too. The Hurricanes in the dugout shout encouragements toward the field; nearly the whole team is leaning on the railing to watch, and the crowd is on their feet too.

The next two pitches are balls, and just like that we have runners on the corners with only one out.

Our odds of scoring three runs are now up to 8.44554 percent.

And it's time to start swinging.

I give our next batter, John Amdor, the signal to swing away. He works the count to 2–1, and then, on the fourth pitch, hits a dribbling grounder toward first. The first baseman charges in and scoops up the ball. He's able to glance at third, keeping Steven there, but has little chance to twist and throw to second. His only option is to reach out and tag the batter for the second out of the inning.

The Hurricanes' very existence is down to just one single out.

Even with runners on second and third, our odds of scoring three runs with two outs are just 4.33863% percent.

As Jes Bradshaw steps to the plate, the catcher stands up and moves to the side with his glove extended away. Even though Bradshaw is just a utility bench player, he's already gotten two hits tonight. But that's not why they're intentionally walking him.

They're walking him to load the bases, because Carla Henderson is on deck.

Her struggles at home are no secret to the rest of the league. At home, Carla's on-base percentage is just .137. And even though she's gone 2–3 on the night, with 2 RBI, the opposing manager is making the smart play to pitch to her with the game on the line. She did hit into a game-ending triple play last game, after all.

But he doesn't know what I know about Carla.

Mustard Park rattles like it might collapse as Bradshaw jogs to first.

The bases are now loaded in the bottom of the ninth. Two outs. We're down by three. This is the sort of stuff that makes up the baseball fantasies of kids all over the country. I know the numbers say our odds of winning the game are now 4.29188 percent.

But those are just numbers.

Our real chances, in the actual moment, are limitless.

Mustard Park gives Carla Henderson a thunderous ovation as she steps to the plate. The 4,884 fans are so loud, I can't even hear my own thoughts down here in the dugout.

I give Carla the sign to swing away.

The first pitch is a slider down near her shins. Just like her dad, Carla is a free swinger. And so she tries to dig it out of the dirt like she's playing golf. She somehow actually makes contact, but it's a foul ball. The next pitch is a fastball up in the zone and Carla fends it off, fouling it straight back into the stands.

It's now 0–2.

Carla is hitless in fifty-eight at bats at Mustard Park after going down 0–2 in the count. That means she statistically has a 0 percent chance to succeed. But she doesn't seem concerned. I wish I could say I know she will pull this off, but the truth is, sweat is pouring down my face as all of my memories of coming to Hurricanes games with my grandpa Ira flash before my eyes. Our late nights talking about tomorrow's matchups, the hot dogs he would always get me, the way he smiled that infectious smile after every game, regardless of the outcome.

It's all on the line.

The next pitch is another slider in the dirt. Carla strides but doesn't swing, bringing the count to 1–2.

I can't even bear to calculate the odds of her getting on base anymore.

Everyone in Mustard Park is on their feet, but it feels like mine might give out from under me.

The Harbor Pirates closer stands tall on the mound, nodding at the first sign he gets from the catcher. He fires a rocket toward home plate. It registers at 94 miles per hour on the radar gun.

I see a white streak approach the plate for a split second.

Then it's gone.

Chapter 40

CRACK!

Carla's swing is so fluid, I don't even see the contact, I only hear it.

The ball is launched so high into the air that I lose sight of it for a few seconds, until it's coming back down—on the other side of the center field fence.

It's a grand slam.

Even more miraculously, it's the grand slam that just won us the game and clinched a playoff spot. It feels like an actual hurricane is happening inside Mustard Park as the town's fans lose their minds.

Carla just saved the whole franchise.

As she rounds the bases, nobody is cheering louder than her father. Eights is the first one out of the dugout. The whole team is on the field seconds later, a huge mob of jumping bodies near home plate—I can't even see Eights or Carla anymore.

I stay where I am, near the dugout, soaking it in.

Suddenly Slips is next to me. He gives my shoulder a few pats and then grins. We don't say anything. We just enjoy the moment for a bit.

Then he tosses Anne of Green Gables aside and sprints onto the field to join the celebratory fracas.

I look across the field as fans from the stands start pouring onto the diamond. Aliyah is in the bullpen, hugging her dad. It looks like she might be crying, she's so happy.

The whole field is filled with celebrating fans, the players and townspeople indistinguishable from one another among the jovial chaos.

But the only thing I'm thinking about in that moment is Ira.

Chapter 41

A WEEK LATER, I'M BACK IN TEX'S OFFICE FOR OUR FINAL MEETING OF the season.

"A valiant effort, son!" Tex barks as I sit down. "You almost won that last one."

He's referring to our *playoff* series versus the Duluth Harbor Pirates. That's the bad news when you squeak into the playoffs as the last seed: you end up playing the best team in round one.

"Yeah, I'm proud of the team," I say.

Nothing could be truer, despite getting swept 3–0 in

the first round of the playoffs. We had at least held our own, losing each game by less than four runs.

"I reckon you're just thrilled you made it at all," Tex says. "What with it meaning I might have to cancel my sale of the team and so on and such."

For the first time, I notice he doesn't have the usual unlit cigarette in his mouth.

"What do you mean, *might*?" I ask. "It says in the contract that you can't—"

"Oh, I know what it says," Tex says. "Lucy assured, the contract is the contract. But, you see, son, the thing is, I got me a whole team of lawyers whose sole function is getting out of flimsy contracts like this one. And who's going to *pay* to legally challenge me? You? Your folks? Lawsuits cost small fortunes these days."

"That isn't fair!" I say. "It's cheating! That's not how things work!"

"Don't kid yourself, son," Tex says. "That's *exactly* how things work, in this world. The sooner you be getting that in your head, the better. I know Ira was telling you all sorts of fairy tales about yonder—"

"No." I think he's as surprised as I am that I interrupted him. "You don't get to tell me anything about what Ira did or said or thought."

Tex looks at me for a moment and then folds massive his hands in front of him on the desk.

"Fair enough, son," he finally says, then laughs that signature laugh of his. "Maybe I was out of line there. But back to the matter at hand: whether you want to accept it or not, I *can* still sell this team if I want to."

"But . . . *are* you?"

"Honestly, son, I still ain't sure," Tex says with another explosive laugh. "It may not be worth the trouble. Especially if these Hurricanes keep making me at least *some* money next season, which seems likely, thanks to you. I can always just sell them the year after. Or the year after that."

It's weird, here I am being faced with the loss of the team again, but this time something feels different about it.

"So, what do you say, son?" Tex says.

"About what?"

"If I let sleeping monkeys lie, and keep the team around next season, do you want the manager job again?"

I'm a bit stunned by the question, and I don't even know what to say at first. On one hand, I already know Aliyah won't be coming back. Shortly after our final playoff loss, the Law reached out to her and told her he'd gotten her a spot the following summer to train at this new high-tech pitching academy. He seems to think she has a legitimate shot to play baseball—*not softball*—in college. And beyond that . . . who knows? There's probably no limit, with her talent. On the other hand, I know that Slips would still be in, because we've already been talking about next season. He said he liked hanging out with his buddy more than he hates baseball, so of course he'd do it again—but only if I agreed to help him fix up a second scooter that winter. A baby-blue 1983 Peugeot Django that he'd named Diva Plavalaguna. Which, of course, I'd already agreed to do.

"Sleeping dogs," I finally say.

"Beg your pardon, son?"

"Isn't the expression *let sleeping dogs lie*?"

"Well, it should be monkey!" Tex bellows with a smile. "Have you ever tried to wake a sleeping monkey? I did once, and let me tell you, they're mighty cranky. It was at this Safari Zoo I used to own a stake in down in southwestern Arkansas . . ."

I sit back, knowing another wild story is coming, but then Tex suddenly stops. "You know what, never mind. The point is, you want the job or not?"

What comes out of my mouth next surprises even me.

"Maybe," I say. "Why don't you ask me again when you figure out whether or not you're committed to this team."

Tex's eyes go wide, but he's still grinning.

"Well, I'll be a goat's great-aunt," he says, punctuating this with a few belly laughs. "Okay, then, I'll do that, son."

I stand up to leave.

"Before you go," Tex says, pulling an envelope from his top desk drawer. "Another note from your grandpa Ira. His will said I was supposed to give this to you at the end of the season. What was with your grandpappy and his cryptic, mysterious letters, anyway?"

I give a little laugh and take the letter from him.

"He was that sort of guy, I guess," I say. "It's what I loved about him."

"His twin sister was the same way," Tex says, nodding. "That was one wild season, eh, son?"

I'm suddenly unable to get out any words, so I just laugh to keep from crying. Tex eventually joins in and is still laughing when I finally turn and leave his office.

I'm sitting in my old seats in an empty Mustard Park.

Ira's letter is clutched in my hand.

I'm still somewhat surprised I didn't push Tex harder

to keep the team. Or assure him I would return as manager if there is a next season. But I think I'm coming to grips with what I finally realized sitting in that office.

Whether the team sticks around forever or not, it doesn't really matter in the end. I love the Hurricanes, so of course I want them to last forever. But I think Ira would say he got everything he wanted out of this season. The whole town of Weakerville united around a baseball team for one unforgettable summer, the way Ira remembered from his childhood. And if he really did have some plan to help me figure out what that means, and maybe even start to have some confidence in myself, it worked. Well, sort of. I mean, I'm never going to win any popularity contests, but at least making *some* friends, and maybe even talking to them without tripping over myself sometimes, doesn't feel so impossible anymore.

But, most important, I know now that what Ira and I had, it doesn't live or die with a baseball team. No matter what happens to the Hurricanes, *that* is going to last forever.

I sigh and finally open the letter:

Alex,

I suspect this was the final season. Even if you

managed to get us to the playoffs, I know Tex and people like him. He'll find a way out of our deal if he wants. But don't be too hard on that old cuss. The truth was, he made my sister happy in her too few years on this earth, and he bailed out the Hurricanes more times than I can count. And he didn't do it because he's generous, he did it for my sister, Lucy. And so for that I have to be forever grateful to him. Because those are the moments and decisions that matter in life.

But that's not what's important. What matters is that you know the truth. The Hurricanes may be a part of my past, my family, the town's history, but it's still just a baseball team. I know that now and have for years. I bet, right now, if the team is indeed about to get sold, you're sitting there thinking: "Man, I really let Grandpa Ira down." But let me assure you: no matter what happened, you didn't let me down.

The truth is, Alex, I was done with this team years ago. I used to love baseball and what this team did for the town, but I realized a while ago that's all gone and probably never coming back. I held on to this team as long as I could just for you,

Alex. Because I knew how much you loved coming to the games. I knew how happy Hurricanes games made you when making friends at school was getting tough. And most of all, because it was our thing, and I didn't ever want to let that go, at least not while I was alive.

So, no matter what happened this season, rest easy, my boy! We can both finally let this team go together! Unless you somehow managed to convince Tex to keep the team around? In that case, well done, Alex, I knew you could do it!

But, either way, you haven't let me down and never could. You're easier to believe in than you know. And if you haven't figured that out yet, you will someday.

For you to be happy is truly all I've ever wanted.

And I know you made me proud. You always do.

Love, your biggest fan,

Ira

ACKNOWLEDGMENTS

[TK]